CW00688366

IMPERIAL PATIENT

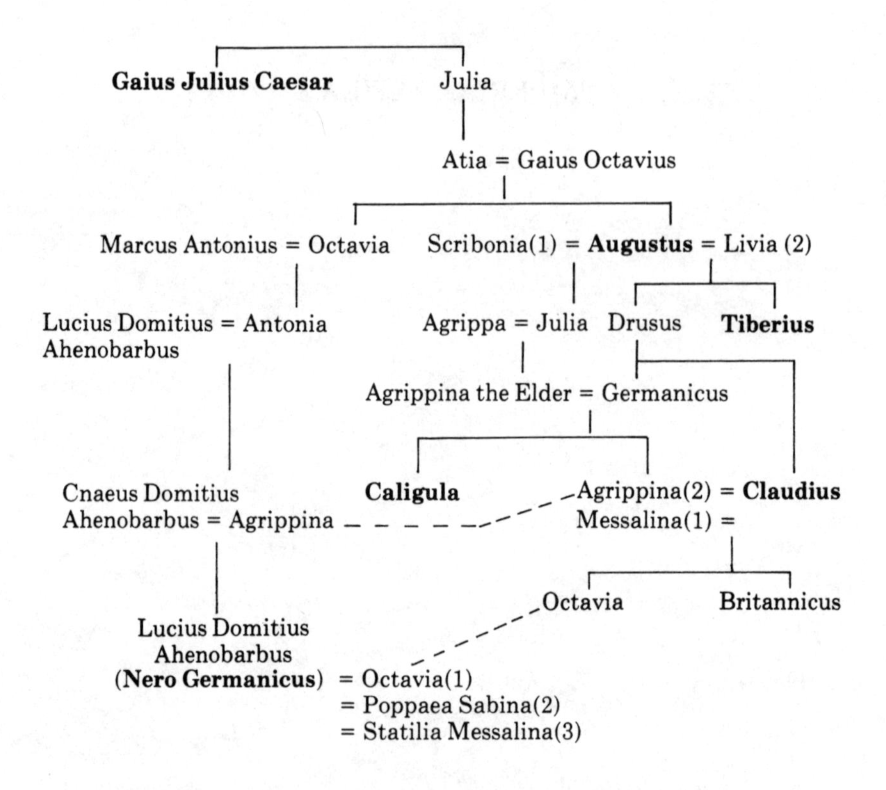

Gaius Julius Caesar
Julia
Atia = Gaius Octavius
Marcus Antonius = Octavia
Scribonia(1) = Augustus = Livia (2)
Lucius Domitius = Antonia
Ahenobarbus
Agrippa = Julia
Drusus
Tiberius
Agrippina the Elder = Germanicus
Cnaeus Domitius
Ahenobarbus = Agrippina
Caligula
Agrippina(2) = Claudius
Messalina(1) =
Octavia
Britannicus
Lucius Domitius
Ahenobarbus
(Nero Germanicus) = Octavia(1)
= Poppaea Sabina(2)
= Statilia Messalina(3)

Imperial Patient

The Memoirs of Nero's Doctor

Alex Comfort

Duckworth

First published in 1987 by
Gerald Duckworth & Company Limited
43 Gloucester Crescent, London NW1

ISBN 0 7156 2168 8

British Library Cataloguing in Publication Data

Comfort, Alex
Imperial patient : the memoirs of Nero's doctor.
I. Title
823'.912[F] PR6005.0388

ISBN 0-7156-2168-8

Photoset in North Wales by
Derek Doyle & Associates, Mold, Clwyd
Printed and bound in Great Britain by
Billing & Sons Limited, Worcester

Author's Note

This novel is an attempt to create a picture of Nero as he might have appeared to his Greek doctor. We have no really good contemporary account of him – Suetonius, from whom the popular, and the Hollywood, pictures of him are mostly derived, was born in the year Nero died: Tacitus, who was born about the time of his accession, recounts the start of his reign, but the bulk of his account is lost. Josephus, the Jewish historian, who was Nero's contemporary, and who may have met him – he certainly met Poppaea – says that the treatment accorded to Nero by historians was 'both favourable and unfavourable'. Whether through censorship · or bad luck, or through the machinations of the Furies of Agrippina, Nero has had by far the worst press of any ruler prior to Adolf Hitler – in fact, if asked to name the most obnoxious Roman emperor, nine out of ten educated people would probably pick Nero rather than Caligula, Domitian, or Heliogabalus.

Readers who wish to see how many liberties I have taken with history should read Michael Grant's brilliant and entertaining book *Nero*, which gives the facts as far as they are known. I *have* taken liberties (in bringing Tiridates on a secret visit to Rome, of which there is no record – in drawing on the apocryphal Epistles of Paul to Seneca, and so on) but not too many. Only a few of these characters – Arbaces, for example, and Callimachus himself – are wholly imaginary: the others may or may not have been as I depict them: for example, Aulus Celsus may have been a compiler, not a practising physician.

One part of the story which requires explanation is the 'experience' to which Callimachus refers in such guarded terms. This 'experience' was initation by way of the Eleusinian Mysteries. The secret of what exactly went on there was so well kept that it never leaked out, throughout the whole of Classical times, but there is now a good deal of evidence that the simple myth of seasonal regeneration, of the Corn Goddess and the Wine God, was supplemented by an oceanic or mystical ‘seeing,’ and that this in turn was facilitated by a psychedelic similar to LSD and derived from wild ergot. We know that the notorious unbeliever Alcibiades stole Eleusinian cakes for use at a wild party. This explains why the Coan physicians are so concerned to ensure that Nero is not liable to mental disorder – and also why, in spite of his ungodlike behaviour, they considered him as a partial avatar or manifestation of the God Dionysus.

The historical Nero almost certainly died by his own hand in A.D. 69. But for years the story was current, especially in Greece, that he was alive – indeed, a pseudo-Nero attempted to reclaim the Empire. If Nero had anything in common with the actor-god and rogue Dionysus, one can never be sure – and that story is as good as any other.

A.C.

1

Because, Herondas, my pupils, being human, are bound to ask some pointed questions about the company I have kept, I have decided to write down for you some account of my practice in Rome – how it came about, how much (or rather how little) part I played in some events now publicly notorious at which I could not avoid being present, and, more important, the principles on which I acted in dealing with the very difficult problems of professional ethics which such an obnoxious society raises. These notes may be historically interesting in themselves, but their main value will be in teaching you something about the practice of medicine which you will not hear in the schools.

Lawyers are sometimes blamed for associating with criminals, because defending criminals is their profession – physicians are liable to the same kind of criticism for treating the good and the bad alike: why take pains to heal disreputable people, whose lives would far better have been cut short? I have even met with some angry criticism because I did not take the opportunity, not merely to let die, but actually to put an end to public figures who survived to kill hundreds or even thousands of inoffensive people. On this count I have no doubts, and nor should you, if you are worthy of the precepts of our College – it is our obligation to treat all sick persons and harm none. The most cursory look at the long-term implications will show that this is right. If physicians were to set up as tyrannicides, they would themselves be tyrants, and if they withheld their skill to punish wrongdoers, no physician could be trusted. Indeed, all the most odious figures with whom I had contact were blind enough to think that they were themselves physicians, or rather surgeons, for the ills of society, and could cure them by letting blood.

My dear Herondas: I hope that start didn't put you off. It was vitally important that the first opening of this scroll should be identical with the published version, for obvious reasons. Not wanting to take risks, I had to wager that eventually you'd read further. By the time you do, there may well be no risk in setting all this down, but one can't be the third man in this kind of operation, however unintentional one's involvement, without getting surveillance-conscious. Why am I writing it down? Well, for a start, I owe an explanation to my residents, even if it is a late one. I've seen you all, courteous as you've been to me, looking at me a little sideways. Stertinius Xenophon told me he never got over being accused of murder: it destroyed his professional nerve. My professional nerve is fine, thank you, but I'd still like you to know the inside story. You may find it instructive: any one of us could find ourselves in like case.

And also, I'll admit, I had to write it down somewhere. The official apologia I wrote for the College's file – well, you just read the first opening. It's for the record, or for the birds. It tells how I got involved, but it says nothing about any of the people. Also it's a public document. This is a professional communication between us, and I can talk about patients. Although most of them are dead I never had their consent to divulge their confidences. Addressed to another physician, it's different. I'd be obliged if after you've read it, you still hang onto it. Don't present it to the College, bequeathe it. In theory medical confidentiality never runs out, but that ought to be long enough to satisfy our oath, and I want these things on record – for the larger benefit, if you follow me. After a couple of hundred years, secrecy is off the boil. Why do I think it's important? Not for reasons of self-justification – I was in a tight spot and improvised, being around some very dangerous people. Some people – one of the Jewish sects in particular – have tried to make Nero Claudius Caesar into an incarnate devil: some of us Greeks have hailed him as an avatar of one of the gods, because he gave us autonomy, and for other reasons. I actually met the fellow, and I may be the only surviving person to whom he ever talked frankly. There are other reasons, professional reasons, concerned with something else we share, which will become obvious later.

I have to apologize for the fact that to save copying time I've left in some bits of the original report – hence the longueurs. Those passages read like sermons from the priest of Isis, or official memos, which they were. You know the College po-faced style. If they remind you that I was your professor, I hope some of the other matter will convince you that I'm human. When all this happened I was in my twenties, like you. I'm also going to start with my life history, which I've never mentioned to you, because what happened later won't be intelligible otherwise. Moreover, as you will have guessed, I am writing this not only for you, but also for my son Telesphorides, your adoptive brother.

You probably do know I was born in Smyrna. My father was Greek, and my mother half-Roman, half-Welsh (her mother was a freedwoman). The record says 'Smyrna was his home.' We did not in fact have a home. Father was a craftsman jeweller who went all over the Middle World and took us with him. The town we spent most time in was Alexandria, but we got as far as Spain and India: the only place we did not go was Rome. Father had been there, but I gather he had for some reason made Rome too hot for him, though I never asked for details.

The point of the family history is that it explains how I came to be a physician, and that in turn bears on other matters. If we hadn't run out of money in Corinth I'd probably now be teaching inlaying, and not to you.

In Corinth, we had to stay in a rather obnoxious inn while Father raised the wind. While we were there, Mother was bitten on the cheek by some insect – a bedbug, probably: Corinthian bugs are an old stage joke. But within twenty-four hours she was really ill. The bite looked angry, she had a painful scrofula, she became feverish, then delirious, and Father was beside himself. The local doctor put a honey poultice on the lesion, said it was touch-and-go, and told us to pray to Isis.

Father prayed to her, and to Apollo the Healer; but I – and I cannot for the life of me remember why, for I can only have been about six years old – prayed to Asklepios. I think I'd seen his statue, with the serpent and staff, healing a child, and that stuck in my mind. I vowed him my personal gamecock if Mother got better.

That night, I dreamed that I saw Mother. She was lying in bed, and a young physician was examining her, very carefully, very confidently. Then he turned to me and said, 'She'll be all right – *you* can heal her. Take the mouldy loaf in the cupboard and make a poultice with milk – cold milk, you understand?' He wrote down the prescription on a tablet (I can see it now) and I woke up.

Next day Mother was worse, and rather unwillingly I told Father, who had had no sleep all night, about the dream. Father was a great one for dreams. He said, 'We must do it!' He went straight to the cupboard, and there, sure enough, was an old loaf, absolutely green with mould, left by some previous occupant and never cleaned away. We made the poultice. In six hours Mother was obviously better, and by next day she was practically well. The doctor put it down to Isis. Asklepios got my pet gamecock: then I learned that Father had gone one better and vowed his son to the Gods if Mother recovered. For a while there was rather a tug of war between Isis, Apollo and Asklepios, but Mother put her foot down: I belonged to Asklepios. So as soon as I was twelve, after we returned from India, I was sent off to Cos, to the College. I worked in the herb garden, copied notes and receipts and stirred ointment. At eighteen I qualified. I still always keep a stock of mouldy bread for similar cases of rapid mortification. Sometimes it succeeds, sometimes not, and I have not been able to determine the indications reliably – but when it works, it works as fast as it did for Mother. She escaped without so much as a scar.

The episode which is the subject of this professional communication happened when I was twenty-two by Father's reckoning, ten years after I went to Cos. It, too, came about through a dream. The third case I had to treat on my own sole responsibility was a barren woman. The profession were clearly at a loss because she'd been fed on eggs and sent on a tour of shrines without ever missing a period. When she came to me it was the last stop. Her husband was threatening to divorce her, and she was going to kill herself if he did. And I couldn't send for the doctor, because blind Diodorus, who was my archiatros, had examined her already elsewhere and told her to pray to Artemis, and that, knowing Diodorus, meant that for once he didn't know what to do either.

So I told her to come back next day, and thought and went to sleep thinking, and I had another very similar dream. I was sitting in the chapel, where we keep the sacred snakes. A young physician came in from the sanctuary, drying his hands, as if he had just examined my patient. He was about my own age, but he had a truly venerable beard, and he grinned at me and said, 'Nothing wrong with the good lady, doctor. She's trying too damned hard. Give her some poppy and henbane to loosen her up a bit, tell her to reckon fourteen days to her next expected period, and then play the lioness on the cheesecutter. That should do the trick.' And he hurried out, as if to get to a clinic.

I knew all about the lioness on the cheesecutter. It's an old joke of Aristophanes, meaning sex from behind on all fours. And here was I, a junior intern, having to give that kind of prescription to a respectable married lady. I lost my nerve and went to Diodorus.

Diodorus listened – as he was blind and didn't watch one, we never knew what he was thinking. He said, 'What are you waiting for, doctor? Tell her – it's the right advice. Should have thought of it myself. And don't be embarrassed, or you'll make her embarrassed. If you hum and haw like a booby she'll take her cue from you. You're her physician. Either treat her or send for the doctor.'

I started for the door. 'Oh, and that physician you consult with in dreams,' said Diodorus, 'He may be Asklepios, but it's my guess he is your daimon. Next time you want to consult yourself, try a mirror. You could take his tip and grow a beard – it will improve your bedside manner with married ladies.'

My patient not only conceived in one, she also talked. In short order I, the junior intern, had a reproductive physiology practice – which was not only bloody ridiculous but quite terrifying, because when I started to read it up the books were congealed drivel, written by people who never attempted to father or mother a baby, judging from their notion of reproduction. I was going to have to do it all myself, on a basis of commonsense, personal experience, and hunches.

Quite suddenly, however, it became much less alarming as the hunches established a record of reliability. I was beginning to learn to trust my clinical third eye – it's a marvellous feeling, provided it's justified by results. Most of them were indeed trying too hard. I gave them poppy, henbane and reassurance. At least one couple literally didn't know how to have intercourse – I lent them an Alexandrian novel which described the procedure. One or two needed minor surgery – quite a few conceived in short order after some sour milk douches to clean up infections. Most, I am sure, were simply impatient and were going to conceive anyway. But here I was, rising twenty, never having to my certain knowledge fathered a child, though I had been through the motions often enough, surrounded by grateful pregnancy and sporting a beard fit for Zeus, let alone Asklepios. The students called me Eilythyia after the goddess of obstetrics; some rival physicians who weren't graduates of Cos put around snide stories that I was doing the work for infertile husbands, which was something I never did, but there was a feeling, I think, even among our senior physicians, that this was fringe medicine and not quite dignified. 'Ignore them,' said Diodorus, 'they're jealous, my lad.' So I did. With men whose seed was weak I was less successful, but nobody gets very good results with these cases. I didn't try any speculative treatments.

Xenocrates, who thinks the source of seed is in the brain, told me he had tried giving sterile men pieces of human brain by mouth as a form of substitution therapy – I told them to cut down on hot baths. Impotent patients, who, as you know, always put their troubles down to sorcery, are of course dead right – one treats them by white magic. Some of mine had made three pilgrimages to Lampsacus to pray Priapus for an erection. I told them to share their woman's bed, eat Lampsacus oysters, since they insisted on having a prescription of some kind, but forbade intercourse for six weeks. With the heat off, few of them lasted out the period of abstinence, though those who could not be suggested out of the habit were tough sledding.

Beside the folk who wanted children and had none, I had an equal number who didn't want any, and here, after reading some books, which were full of spells and general garbage, I used my head and did the sensible thing, which none of the panjandrums had done – I asked my mistress. I was living with a Coan girl, a silk weaver. Her name was Acte – a funny coincidence, because the Caesar's mistress was an Acte, too. Her mother had been a curandera, a wise woman, and Acte had some powers as a healer herself. She was a good deal older than I and looked after the young doctor beautifully. So the young doctor asked her how sensible girls handle such matters. Acte told me her mother had started her off using half a lemon, squeezed first, but her men didn't like it, because it was hard and got in the way, so she had cut a half lemon from a sponge and dipped it in lemon juice. That worked as well, and I'd never noticed it. Acte giggled when I told her about the clinic – all working girls knew about lemons, though the sponge was her own idea. She made a supply for my patients. Once I told Acte about the mouldy loaf which had cured Mother. 'Oh yes,' she said, 'my mother used that, too. Didn't the College know mouldy bread cures suppuration? They should put a curandera on the staff.'

It seems reproductive medicine needs no bush. I was summoned via Diodorus to attend on a Roman-Spaniard called Lucius Annaeus Gallio, who had been governor of Achaea. He was touring Greece and summoned me to consult in Athens. 'Damn his impudence,' said Diodorus, 'stop packing, and tell him to come here if he wants to see you!'

I was a bit dubious, but Gallio came, bringing his wife, and took her back to Rome pregnant. 'That,' said Diodorus, 'is big medicine. Gallio is Seneca's brother. I hope with all this baby business you aren't neglecting medicine. You're a physician of Cos, not a man-midwife, doctor.'

I wasn't. The fertility clinic took only two afternoons a week. I did ward rounds and operated regularly. When we sent a team to deal with the plague in Cyprus, I was chosen to lead it, and in Cos one was never short of general experience. And so the Gods manoeuvre us into position, Herondas, before creating lives for us.

In the year of his joint Consulship with Lucius Calpurnius Piso, Nero Claudius Caesar sent a confidential messenger to the College in Cos, requesting the services of a physician.

I was coming back from the clinic in Rhodes, and I wondered what the smart Roman packet ahead of us was doing. I was in no hurry. I collected my gear on the dockside and was looking forward to Acte, lunch and a bath, when I heard the College messenger. He was shouting 'Doctor Callimachus, emergency! Doctor Callimachus, emergency!' I left him to see my bags home and ran to the College, bumping into Charmides, my junior-apprentice, at the entrance.

'Hail, Caesar, those about to die salute thee!' said Charmides.

'Knock it off, they're paging me. Where's the fire?'

'Diodorus wants you,' said Charmides, 'They're all in there with him. You've got a new patient – bloody Caesar.'

I pushed past him and went to Diodorus' office. Nobody was around but all the office doors were ajar. And indeed they were all in there, Periander, head of Surgery, Hermodorus, head of Internal Medicine, Anaxagoras, head of Psychiatry, and Diodorus himself. Hell, I thought, someone must have complained. This is a kangaroo court. 'Sorry to waylay you,' said Diodorus, 'but this won't wait. Sit down, Callimachus. We've had a letter marked "Top Secret." ' And Hermodorus passed it over – or rather, passed them over, because there were two – holding the tablet as if he'd just taken it out of boiling water.

Caesar wrote very good Greek. The letter was in his own hand. He presented his greetings to the illustrious College and requested their assistance. His wife Octavia remained unfortunately barren, and before consulting oracles or performing any rites of a religious character, he felt it incumbent on him to exhaust all secular resources, and would esteem it a great favour if the College would dispatch to him its physician most skilled in such cases. He would welcome their nominee as his guest, reward him and the College, and all expenses would of course be paid.

Since Caesar, according to gossip, hated his wife's guts and probably no longer slept with her, this letter raised a number of questions it did not answer. The second letter was from the head of the Medical School in Rome, Aulus Celsus. He wasn't a graduate of Cos, but he was quite the best doctor in Rome now that our own archiatros, Xenophon, had retired from practice to go into politics. He would be greatly obliged if we could provide him with the benefit of a consultation in the case of a childless woman, the case being of sufficient importance to reward the expenditure of the time of a physician of Cos in travelling to Rome. Under his signature was a little Coan prescription seal. It belonged to Stertinius Xenophon, and under it he had written 'Callimachus?'

'You see,' said Diodorus, 'your merits are recognized.' In other words, I had brought it on myself. Our archiatros had fingered me personally.

The letter was in highly deferential language, but coming from Caesar, it amounted to an order. You need to know the background to understand why the Faculty looked so glum.

Our intelligence was then, and probably still is, better than that of anyone but the cornmerchants, and nothing which we had heard in the previous twenty years had made any member of the College particularly anxious to go to Rome. Whereas during the time of Augustus there had been regular lecture tours, two reigns of terror, the first under Tiberius and his chief of police Sejanus, and another under Caligula, had made Rome an unhealthy place for any professional man, and particularly for a physician. Not only is he the first and most convenient scapegoat on poisoning charges, but since, like the eunuch or the chambermaid, he is a constant witness of private and confidential matters, no conspiracy charge is complete without his testimony. Conspiracy trials were originally the invention of Sejanus, but even after he himself was executed they remained, and were still within living memory, one of the chief instruments of Roman life, for the removal of political opponents, inconvenient husbands, rich men who attract informers, and personal enemies – one could call them a national sport, second only to the arena. Only the fashionable or the greedy among physicians (which often comes to the same thing) were anxious to try their luck in Rome with this kind of threat hanging over them, and even the prospect of a quick fortune had ceased to attract quacks because of the growing practice among wealthy patients of buying a slave-physician, or consulting one of the excellent young Roman practitioners whom Aulus Cornelius Celsus was training, under considerable difficulties.

I don't for a moment imagine that you people know what the Claudian period was like. You know in theory, but history has a short memory if you weren't actually there. Men saw a little of what I mean under a Caesar whom I will not name,* but you've lived nineteen of your twenty-five years under Trajan: for you 'Caesar' means a good administrator and a competent general. Now he has gone, he has been succeeded by another Caesar in the same mould. If you'd been born twenty years earlier, and seen the accession of Nerva from years of discretion, you'd have some idea, perhaps, of the atmosphere which existed when I was in Rome, except that in my time it was far worse, and the gentleman I won't name was more private about his abuses. In Claudian times, everything was public knowledge, and what was worse, the public – the Roman public – loved it. As for those solid citizens the Senators, they still scrambled for pickings even when they were in fear of their lives. Don't let the fine old rectitude of the patricians fool you. Led by a decent, upright wolf, they can be Roman wolves, but led by a jackal they are jackals, and that was how it was then. Did you ever meet a professional informer? No. In Cos you wouldn't in any case – in Rome, spying was the most lucrative, if dangerous, profession. I won't expand on this theme. You can read, and you have access to all the histories of those unpleasant times.

About the time I went to Rome (this isn't in the books or not in detail) there had been for some time a private war, or rather a series of them, conducted by Claudius Caesar's womenfolk against all manner of persons, with the traditional weapons, poison and judicial murder. Caligula was a sick practical joker, with a grudge against Rome, who had become really dangerous after an attack of encephalitis turned him from a hoodlum into a psychopath; his final sick joke was to marry off his inoffensive uncle Claudius to a teenage prostitute called Messalina. Messalina drafted slaves, senators, charioteers and everyone else in sight as lovers, and anyone who said no was due for early

* Callimachus is referring to Domitian (A.D.81-96). He is writing in A.D. 118 or 119, two years after the accession of Hadrian.

burial. When Claudius' freedmen finally had her executed (she had just gone through a form of marriage with an ambitious young senator), the old man married Agrippina, Nero's mother, who was, if anything, worse. At this point the College was directly involved, because archiatros Xenophon was Claudius' doctor. Whether Agrippina poisoned Claudius was anyone's guess, but he was poisoned – Xenophon tried to make him vomit with a feather and was accused of trying to finish him off: at one point he had to run for his life. Xenophon swore to me that Agrippina was innocent. Claudius fancied himself among other things as a botanist, and used to pick magic mushrooms for his own table, but his eyesight was failing and he picked a death cap, or something similar – those fungi produce a couple of dozen deaths in Italy every year. Xenophon was so shaken that he retired from practice and became the young emperor Nero's Colonial Secretary, but he kept in touch with Cos, and evidently he'd heard about me. You know his monument here in Cos. The inscription originally said 'by appointment to Claudius', then 'by appointment to Nero' – now both legends have been scratched out. That just about fills in the background. No wonder the faculty weren't overpleased with their junior member.

'Well, gentlemen?' said Hermodorus.

There were no volunteers. Everyone was looking at me.

Periander, the Head of Surgery, got up, opened the doors carefully, looked outside to make sure nobody was listening, and rejoined the group.

'Gods,' I thought, 'we might be in Rome already!' The wretched piece of wax seemed to have brought a cloud with it, even here in the bright sunshine of Cos, where people didn't often listen at doors.

'Well,' said Periander, 'we shall need some time to think about this one. We could stall, I suppose. Ask him if she's tried sleeping on the Island.' The Island is the site of a medical temple, in the middle of the Tiber, where people go for a 'dream cure'. Some of the dream analysts there are said to do good work with mental illness, and it has become a fashionable place to send sick slaves, but the cure is so long that some masters got tired of paying fees and abandoned them there, until Claudius made a law against it. Not quite the thing for Caesar's wife. Our Head of Psychiatry, Anaxagoras, who doesn't work with dreams, ruffled up like a wet bird and said we shouldn't validate that sort of quackery, even to gain time. I said nothing about dreams.

'You know what it is,' said Periander, 'either Caesar is going to get rid of his wife because she is barren, or he's simply about to get rid of his wife. Gentlemen, we are in the middle.'

'Oh no,' said Hermodorus, 'I don't think so. I agree it's an odd letter for Caesar to write, and I know he is said to hate Octavia. But he may need a child for dynastic reasons. And this, Gentlemen, is a new Caesar. *I* don't know any ill of him – he is said to be dissolute, but he's young and a Roman – my reports say that he's a poet, a reasonably good musician, and he was raised by philosophers. Aren't we overreacting a little? At least he hasn't written us an Imperial Order, simply a civil request in very good Greek and in his own handwriting. Someone will have to go.'

'Oh no,' said Diodorus, 'Callimachus will have to go. Nobody else knows the stuff. And Callimachus speaks fluent Latin.'

'They all speak Greek,' said Anaxagoras.

'The women, too?' said Diodorus, 'You may be able to discuss such delicate matters with a lady, Anaxagoras, but wouldn't you prefer to do it in her own language?'

I didn't say anything, nor did anyone else.

'Or do you think I should go myself? Even the Romans won't execute a blind man,' said Diodorus.

'No, of course I'll go,' I said.

'Actually,' said Diodorus, 'you don't run any risk. You and Nero are the same age. I have a feeling you may be able to – er – communicate. I don't need to tell you, my boy, that it will be a profitable mission, medically and, if you care about that, financially. Also, you'll be carrying the reputation of this College. I don't need to tell you to stay away from liquor, and women, and courtiers – particularly courtiers: *all* Romans are dissembling sons of bitches nowadays; oh yes, I know your grandfather was one, but that was some time ago – they've gone downhill since. The best of Greek luck to you, and try to come home in one piece.'

The worst of it was that I knew what they were thinking – that I'd got above myself, with my questionable counselling practice, that now I'd involved the College in an embarrassing situation – something that was simply not done. It would be remembered: I could say goodbye to any idea of being archiatros one distant day, because professional colleagues have long, long memories.

'I'm sorry, Diodorus,' I said when the others had gone. 'I'm afraid this is my fault. It was due to excess of zeal.'

He looked at me, unseeing, but at me still. 'No, no, certainly not,' he said. 'We should be complimented. Never apologize for curing people. And use the opportunity. I'm perfectly serious – I'd go myself if I could talk to the lady in Latin. I suppose it's a dangerous assignment, but you tackled the plague, didn't you? We're a bit like soldiers in this kind of situation. I can't assess the risk, but you know enough to be careful – besides, you're not only a good doctor, you've got a sixth sense for trouble, and your footwork is a joy to watch.' I report this compliment because of what followed. 'Just make sure you aren't too clever by half; if you get into unnecessary trouble, that is how you will do it. Romans have little sense of humour and Roman emperors none whatever. So if you want to be sure of keeping your head on your shoulders, keep you mouth shut and your eyes open and play it strictly by the book. With any luck you'll find it a very interesting assignment, and you'll meet Celsus. I want to know what his group is doing.'

'Come clean,' I said, 'why did archiatros Xenophon arrange this? Normally the College would consult and send Caesar advice, or tell him to consult an oracle – or Aulus Celsus.'

Diodorus didn't answer, but focussed his disconcerting blind stare on the window.

'Ever since the Xenophon affair,' I said, 'it's been College policy not to risk our people in Rome.'

'Yes,' said Diodorus, 'but now we have to know the score.'

'About Caesar?'

'About Caesar. We need a first-hand report on his medical condition.'

'You mean, is he dangerous?'

Diodorus nodded.

'Well, couldn't the archiatros make a diagnosis himself?'

'He could,' said Diodorus, 'and he has, and he wants a second opinion.'

'He thinks Nero is another Caligula?'

'No. But remember, it is on the archiatros that the future of this College, and of Greece itself, depends. He's doing his share. He wants a second opinion.'

'Mine?'

'Evidently. You have an opening here to unofficial observation which he doesn't have. Plenty of people in Rome recognize that the archiatros has nationalistic ambitions in mind. He has to be very cautious. And so will you have to be.

You will be the eyes and the ears of the College.'

'So he picked me?' I said.

'No,' said Diodorus, 'I did. Say, if you like, that you've been my eyes – and very successfully. You may blame me.'

I didn't blame him, but the sheer complexity of this whole double-agent operation struck me as overwhelming and a bit unmedical. Caesar was playing some kind of game – so much was clear. Xenophon, who was working for the independence of Greece and the privileges of the College, was playing another. The College itself was trying to plant me on Caesar to see if he was unbalanced. I was on the point of saying that this wasn't medicine. But at that point Diodorus looked at me as if he saw me, and repeated a phrase which, if I were to set it down, you and many others would recognize, and also the occasion on which it is spoken.

I didn't understand. 'How,' I asked, 'are those matters related to these?'

'Only,' replied Diodorus, 'that it is not Caesar's sanity that interests us. We need to know if by any chance he may be worthy of a particular step he intends to take. If he is, it might be extraordinarily important for Rome, and, of course, for us.'

At last I saw what was in the wind. 'Do you mean to say that he has applied?' I said. 'After all, he need only present himself at Eleusis.'

'Which being Caesar he could hardly do incognito. And with his family history, we have to be extremely careful,' said Diodorus. In writing for your eyes, Herondas, I don't need to explain what was worrying him. We all know that there are those for whom the experience of enlightenment, by reason of the means we employ to attain it, can be harmful. Xenophon was worried, and with reason. If Nero was unstable, and if he insisted on pursuing spiritual goals unfitted for him, we were in line for some bad trouble.

'We can talk frankly,' said Diodorus, 'and we ought to. Wouldn't want you to go into this without your eyes open – it's a literal den of lions. You know what Stertinius Xenophon is doing?'

I said I gathered he was trying to preserve some privileges for Greece, which wasn't an over-popular project in the Roman tax-farming industry.

'Xenophon,' said Diodorus, lowering his voice, 'is out to get independence for Greece. As much independence as one can get without threatening the pashas in Rome.'

'How much independence will that be?'

'Don't ask. He doesn't know. But that's the Great Project.'

'Nero likes Greece, I gather.'

'He does – in fact he's gone overboard for being Greek himself.'

'Hence the application to Eleusis?'

'Precisely. Now, we have to know. A and 1, Nero's religious enthusiasms are pretty ill-focussed. There are other people out to fill the philosophical vacuum – he'd be a catch. Imagine an emperor in search of an affiliation, with an empty head that needs filling.'

'Who else is trying?'

'Well, the Jews for one. But we're in touch with them. Talk to Dr. Bar Cochba, before you go, about that. He'll fill you in.'

'He can't be a Jew and an initiate,' I said.

'They know that, and he can't be a Jew in any case. Can you see a Caesar getting circumcised and keeping the dietary laws? All they want is to get recognition – and see he doesn't let his colonial officials start a religious war by deifying him. That *would* put the fat in the fire.'

'And the other thing?' I said.

'B and 2,' said Diodorus, 'is the other thing you refer to. It's his idea, not ours. He's been sending feelers to Eleusis.'

'Good for the Project, or bad?'

'Depends how you might look at it, said Diodorus. 'If he's in his right mind, it might cement his allegiance to Greece. It also might be a handle for some of the hardline opposition, but we think he can handle that. But if he's unstable, or borderline, we'll have to warn Eleusis. They can arrange some kind of mummery for him – we can't risk the genuine experience. It's an extremely tough choice. Bar Cochba's worried about it even more than I am. Roman Caesars who have – unusual – experiences are apt to discover that they are gods. Caesar tells all his friends how like Dionysus he looks. You follow?'

'I follow,' I said, 'and I wish I'd known about this before I came back here. I'd have shammed sick, or dead.'

'You wouldn't,' said Diodorus. 'You've got a well-developed sense of professional duty.'

'Anything else?'

'Yes. The Project also wants to provide Caesar with the right woman. It'll help.'

'Who's the right woman?'

'Well, not Octavia, and she's on the way out in any case, poor child. Never had a chance. Bar Cochba thinks it should be a lady called Poppaea. She's the wife of a crony of Nero, and they share her. We think it's Poppaea you will be treating.'

'What a delightful bunch!'

'I agree, I agree. It's not a pleasant assignment. But both the College and the Project have to depend on your ingenuity. It's a providential opportunity.'

'How about the rest of the Faculty?' I asked. 'Do they know the score? It didn't sound to me as if they did.'

'Oh no. They, as you recognize no doubt, are an ordinarily skilful and thickheaded lot of doctors. You and I are the only two who have eaten from the tabor and drunk from the cymbal, Callimachus. And have consequently learned to keep our mouths shut.'

'Is there *anyone* I can talk to?'

'Talk to Bar Cochba. He knows. And he's our liaison with the rabbinate – they have to be kept briefed. Nobody else has any need to know.'

I thought about Acte. Obviously I wouldn't tell her. But Diodorus was a natural mind-reader.

'Your lady is one of us, I know, Callimachus,' he said, 'but I think even so I wouldn't tell her much.'

'I won't,' I said, wondering if she would worm some of it out of me – Acte had a way of making good guesses: it must have been inherited from her wise-woman mother.

'How about Seneca?'

'He's obviously our link, but don't trust him. Xenophon doesn't. He's pro-Greek and he's been told a bare minimum.'

'Not about the Project?'

'Indeed not. You'll have to case him for us, but don't let him pump you – he's a Roman, for all his philosophical airs, and Romans are bad news. Mind you, I'm not a racist, but – well, you know damn well that it's true. That place gets to people – the money, the atmosphere. You'll understand when you go there.'

'So trust nobody whatsoever?'

'Absolutely right.'

By now, Herondas, I was in over my ears. It wasn't as frightening as you'd think, because I was young, and Diodorus had convinced me that the job had to be done. I didn't fancy the sub-plots, but clearly the interest of the College was involved, so it was a proper and ethical mission, and any information I got would be communicated only within the profession.

A genuinely enlightened Roman emperor on a spiritual quest would be one thing, especially if he was a Hellenophile. A borderline Roman emperor who already had delusions of divinity was going to be a disaster, and his search for enlightenment by inappropriate means was going to be hard to resist.

'It is our rule,' said Diodorus, 'that one may not speak ill of initiation, and that it is still better to speak neither good nor ill. But if in your judgment Nero Caesar is a bad risk, I think you are absolved – speak as ill of it as you like, tell him it's contemptible mummery. You understand?'

'I understand,' I replied. 'Who put him up to this? Seneca?'

'Possibly,' said Diodorus, 'but possibly not – Nero Caesar likes to think of himself as a Greek. He's on a number of Hellenistic trips. He's also a spiritual glutton, hungry for every sort of enlightenment, provided it's exotic – he talks at length to Babylonian rabbis, then worships Atargatis and thoroughly offends the Jews.'

I told him that if Nero wanted enlightenment he had better go and chop wood for Kapila.

Kapila had been my old guru in India when I was only a boy. It was he who had sent me to Eleusis.

Bar Cochba, who was about my age, was washing his hands in his office.

I told him Diodorus had briefed me and told me to see him and asked him what in Hades was going on. Also why it was I who had to stick my neck out.

'Obvious reasons,' said Bar Cochba, 'You're the one they wanted. Also any Jew in Rome is sticking his neck out, and I'm delighted to see a gentile taking his share.'

'What are your chaps up to?'

'Limited objective. Sooner or later the bloody heathen try to deify Caesars for state reasons, or the Caesars do it themselves. Then they defile our Temple, there's a riot, and Jews have to die for their faith. Simple as that.'

'What's the plan? Convert this Caesar and head him off?'

'Not convert him – *we* don't want him. But we were on good terms with Claudius. We simply want him to be educated. Then he won't make ignorant blunders we have to bleed for.'

'Give him a Jewish guru?'

'We should be so lucky. But as a matter of fact, his dissolute friend's wife, with whom he commits adultery, has a rabbi as her spiritual adviser. No, he isn't preaching to her – it's not her fault, and God looked with favour on Rahab and spared her house. We gave up trying to inculcate morals into pagans years ago. We simply live alongside them and keep our own counsel. I told Diodorus I thought this was the lady Caesar really wants you to check. He couldn't care less about his wife.'

'This is Poppaea?'

'Correct.'

'And she'd be a plus for you?'

'Hopefully. And for you.'

'Better give me the rabbi's name,' I said. 'Can I talk to the Jews in Rome?'

'Only the people I list for you. They're all physicians. And mind you, talk to the right Jews – the people Annaeus Seneca corresponds with are a sect of messianic heretics.'

I told him I'd like the list. I couldn't tell Jewish sects apart.

'Nor can the Romans, unfortunately. When the heretics make trouble they kill the orthodox.'

'You want me to take any action?'

'No. You'll do the wrong thing. Leave Judaea to us. As for the messianists, leave them alone – at least they won't encourage Caesar to demand divine honours.'

Bar Cochba sat down and started writing the list – Greek on one side, Aramaic on the other, so there wouldn't be any confusion over the names.

He passed it over. 'God bless you and keep you, colleague,' he said. 'Some of our best friends are gentiles. They have public baths in Rome where men and women are as naked as dogs. Your lack of modesty and your uncircumcision will be a real protection. Don't get that or anything else cut off, will you? Those bastards are dangerous – we should know. You just come back in one piece, and you shall share shabbat with my family.'

I told him I'd be honoured, and went to find Acte.

Acte was where she was supposed to be – in the store, laying out the bundles of herbs on drying racks. She didn't put down her plants to kiss me, and I might have been with her the night before and only slipped out to go to the College, instead of having been away for weeks, but Acte is like that.

'Are you well?' she asked.

'Yes, well. And you?'

'I am well. Apart from missing you – but I've been busy. Don't tell me,' she said, 'you've got to go away again.'

'I'm afraid so.' She always knew, which saved me the trouble of telling her.

'For long?'

I told her I hoped not, but couldn't be sure how long it would take.

'Where?'

'Rome this time. It's for the College.'

'The College,' said Acte, 'doesn't send people to Rome.'

'They do this time. They have a consult.'

'When?'

'In about five days.'

'Then,' said Acte, 'that gives us five days.'

'And five nights.'

She smiled and said, 'It isn't much time.'

I took her out to dinner, and we ate looking over the harbour. She was the only woman in the inn, but Acte was used to that too, and nobody ever passed comments. I told her I was going to need her help to get ready – after all, we couldn't make love all the time – and I wanted to be sure my medicaments were fresh, not trusting the stuff I might be able to buy in Rome. I'd be taking the minimum, including the old poppy-and-henbane, plus some of the standard medications, and Acte was going to have to do some dispensing, because I wanted to take a good, fresh batch of nepenthe.

'Nepenthe,' said Acte. 'You aren't going to perform any surgery, are you?'

I told her I wasn't, so far as I knew.

'Then,' said Acte, 'there's more to this visit than you've told me. I'm not going to ask questions. But be very, very careful – please.'

I assured her that it was all right, that I was going to consult with the great physician Aulus Celsus and he'd look after me.

'Then who's the nepenthe for?'

'Nobody in particular. But Rome is Rome, and it's easier to make a rear exit if everyone's sound asleep.'

Acte didn't pump me. 'When you come back,' she said, 'you can do something about my infertility.'

'Any time you say – but let's both digest our meal first.'

'I don't mean that. I believe you don't want me to bear a child.'

I didn't, but it was hardly the time to say so. 'Try taking out the sponge,' I said. 'I hope you won't be too lonely.'

'I have plenty of company,' said Acte, 'but only one Callimachus. And I haven't used a sponge for some months when I'm with you. Be careful, Callimachus. With what you say, with women, with Romans.'

'I will indeed. Either I'll be back or I'll send for you. Celsus will pay your passage.'

'You'll be back,' said Acte. 'If you wouldn't, the omens would show it, and I'd warn you. But I want your child first. At the moment we're wasting time.'

As it was we waited for the sunset. When it was dark I lit a pine splint from the grill, paid the account, and took her home. When I woke next day I was alone. She'd gone out early to pick the ingredients for nepenthe. When she came in she put them to steep in wine and came back to me. And when I finally left, there was no fuss – in fact, we said a sober goodbye in the storehouse among the bundles of drying herbs. She was matter-of-fact and rather pleased with herself, because she'd dreamed she had given birth to a boy. I was arranging how she could let me know if the dream was accurate, but she said, 'No need – it's true. I'm telling you now, so I don't need to send messages.'

'If I'm not back when he's delivered, tell Diodorus. The College will enroll him.'

'As young as that?'

'He's the son of a physician.'

'And,' said Acte, 'of a healer mother. The Gods go with you.'

I went to the College, and the whole damn Faculty escorted me to the ship as if I were on my way to burial. The ship they sent was not, in fact, a packetboat, but a royal yacht which had belonged to Tiberius. My cabin was sandalwood, containing a king-sized bed with some interesting carvings, chiefly homosexual – anyhow the venue was wasted, since Acte wasn't coming with me. In fact I took nobody, not even the personal scout provided by the College to press my clothes; there were two imperial bat-boys allocated to look after me, and I wanted to look austere. The boys looked as if they doubled as concubines, but I didn't enquire, and they did their job. Most of the voyage I read the books I had brought.

I suspect, Herondas, that you know as much about Romans as I do, even if you never saw them at home. Menippus called them 'the locusts', because they have swarmed all over Greece. It is hard to sum them up, because of all people they are the most contradictory – I don't know any other nation which manages to be both stuffy and debauched, or both unimaginative and devious, at one and the same time. I'm not a racist, and I had a Roman grandfather; also I have been in a great many places where customs were uncouth and life cheap. So my main reaction, when I was dropped into Rome, all raw, wasn't so much dislike (that has come later) but rather blank incomprehension. One of the first things I saw was a poster – which I took down, and have today: you can say I stole it, though I prefer to regard it as a specimen. It reads:

Cn. Vatinius, Praetor, in honour of
the Shades of his father and the
Divine Caesar Augustus
presents

A GALA PERFORMANCE

200 SWORDSMEN 200
NO QUARTER
S50,000 in audience prizes
Morning:
Killing of Lions and Getulian Elephants
Acrobatic sex show

Well, thanks to the civilizing mission of Rome we've now got similar shows in Greece, and people apparently enjoy them. They are Rome's thumbprint. But a square Roman would have strongly disapproved – of the sexual acrobats, not the 199 dead men. People like Seneca were as disgusted by that as any Greek; so, as a matter of fact, was Nero (both of them would have preferred the sex show, which was harmless and instructive, if sleazy), but Rome isn't about to change. It arranged matters so that they destroyed each other, and the shows go on.

Another vignette: You've been to a few executive stag parties in Greece, as we all have, and you probably found them as cheap as I do – too much to eat and drink, whores, but at least music and a certain amount of pseudo-intellectual conversation to go with them. Not my taste, but harmless enough, if you enjoy that kind of thing. Romans, by contrast, don't engage in clever talk when drinking. Worse still, they have no sense of fun. Picture a middle-aged Roman executive playboy in a tax-collecting corporation entertaining his friends and his competitors, and their wives, at dinner. His drinks are poured by a painted, naked Syrian boy with a gold wig and gilded genitals, who kneels beside him, lies on top of him, or climbs all over him. One minute they are engaged in heavy petting – the next, the boy is ferociously beaten for spilling something: all this before the entire company and the host's wife. The point is not that it's typical (I've been to some decent, and dull, Roman occasions), but that when it happens nobody leaves, and they'll all accept the next invitation. Seneca complains that the poor boy will be kept artificially juvenile and his beard plucked into his twenties, and that his growth will suffer from late hours and being awakened constantly to service his master. Precisely as the executive's rich friends will come to his next party, even while laughing at him, we Greeks, between laughter and scorn, still go to Rome to make fortunes. So I suppose we are not in a position to talk.

Some things they do splendidly – war, of course, engineering, public architecture (the heavy kind – anything at all spirited is usually Greek).

The thing I can't stomach about Romans isn't their brutality but their seriousness. They have this incredible, bovine, po-faced approach to everything. Whether it's poetry, debauchery, administration or architecture, there isn't a spark of humour in it. In consequence, they get the rulers they deserve – either flatfootedly righteous or frankly psychopathic, and they're equally serious about both kinds. Caligula's jokes were Roman jokes, and Roman jokes are not funny. Neither, I assure you, are Roman patients, especially top Roman patients. One of the pathetic things about Nero Caesar when I followed his case was to see Rome swallowing him up – a process which he was too disorganized to resist and which I couldn't stop.

What Romans do raise in a particularly acute form, since they will not go away, and we have to live with them, are the basic issues of medical ethics: not just cross-cultural, but general. How does one doctor a nation of serious-minded gangsters who have no imagination and no sense of fun? I've been criticized by some people in Cos for trying to treat them at all: leave them to soothsayers and quacks, some physicians say – you can only treat human beings, not imperialists who are something else. I don't agree, however, and I don't think we should let distaste for our patients get in the way of healing. If one starts to ask which patients are worth healing, one risks becoming a Roman oneself.

The middle-aged doctor standing by the couch had to be Aulus Celsus. The plump senatorial figure, fat face, weak chin, executive responsibility wrinkles, was the owner of this vast establishment, Lucius Seneca. Every so often one meets in the flesh someone whom one has known as a public reputation and is flabbergasted by the bad casting: the lyrical poet who looks like a pugilist, the great surgeon who looks like a bath attendant. Seneca was the finest example I can recall. When I was a child I used to trace figures from books and cut out paper clothes to put on them – making Alexander the Great into a fisherman, or Cato into a centurion. Seneca was the figure without the clothes. I looked more like a Stoic philosopher than he did. As a tycoon, he would do – tycoons come in many kinds – but he had far more the look of a browbeaten employee. As a dramatist ...

'Doctor Callimachus,' said Seneca. 'Welcome. We're most grateful to you.' And the voice didn't fit either – a fine rhetorician's voice: how could it come out of that face?

'My family owes you a great deal already. Lucius Annaeus Gallio is my brother, you know?' The toga, too, didn't belong on that fat Spaniard. I greeted him, as host, then Celsus.

'I hope you had a good journey,' said Seneca. 'Make yourself at home. I'm going to make my excuses, so that you and Aulus Celsus can consult – we're expecting the Caesar in about an hour.' The man positively fled. I was left staring at Celsus.

'Yes,' said Celsus, 'it's been a difficult time for Lucius. I'm delighted you got here so quickly. We ought to talk medicine before Caesar gets here. Do you mind getting rid of the formalities?' And he handed me the little soft wax tablet, like a triptych with two of its leaves closed. I pressed my thumb on it and gave it back – I remember being surprised that someone not of our College knew our mode of recognition. Celsus opened the closed leaf and carefully compared the print with that of the sealed part of the tablet, and then visibly unwound.

'I'm sorry to spring that on you,' he said, 'but we can't take chances. We must consult now and keep civilities for later.'

'I'm ready,' I said, and moved towards the couch. I imagined we'd sit down.

'We'll talk while walking,' said Celsus. 'I like to consult while walking.' He steered me into the garden, but when we got there he said not a word – he was headed out into a circle of lawn with a fountain in the middle. When we got to it, he planted himself facing the vomiting dolphins, put a hand on my shoulder and manoeuvred me alongside. There was enough white noise from the water to prevent eavesdropping. 'We'll talk towards the fountain,' said Celsus, 'some of 'em can lipread.'

'It's as bad as that?'

'It's as bad as that. Now, listen carefully, because I'm going to give you the whole background – no, don't take notes, you'll have to remember it. Never take notes here. Claudius used to write notes in Etruscan, but they still got read.'

'I'll have to get used to this,' I said.

'You will – I'm still getting over my relief that the real Callimachus got here. Seneca was scared breathless that you'd turn out to be a ringer. That was what was wrong with him.'

'Where did you get my tablet?' I asked. I nearly added, how do I know that you're Celsus, since we're playing games.

'From Stertinius Xenophon, your archiatros. Now, listen, because we don't have much time. Nero Caesar is twenty – ye Gods, you can't be much older – his real name was Lucius Domitius Ahenobarbus. He's got a red beard and body hair like all the Ahenobarbuses, it's dominant. *Never* call him that if you want to stay out of trouble. His mother is Agrippina, Caligula's sister. She married Claudius, and Claudius adopted him. You're about to meet him. Don't ask the question – yes, he's got problems, but he's handling them well. Far better than I thought he would. He's extremely intelligent, and he's letting Seneca and Burrus run the Council – Rome is better governed now than at any time since Divine Augustus died. It's absolutely vital that doesn't get upset, and Nero Caesar doesn't get upset, and that's why you are here. Even though nominally he isn't your patient.'

'What problems?' I asked.

'His mother, for one. She's Medusa with a taste for being Empress. You've seen the coins – obverse, divine Agrippina; reverse, in homage to Nero Caesar. That about sums it up. Nero slept in her bed until he was fifteen. After that he slept in Seneca's. Seneca was his tutor.'

'I thought Seneca was an ascetic philosopher,' I said.

'He is,' said Celsus. 'He's also a millionaire and a

guilt-stricken libertine. His interests are ambition, money, philosophy and impulse gratification, in that order. Odd chap. Don't you know anything about his pass at the Caesar? It's ancient history, but it did a vast amount of harm. Caesar panics over women, and every time he panics he goes back to boys or father figures. We're trying to build him up into an adult.'

'His wife?' I queried.

'She's your patient. Daughter of Claudius and Messalina – saw her mother in action: it was one of Messalina's kicks to make love in front of her kids. Then she stood by while her mother was told to stab herself, and failed, and was finally dragged out and stabbed by a top sergeant.'

'So Nero and Octavia are a couple of psychiatric accidents looking for a place to happen,' I said.

'They've happened. Agrippina married them off when Octavia was fifteen,' said Celsus. 'His mother encouraged him to rape house-girls to make him manly: when she found out about Seneca's tutorials, that is – he tried to rape the child on their wedding night, she got vaginismus and is terrified of men, he's obsessed with his mother and terrified of women.'

'This I have to cure?' I asked, 'Why?'

'Nero asked us to arrange for Octavia to see a counsellor. That's why,' replied Celsus.

'You mean he wants to get her functioning?'

'That's the odd part – no, he doesn't. His mother's taken her over, and they're both tarred with the same brush in his eyes.'

'So?'

'You'll have to find out what he wants. It isn't Octavia as a functioning spouse. He's got a very sensible mature lady called Acte who has done him a world of good – used to be a very good singer, too, in her stage career, and Nero loves music.'

'My mistress is called Acte,' I said. 'That's funny.'

'Not funny, reassuring – when they told me about you I was afraid you were a wonder-boy with a medical scroll instead of the usual equipment,' said Celsus. 'You need a sex life to understand Claudians. I'm glad you've got one, but don't exercise it here, or you'll be got at.'

'If it's Acte not Octavia he wants me to see, it should be much easier. With Octavia's heredity ...'

'Don't ever theorize about Claudian heredity. Nobody knows who fathered whom in their family. Let me go on, and you'll see what I mean. Octavia had a brother, out of Messalina, ostensibly by Claudius – I think she was in foal when they married. The horse could have been anyone, but it was probably Caligula himself. Nice picture.'

'That was Britannicus?'

'Right.'

'He was supposed to be the next Caesar, not Nero.'

'Right.'

'And he's dead.'

'Right. He died at Nero's table. I didn't see the body, but he either choked or had a cerebral haemorrhage. Agrippina thinks Nero poisoned him.'

'And did he?' I asked.

'At his own dinner table in front of his mother?' said Celsus.

'No, I suppose not.'

'Nero would gladly have strangled him, because the little beast called him Lucius Domitius all the time. They hated each other, when they weren't seducing each other. But Nero hates violence. Dead puppies, or swordfighters, make him physically sick.'

'And he's a Roman?' I said.

'You don't like us much, do you, doctor?' said Celsus. 'Between ourselves, neither do I. And neither does Caesar. He wasn't born in Rome. His father threatened to dress him as a girl, and Nero says he preferred that to being the kind of Roman his father was. He was brought up to be a mime artist, by a Greek mime artist. He speaks Greek and dresses as a Greek. You'll like him.'

'And in fact,' I said, 'Nero is my patient. You and Seneca want me to keep him Greek but give him enough confidence to stay alive in Rome. Is that about the size of it?'

'They teach well in Cos,' said Celsus. 'None of my students would have said that. They'd have wanted to make a man of him, meaning a Roman goon. They have crew cuts and get jobs as army surgeons. They volunteer to treat gladiators so they can get tickets to the swordfights. You see why Seneca wanted a Greek physician.'

'I know what you're thinking, however,' I said.

'What's that, doctor?'

'That you've got a boy to do a man's job.'

Celsus put his hand on my shoulder. 'Hercules, no. I was dead scared I would get that, when I heard you were his age. But Seneca thought it was an advantage. And now I've had the pleasure of this consultation, I know what I have. And not just the beard – you talk as if you've been treating Claudians and dodging transcervical cephalectomy all your life. Just don't be too smart, however. These people have live ammunition, remember. You aren't in Cos now. Don't trust anyone. Not even me. Don't talk. Don't have friends. Don't make notes. And for Isis' sake take this seriously.'

'I do,' I said. 'Who's the opposition? The mother?'

Celsus nodded. 'Mostly. There are other operators. You'll have to pass her to get to Octavia, if that's going to be the play. That's probably your cover, so you must do it according to the art.'

'You don't think,' I said, 'that Caesar wants a physician to waste the wife for him? Or the mother? Or both? Because if so, I'm not going to oblige.'

'Caesar may do that one day,' said Celsus, 'but not now – he's like Catullus' lover where Mother is concerned. He hates and loves.'

'And later on?' I said.

'If it ever did happen, or anyone else tries any similar propositions on you, stall them and run for it. Don't stop to pack. Just send word to Seneca that your father is ill – he'll know what to do. And one more thing – I'm honoured to present you with a copy of my *Principles of Medical Practice*. Here you are.'

I thanked him with suitable deference.

'Never mind the thanks,' said Celsus, 'just listen. If ever I send you a second copy of the same work with my sincere regards, be out of Rome and at sea within three hours. Don't pack, don't argue, and don't contact me. Just run. Understood?'

'Understood.'

'Good. Seneca's signalling back there. We have an audience. Come on. And I hope you have a good memory.'

I assured him I had.

'And incidentally,' said Celsus, 'don't be scared if you're shadowed. Take no notice. Burrus is laying on a babysitter for you. We think it's wiser. Shall we go in?'

We went back into the house, and without the slightest warning I came face to face with Caesar.

He was a stout, chunky young man, built like a wrestler, or a big child. His hair was curly and bronze-yellow, the Ahenobarbus colour. He had the slightly varnished, over-clean appearance of persons in office or stage performers, but it was a stage performer he most resembled, a popular music singer or a mime. I'd expected the senatorial toga, but he wore a flowered shirt with a gold lion clasp at the shoulder. Round his neck was a thong, from which hung a gold charm of the Syrian mermaid-goddess Atargatis. He was hot and smelt of lotion.

I said, 'Hail Caesar.'

'Callimachus,' he said in Greek, 'I'm so grateful to you – coming all this way at such short notice.' And he embraced me. It was odd: we were about the same age but I felt him treating me as much his senior. Everyone switched to Greek (Celsus spoke it very badly) and Seneca sent for refreshments. Celsus drank wine, Seneca water. I took hydromel, unfermented, according to our usual practice. Seneca said to Nero, 'You'll take your special brew?' Nero nodded, and quite a performance began. The servant had a big bucket of ice, and water boiling in a copper kettle over charcoal: a glass was put in the ice, the boiling water poured in, and the whole thing left to cool. Nero waited patiently for it. 'It's my invention,' he said, seeing that I was staring at the operation, 'for my voice, you know.' We all stood round waiting for someone to jump first. Celsus finally did.

'I've been talking to Doctor Callimachus,' he said, 'but of course I couldn't tell him exactly what was in your mind, Caesar. Will you do that now?'

These middle-aged men were horribly uncomfortable before this young man – they were stretched, trying to treat him as one of themselves while their eyes said 'child', and Caesar himself responded with a kind of uneasy surliness.

'You couldn't tell him, Celsus, because I didn't tell you, did I?' said Caesar. 'I want to talk to the doctor myself. Callimachus, you probably think we're bewitched: Hercules, I can feel the tension in this group. Do *you* know why I asked you to come?'

'I understand you want me to see a barren woman, Caesar – your own wife, I imagine,' I said.

'Right, right, I do. I'll talk to you myself about it privately in a couple of days. It's better that way. Celsus thinks I ought to have consulted him, but this is a family matter, and I wanted a stranger. You understand that? It's easier with an out-of-town doctor; Rome's too like a village – if your wife's barren you don't want to talk about it to the village midwife. Not that Celsus is the village midwife – it's all right, Callimachus, don't look shocked, I'm not insulting him; Lucius Annaeus and he have been through all this with me – no professional feelings being hurt. Stertinius Xenophon suggested you, I asked Celsus to invite you.'

'And to make sure I wasn't being impersonated, Caesar,' I said.

'Right,' said Nero. 'I'm not crazy – Lucius will tell you it was quite possible. This is a horrible place to live, Callimachus – particularly when you find yourself responsible for it. I wasn't to come until they'd made sure you were yourself.' He put his finger in the iced water, then drank it. 'And forgive me, I wanted to see if you were someone I could talk to.'

'Well, Caesar, can you?' I asked.

Nero suddenly took me by both hands. 'Hercules, yes. We're of an age, aren't we? Man, I thought they were sending a high-powered greybeard.'

'A high-powered beard, Caesar,' I said, 'but not a grey beard – at least not yet. I'm at your service.'

'Right, right,' said Nero. 'I was terrified of you. You're a load off my mind, doctor. We can talk, yes.'

'We'll talk whenever you wish, then.'

'We can't yet – I'll explain everything later. Lucius is going to make you comfortable for tonight. Come up to the palace if you want, and conduct me to the Games, but I've got to be official, so don't be offended if I never met you before. You know your cover story?'

'No, Caesar – I take it I need one?' I said.

'You need one,' said Seneca. 'You've come to Rome to set up briefly in consultant practice, bringing letters to me from my brother Gallio, and I've introduced you to Caesar so you can solicit custom from the Imperial household.'

I told Caesar that that was acceptable, so far as I was concerned, but I would prefer for practical reasons to know against whom the cover was directed. He wasn't offended. Obviously we had established rapport.

'My mother, for one,' said Nero. 'I'll tell her the tale later – Octavia lives with her, and you'll have to get past her eventually. You need a cover so that I can let her into a secret – then she won't go prying. If I told her you were coming to see Octavia in the first place she'd think I was lying and start to poke around – isn't that right, Lucius?' Seneca nodded. 'Very well,' Nero added, 'we haven't met today. Callimachus, my friend, we'll talk when the time is ripe.' And he left.

It had been odd, brittle and unreal. Emperors are not men of one's own age. They do not dress like entertainers. They do not blush when they talk to another male and telegraph reassurance, seductiveness, and dangerous personal emotions. I could see that there would be a narrow line here between supportive friendship, impossible demands, political danger, and homosexual transference – all bundled up in one relationship with a patient who was not ostensibly my patient at all, and who could order my execution if I misplayed. On the other hand, I thought I had gained control, in a genial way, but sufficiently to establish safe distance. The first five minutes of the first psychiatric interview are the most important for what follows – mess them up, and you are in trouble, but I was satisfied on that count. What made me anxious was not this imperial hazard-patient, but the resemblance Acte had seen – probably on a coin, for she had not seen the man. Steady, I thought, it's the man you are to deal with. He drinks iced water, not wine. He wears a flowered shirt, not a leopard-skin. I put the pattern out of mind. It belongs in good psychiatry, but one has to control arbitrary associations, and I had done. Nero wouldn't have read back subliminally what I saw looking over his shoulder.

It had been a far odder interview than it sounds in telling. They all appeared to be playacting to one another and to me. You could have cut the air with a knife, but when Nero left so did the tension. Seneca became human – he picked up Nero's iced water glass and finished it.

Celsus took his leave. 'I've got quarters for you,' he said, 'a doctor's office. If you stayed here with Lucius it wouldn't square with the story about going into practice. I think you'll like it – you've got a cook, a housekeeper and a pharmacist. They're all screened, but still be careful. You're just a visiting consultant drumming up a practice. Be suitably surprised when Caesar sends for you. Good luck.'

When Celsus had gone, Seneca took me into his study. It was a pigsty of books, papers, statuettes, accounts. He pushed them into piles to make a place to seat us.

I watched his fat, anxious face relax. He was in his burrow here, evidently.

'This is where I write,' he said.

I told him I knew some of his work.

'The plays, or the letters?'

'Neither. The doctoral thesis you wrote on Indian ethnology. I read the letters afterwards,' I said.

He seemed pleased and a bit defensive. 'Didn't know anyone still read my writings on India. May I guess what you are thinking? he said. 'You're thinking that a Stoic philosopher has no right to be a millionaire. My brother Gallio thinks that. You're thinking, I don't hold together.'

'I don't,' I said. 'Perhaps you think that yourself?'

'No,' he said, 'I don't think it myself. I think we have to live in our time and according to our duty. Believe me, I could lose all this and never care, but while it is here I must administer it prudently. And mitigate things I hate – slavery, for instance. Swordfighting. Palace intrigue. You're a Greek, Callimachus. One can be a general and detest war. But then one looks like a hypocrite.'

The room was full of junk – not only scrolls and papers but expensive junk; beautiful, some of it, two strong boxes and an abacus, a Greek cup, among the papers, on which were thyrsi and masks, dancers with the tambourine, that fell in with my thoughts: on one of the darker shelves a beautiful set of Alexandrian ivories – erotic postures. This room was the inside of Seneca's mind.

He went on talking nervously, justifying himself for being rich, for being Nero's tutor, for being alive and here, in fact, not withdrawing, not opening his own veins. He had no reason to apologize to me, a young, foreign physician, but he desperately wanted me to understand – that he was not a pious fraud, that he was doing his duty, that it was disinterested, the money and the indulgence as well as the politics, though he did not say it in so many words. And I tried to look attentive, as Diodorus had taught, and yet I stared as blindly as Diodorus. Piece by piece I went through the contents of Seneca's mind arranged on the shelves.

Next to the ivory lovers I saw a small brass figure, not Roman, not Greek. With its legs easily crossed, in a pose of divine rest, it was playing, eyes closed, upon a makara-headed flute and I knew what next to say to its owner.

There was a warrior king,' I said, 'whose charioteer would have agreed with you.'

Seneca looked hard at me. 'If you know that too, I *can* readily talk to you,' he said. 'I knew the school of Cos was good, but I didn't know how good. Where did you read of Krishna and Arjuna?'

'I didn't,' I replied, 'but we have Indian physicians on our faculty. Where did you?'

'The same place Zeno read Indian philosophy,' said Seneca. 'In books my father brought me when he travelled. But I took it further. Zeno's master was probably Pañca Sikha. Mine was Varsaganya. My guru was called Kausalika. I was incredibly lucky – their religion forbids these sages to travel, but he was carried off by pirates. I met him in Alexandria. After I'd worked with him I helped him to get home. He had second sight, you know – he told me my life would be the mirror of his. I used to think I would be carried off by pirates and I wondered then if I could treat it as he did, as part of the universal play. Well, I have been, and you see I do. You Coans have to be sages too, or wizards. I can talk to you, Nero can talk to you: you saw that for yourself – normally he's shy, or stubborn, or arrogant, but he talks to you.'

'He talks to me because I'm his age and he's surrounded by senior advisers,' I said. 'And you talk to me because I'm a physician, and being able to be talked to is the name of the game.'

'Celsus is a physician,' said Seneca, 'and a bloody good one. But if I told him that I had diksa from an Indian ascetic he'd probably prescribe cold baths and hellebore.'

I asked him if he had taught Sankhya philosophy to Caesar.

Seneca shook his head. 'I wanted to,' he said, 'some of the basic ideas, yes – the meditative techniques, no. Caesar couldn't survive a meditative experience and stay where he is. He'd go overboard on mysticism. It's not for people with weak heads.'

'Would it matter if he didn't stay where he is?' I asked.

'It would matter,' Seneca replied. 'We would get a Roman instead of a Greek – a swordfighting, slave-killing goon. You saw Caesar. You saw his clothes. He was brought up to be a popular singer. He wants to be a popular singer, but *he's* been carried off by pirates and they've made him their chief. There's an outside chance that he is stronger than they are.'

'You think it will work?' I asked.

'No. Rome will probably destroy him. But it has worked for four years. He's survived. This city is beginning to be decently governed and to look civilized, for the first time since Divine Augustus, and its style is starting to change – that's Nero's doing.'

'And yours?' I asked.

'Not really. If he'd turned out Roman instead of Greek a Spanish philospher couldn't have altered him.'

'Who are the opposition?' I asked.

'Rome generally, the old guard who think he's a pansified, lyre-playing scandal, but who have to put up with him because he's a Claudian by adoption. His mother. She thought he was her dutiful boy. He still doesn't dare to tell her where he stands. When she finds out, one of them will kill the other. Pirates, I told you.'

I said that I thought that would be the turning point.

'Yes,' said Seneca. 'That's why you're here.'

Celsus' apprentice took me to my office. It was the first chance I had to walk in Rome. When he left me, I took barely a glance round the office, then walked alone to the end of the alley and back.

I'm not in the business of writing travelogues. But Rome is simply not what we understand by 'town' or 'city.' It is crowded, topheavy – enormous warrens of apartment houses many stories high, built far too close to each other because of the price of real estate, dwarfing the public buildings. And it was far worse then than it is now. I classify cities by my nose. In Cos one can smell seaweed, in Corinth it's chiefly tar. Rome smells of fish – stale oriental fish, like an enormous grocery. Romans smell of fish, especially the establishment, who wear Tyrian cloth dyed with shell-fish juice, but that's different. The smell which comes through in the first few minutes is anchovy-sauce, garum. In Cos, the street where my high-class medical office was situated would have passed as a slum, but Celsus told me it was expensive, and fashionable. I took several dozen deep breaths to register the smell of Rome. To this day if anyone opens a pot of garum, I'm back there.

Then I went in. The office wasn't bad. It had pleasant wallpaintings of healers and serpents, a desk, a lectica, books, a chair for me, no waiting-room, because in this class of practice people come by appointment and one operates like a barber in a front office.

There was a back dispensary full of tidy jars, with a

dispenser in it, an ancient one-eyed slave who respectfully took me for granted, and whom Celsus, meaning Burrus' security people, had handpicked. He also, I found, knew his job. My quarters were not exactly over the shop, but upstairs across one of those little Roman gardens with a tank it it – which meant that I was spared living in a villa, or in one of the apartment blocks. The Romans, for all their splendid water system, have no sanitary plumbing. Ten stories up one uses a chamberpot, empties it in the street, or goes down to a rather sumptuous street latrine where the Romans sit and defecate in rows, swapping market information. I went into one once and came out again without transacting any business. Seneca and Celsus had laid on a couple of house slaves, a housekeeper, that is, and a cook, who, thank the Gods, was Greek, and who was getting me a decent meal when I arrived. There was a good deal of noise from the blocks overhead, but they were out of my sight. I had the feeling of still being in a ship, and the whole place seemed to creak and be on the move. Once I was alone I unpacked my kit and gave Acte's jars to the dispenser, all except the nepenthe, which I stowed in a safe place. The evening I spent reading Celsus' book, with quite a decent lamp. Then I went to bed. That was the end of my first day in Rome. There was an uproar in the middle of the night, when fire broke out down the road, but they put it out, and I slept soundly enough.

We all know what it feels like to sit in a new office and wait for patients. The difference here, of course, was that I knew there wouldn't be any, though there might be some instructions. I made a quick survey of the facilities, however, in case a stray should come in to see the new doctor: the place looked very much in business. There was a vaginal tray – speculum, bronze mirror, vulsellum, tow. The instruments were not mine and were brand new – Celsus, presumably. The one-eyed dispenser had put out all my pots and a few of his own, as a tactful hint about local prescribing preferences – bryony, for example, which I never use. I sat down at the desk, feeling more like a student than the emissary of the College, and took the chance to check the most important part of my gear, which wasn't strictly therapeutic. The code book we'd agreed on was the *Odyssey* – two books only, because the whole thing is far too bulky, numbers 1 and 12 – and that was to hand. My prescription seal is on a ring – no risk of losing that. And one can't lose a thumbprint. From the communications point of view, I was in business: and in any case, I wasn't likely to get any messages yet and had none to send. So having nothing else to do I went back to Celsus. When I'd had enough of that I took a turn round the dispensary, asked One-eye his name (it was Sosibius, a well-omened name for a druggist), and got a brief conducted tour of the dispensary stock. Then I went back to Celsus.

Chairs and litters kept going past, but I kept my door shut – it wouldn't be professionally dignified to stand at the door and watch the traffic like a shopkeeper, though I was keen to see Rome on the move. Around midday I did, by going out and walking to the corner eatinghouse and having some pork cutlets out of one of the pots set in the counter. (That was before fast-food restaurants were barred, and restricted to selling vegetables.) They didn't have any of my hydromel and I didn't intend to start on Roman wine. The pork wasn't bad, but my exit upset both Sosibius and the middle-aged housekeeping lady, who both told me that all my meals were provided, and the stuff in the eatinghouses was stale, which was probably true, so I ate a second lunch. I'd seen plenty of litters and porters but no highclass Romans – I found that people inside the litters kept the curtains drawn, so there was nothing for it but more Celsus. When I'd finished reading him, and made some notes for Diodorus, I started on the other books in the office, and found that the first three were on astrology. So I put those back – number four was much better value, a treatise on drugs by a young military doctor called Dioscorides, but I wasn't destined to get very far, because a chair stopped at the door and a woman came in.

'Callimachus?' said the lady. I nodded.

'I am Acte.' She pushed back her veil. I thought – watch it, the devil you are. Not at all like my own Acte – short, very dark bright eyes, rather hard features, but handsome, and a lot older than Nero.

'Can I help you, madam?'

'No,' said Acte, 'I can help you. I have a prescription.'

It was from Celsus, the seal was authentic, and it said 'Nostra: tutus loqueris' – one of ours, safe to talk.

I gave it back to her. Presumably she knew the ropes. 'Can we talk here?' I asked.

'Yes. My man will watch outside.'

'I think,' I said, 'that you're my real patient. Is that right?'

'No,' said Acte, 'I'm not. But I know who is.'

'I wish I did,' I said. 'Did Celsus send you?'

'No, Caesar sent me. Celsus did as he was commanded.'

'Well, I had an audience with Caesar yesterday ...'

'I know, and having had an audience with him I think you may understand why he preferred that I should speak to you. About what he has in mind.'

I told her I thought I could guess. 'And you suggested it, because you wanted to talk to me yourself.'

'You're right,' said Acte, 'and you read my mind like a good physician.'

'So there are two messages – Caesar's and yours.'

She nodded.

'We'd better start with Caesar's.'

'It's simple. Your mission here for Caesar is to remove a spell of barrenness on the lady Poppaea, because if she can bear more children, Nero Caesar intends to make her his queen.'

'And how,' I asked, 'does Acte feel about that?'

'I accept it. Poppaea shares Caesar's bed with me already – it will make no difference to me. In fact I shall be happier.'

'Because Caesar will be safer?'

'There is not much,' said Acte, 'that I needed to say to you. You seem to know it all already.'

I told her I didn't know it all, but one did not need to be a sage to read her mind. 'You love Caesar, and you think he's in danger,' I said, 'and you took this chance to ask me to look after him. Well, I'm not a very effective bodyguard – he has got Seneca and Burrus, who seem loyal; I'm a physician and a total stranger, so what do you expect me to do? I wish Caesar well, but he's in a dangerous place at a dangerous time.'

'I wasn't thinking of his mother,' said Acte. 'Caesar's enemy is Caesar. And he wants a friend, not a bodyguard.'

I told her that was perfectly obvious.

'You make it easy,' said Acte. 'I thought that it would be difficult to explain to a physician. Caesar is still a boy.'

'He's about my age,' I said.

'But you aren't a boy,' said Acte. 'I feel better for seeing you – at least you'll do what you can.'

'Do you know what Caesar plans?'

'Well, you have to see Octavia, because that is the reason given for your visit. To see her you'll have to pass the mother, which will require great care and discretion, Callimachus. Then

Poppaea will consult you privately – Caesar will arrange it.'

'If I'm his doctor, Acte, I'm going to have to know the lot about him.'

'What I know, I'll tell you.'

'Is he sexually normal?'

'No,' said Acte, 'how could he be?'

'In what way?'

'Addicted. Don't take notice of the mistresses and the pranks and the bed-boys – that's not abnormal in Rome. And he can have anything he wants, when he wants it. It's the other Romans who are abnormal. They prefer bloodshed to sex. And mix them. But he's got no other way of touching people. So he has sex with everyone – if that's the only way you know to make contact, I suppose it makes sense. If he can find other ways...'

'If he can, you reckon he'll grow out of it?'

'It's not important. It's how Caesar and I came together, after all. I suppose I shouldn't complain. Except it makes him vulnerable. His mother and his tutor both seduced him, you know? If he likes someone, it's apt to make that turn. He gets himself seduced. You can handle that, I'm sure. But it's a difficulty.'

I told her that was a far deeper answer than I'd expected – it was Caesar's fertility I was thinking about.

'There he *is* normal. I've had to drink pennyroyal twice. And he's normal otherwise – for anyone but a Roman. The first time he had to sign a death sentence he wished out loud that he'd never learned to write his name. Tomorrow he's got to open the Games. It makes him sick to his stomach, to see slaves killing each other. You've got to go with him tomorrow, and it'll probably make you feel sick too. We're both of us Greeks. Caesar is a Greek.'

'Where are you from?' I asked her.

'Rhodes,' said Acte. 'I sometimes dream Caesar has been deposed and let live, and I take him back with me there.'

'Tell me about the people around him,' I said. 'Seneca I've met. Burrus I've heard about. Those two are substitute fathers. Who are his companions?'

'Otho – he's Poppaea's husband – he introduced them. And Tigellinus. Tigellinus is Caesar's right hand, and often his left hand as well.'

'Any opinions of them?'

'Otho's goodnatured, lazy, a playboy – he wants a province and Nero will give him one in exchange for his wife.'

'Tigellinus?'

'Frightens me – ambitious, a dandy with a yahoo inside him, a typical Roman swinger on the make.'

'I like your portraits, Acte. Both of them bad for Caesar?'

'Yes.'

'Likely to kill him?'

'Not now. Yes, if he slips.'

'Poppaea?'

'I like her,' said Acte. 'She's promiscuous, but who am I to talk like a matron? I have been a prostitute from my childhood. She does as Otho tells her. And she cares, in her way, about Caesar – not simply to be empress, I think. They're both confused children, but Poppaea is growing up.'

'Anyone else?'

'Who, really, can be a friend to Caesar? Drinking companions, though Caesar no longer drinks, actors, swordsmen – Burrus sees that swordsmen and prize fighters go about with him, because he used to go looking for trouble at night with Otho and Tigellinus, dressed as a street person, and getting into fights. There was terrible trouble once when they beat up a senator – not for any good reason, either.'

'Who's on your side, Acte?'

'Well, Otho is. He introduced me to Caesar – as he did Poppaea. And Caesar has a boyfriend called Doryphorus who's been kind to me. The mother hates me. Probably if she felt strong enough, or Caesar tired of me, she'd kill me. I'm Caesar's cover – she thinks that I'm the one he intends to marry, after Octavia. I wouldn't do that to him.'

'It looks to me,' I said, 'as if you need protection more than he does.'

'No, thank you, he looks after me. I'm a rich woman. I'm the official mistress of Annaeus Serenus – he's another smart young man, head of the Fire Brigade, and Seneca's cousin. I don't even have to sleep with him. Nero told his mother that I'm descended from a Greek princess, and worthy of an emperor, as part of the marriage story. Then he made Tigellinus give me a twenty-four-hour bodyguard, and so far they've killed four trespassers at my villa in Puteoli. So you're right and wrong, Callimachus – I'm in danger, but it's deliberate danger. I want to do what he wants.'

I asked her if he was worth it.

'Caesar is worth it. Forget about the sexual capers, and the silly, schoolboy stuff. How would you be if you were where he is, born of such a mother? Either he will be the greatest Roman, because he is at least made of flesh, not cast iron ...'

'Or the cast iron party will get him?'

'That's what I'm afraid of.'

'Or drive Caesar mad?'

'That,' said Acte, 'they won't manage to do. If Caesar were what he wants to be, given free choice, I would marry him and no other.'

'What does he want to be?'

'A musician. He is a musician, a very good one.'

'That's extraordinary,' I said. 'I've got a feeling that Caesar and I may get on rather well.'

'I think so,' said Acte, 'but go slowly. Inside that boy is an incredibly bruised person. He hardly comes out and shows himself to me, and when he does I feel incestuous, because I'm being a mother, not a mistress, and I'm not used to that. Callimachus, I believe you understand.'

I told her that I believed I did – it was an extraordinarily useful interview, in fact, and widened the scope of my thinking about Caesar a great deal. Clearly, *he* was going to be the patient. Also I saw why Xenophon had been worried about Eleusis – anyone having as difficult a growth-period as that was going to be at risk from religion as well as from daggers.

Acte left, and I thought a great deal. Shortly after the door closed, I got some more to think about.

This time it was a boy. He looked about fourteen, thoroughly rude and spoiled, with bleached, curled hair and a ridiculous padded-out jock-strap.

He said, 'You the doc? I thought this was the place. I've got a message for you.'

And he gave me a tablet – no seal, not from Celsus, obviously not from Caesar, who wouldn't send a little horror like that, I thought.

'Who is it from?'

'Read it and see.'

I didn't – I wasn't opening it in a hurry. I put it down.

'Also, Nero Germanicus told me to give you a present, if you want it.'

'All right,' I said, 'hand it over.'

'You mean here?' said the boy, and giggled.

'You mean, you are the present?'

'Sure. I'm a very valuable present. I am Caesar's best concubinus. I was trained by Doryphorus. What do you like best?'

'You normally call Caesar "Nero Germanicus" when he sends you on errands?'

'I'll call him what I like. He calls me Flute-Fingers. Do you want to know why?'

'I want you to thank Caesar very sincerely for his gift, and tell him I cannot take advantage of it, but I deeply appreciate the thought. Got that? I want it said right.'

'Then write it down,' said the boy. 'You've got to answer the letter, haven't you?'

The letter said 'Callimachus: Lucius Domitius Ahenobarbus sends greeting. Let us dine tonight at the Wolf's Head. All the chairmen know where it is. I would appreciate it if you didn't show this to Nero Germanicus. Reply by my messenger. If my gift to you is welcome, good. If it miscarries, I apologize.'

I thought about that for some time. I was thunderstruck.

'You going to write or not?' said the boy. 'I'm getting tired standing. I'm not supposed to get tired – I need all my strength.'

Finally I wrote: 'Dear Lucius, I'll be delighted. Your gift was very kind, but you were quite right in thinking that it was not really for me – you do have to remember I'm new in Rome, and I doubt if I'd make very good use of it. But thank you all the same. I look forward to our meeting.'

This I sealed with my prescription seal, and gave to the boy. 'My name is Pythagoras,' he said, 'after the philosopher. Ask Nero Germanicus to let you try me if you change your mind.'

There was quite enough to bother me without arguing with a juvenile concubine. First – Acte was right: this was uncommonly like seduction by proxy. Hopefully it meant that Caesar realized that he wouldn't get anywhere with me himself, but that would have to come out during the sessions. Second – and this was the big surprise – here was an invitation in Caesar's real name, the one which usually threw him into a rage. So I was meeting Lucius, not Caesar. That struck me as hopeful, if I could handle it. You've got to remember, Herondas, I'm not a psychiatrist – I just had to reckon that I would do better if I played it with feeling than Anaxagoras, my Chief, could have done, with his hellebore pills. This kind of psychotherapy was never his mark.

The Wolf's Head was some way out, towards the marshes –

the chairmen trudged for a good hour. It was nearly dark when we got there. I could see poplars, a big vine, lights inside, and a couple of gorillas from Tigellinus' Secret Service standing one on each side of the inn front, discreetly out of the way, taking no notice of me. And it was Caesar who ran out and embraced me.

'Callimachus – I was afraid you'd be afraid to come.'

'Not a bit,' I said. 'I don't think Nero Germanicus can hear us out here, Lucius.'

'No, he can't, he can't,' said Nero. 'You've got the idea. And I didn't offend you, physician, by sending the boy?'

'Not at all, Lucius. If I didn't offend anyone by sending him away. You know, I think that boy belongs to Nero Germanicus.'

'He does,' said Nero. 'I should have thought of it. I'm clumsy. It was insulting to send him – insulting of Nero Germanicus, I mean, and Lucius apologizes. Actually you missed something – he's fantastic. You despise me, don't you? In my position one takes any sort of pleasure one can get, Callimachus.'

'Certainly I don't – I entirely understand. But it's Lucius who is going to have dinner with me,' I said, 'and I don't think he's got problems. Let's go in, shall we?'

We did, and the host seated us as if we were two rather ordinary diners, but I noticed we were the only diners, and he brought my hydromel and Nero's iced boiled water, and called Nero 'Lucius Domitius'. So he was in the charade too.

'You know,' said Nero, 'Lucius Domitius hasn't done this in years. Now we can talk. I wanted to talk to you. But not in front of holy Seneca. Or in front of Nero Germanicus. I like to talk before I eat, if you agree. When I'm not heavy with food. I eat too much.'

'One question,' I said. 'Can one talk to Lucius Domitius about Caesar?'

'We have to,' Nero replied. 'If Lucius Domitius could stab Claudius Nero Germanicus without stabbing himself, he'd have done it long since. But he can't.'

'Then tell me about both of them, Lucius. As a Roman to a Greek.'

'I'm not a Roman,' said Nero. 'I'm a Greek too.'

I told him Ahenobarbus was a pretty good Roman name.

'Roman – I don't know about good,' said Nero. 'My father was a thug. I remember when he got into trouble for deliberately driving over a pedestrian. And he hated me. When he found I could play the lyre, he dressed me as a girl for six months.

Father used to point to me and tell people that anything he and my mother did together was bound to be a fiasco. Those two deserved each other. I'm a Greek like you,' he went on. 'I love music: it's about the only thing I do love. I hate bloodshed and Roman thuggery. I didn't want to be Caesar – that was mother's idea. I wanted to work in music drama. That's what I was trained for. I'm good. If she hadn't ensnared old Claudius I could have been emperor of music drama. Oh well, if ever there's a revolution I can still make a career there. People don't kill musicians.'

'You still manage to practise, in spite of your political duties?'

'I do, and damn the political duties. I leave all but the top decisions to the Group. I'm not irresponsible, Callimachus. Caesar is deadly serious. Music is a political duty, to me. The one chance I've got to civilize this bunch of gladiatorial half-wits is to be Caesar and an artist, but I've got to succeed brilliantly at both or they'll have my head. The old guard and the Families think an artist is a screaming faggot. Caesar is the only person who might just pull enough rank to get away with it. It's probably not going to work, and they'll kill me, or my mother will kill me, and I don't want that. Have you ever been scared?'

I told him frankly I was scared stiff then, by Rome, by what I'd got into.

'Not as scared as I am,' said Nero.

There was a long pause. I looked at him, because quite obviously he wanted me to put a hand on his shoulder, and it might have been the wrong thing to do, for obvious reasons. And I saw Nero reading back what I wasn't saying to him.

'An artist needs constant criticism,' said Nero. That, luckily, was over. 'If Caesar performs, everyone claps madly out of sycophancy. It's unnerving. I don't know if I gave a professional performance or made a fool of myself.'

I told him that if he was going to be Lucius, he could let me hear one of his performances and I'd tell him quite frankly what I thought of it. 'Provided,' I added, 'Lucius doesn't turn into Caesar and have me flogged if I don't praise a bad performance.'

'You mean that?'

'Certainly. You've got to be Lucius to somebody. Try me.'

So he got his instrument, fiddled around a long time tuning it, looking at me from time to time, as nervous as hell. Finally he started – playing and singing. And to my intense relief he was good – not much of a voice, but a first-rate lyre-player. I told him exactly that.

'You're so right,' said Nero. 'I know. I'm working on my voice.'

'Look, Lucius,' I said, 'I'm a doctor, and I have to stand off a bit, exactly as Caesar has to stand off a bit – we've both got jobs to do. Obviously, I'll try to be a friend as well, circumstances permitting. Is there anyone else you can talk to?'

'Acte,' said Nero. 'I can talk to her.'

'Then do.'

'Oh, I do, but there are problems there too. I can't be Caesar with her, only Lucius.'

'Anyone else? Friends?'

'You must be joking.'

'Otho? Tigellinus?'

'They're all right. When my guard's up.'

'Seneca? Burrus? Aulus Celsus?'

'Look,' said Nero, 'I don't want any more fathers. Or any more mothers. Burrus is a Roman Roman, or would be if he wasn't a Gaul. Celsus is another doctor – I don't need a dose of hellebore. Seneca I used to trust, but that was a mistake. That man taught me most of what I know, then fucked me in the ass. Told me it was a Greek custom. Now he's scared of me. I think he's a fraud. You can't be a philosopher and a millionaire. But I've got the whip-hand because of what he did, and he's useful. Also he hates Roman Romans.'

'You,' I said, 'have had a hell of a life.'

'I still have,' said Nero, 'while it lasts. Now if you don't mind, Callimachus, I've got to talk to you a bit as Caesar. I didn't mean all this to come out. I'm going back before you come to despise me. Right?'

'Right, Caesar. And I certainly don't despise you.'

'Very well. Let's talk business. You know why I sent for you?'

'Yes,' I said, 'you sent Acte to tell me.'

'I ought to have told you myself.'

'Not if it was difficult. She did it very well. She's an extremely intelligent woman who loves you very much and wishes you well. Now, since we're here, is there anything you want to tell me?'

'She told you whom you are to see?'

'Yes.'

'And why?'

'Yes.'

'And that Medusa will probably kill her, and Poppaea, and you, and me for all I know, if she gets a breath of this?'

'That was my general impression. It can be avoided if we all keep our heads cool and our mouths shut.'

'Has the College been talking?'

'They didn't know what you had in mind, but they made some intelligent guesses.'

'Then everybody knows, and my mother knows.'

I explained that the College had a tradition of total confidentiality, and it was the one place where nobody's mother had spies.

'I hope you're right. I wouldn't bet on it. You don't know her. Well, that's settled. Talk about something less ill-omened,' said Nero, 'or better, let's eat. You like sow's womb with the sucking-pig inside? It's special here.'

So the eggs were brought, and the salad. I saw Nero enjoying the plain wooden table and the country platters, simple-lifing as Lucius. He was getting natural. He started talking about his interest in Egyptian religion (his second tutor was a leading authority) and I wondered where that was going.

I said a little about living in India and let him talk – I'd have liked to ask more about the mother, since I had to pass that formidable lady, but decided it was better to get briefed elsewhere, by Seneca, or Acte, or preferably both. Mistakes could be rather serious at that interview. But the subject was far too sore to open unless Lucius did, and I'd bitten my tongue to avoid saying, 'Tell me about her,' because I'd have got, not information, but a tirade of confidences. Then Lucius brought me up short by asking me if I thought we live more than once.

'Because if we do,' he said, 'all this wouldn't matter: Caesar one time around, musician the next. Our stars wouldn't matter, because they'd be different next time. Do we?'

You can see, Herondas, what tricky ground this was, because one can't pass on everything one has learned. So I told him my master Kapila thought so: but if we did, we wouldn't know it, any more than we remember being infants.

'I know it,' said Nero. 'I have been a musician before. I shall be one again. How did I get trapped as a Caesar?'

'Perhaps so that you may be a better musician,' I said, 'for having had the experience you're having. Kapila thought so.' So that was all right. Probably it was simply the Roman obsession with Fate – I remembered all those idiotic astrological books in the office – one gets born by the stars, sickens by the stars, accedes to be Caesar or gets killed swordfighting by the stars, the whole sorry, mechanistic trip which makes simple psychotherapy with Romans near-impossible, and Romans themselves quite impossible. I'd have thought Seneca would have cured him, but he hadn't.

'As to stars,' I said, 'we're born with what we've got – music, and a very good mind in your case, Lucius – what we make of it depends on us.' He nodded at that, and I hoped it registered. The transference was in hand and going quite well.

'That hurts,' said Nero. 'It means we're responsible.'

'Well, aren't we?' I said.

'Tomorrow,' said Nero, 'I have to open a swordfight. You have to sit through it with me. As it is it's humiliating and disgusting. If I'm responsible, it's unbearable.'

'I did say responsible, not omnipotent, Lucius. In your place I'd say, Lucius detests all this barbarity but Nero Germanicus has to officiate at it to save his skin. But with age under your belt, and a free hand eventually, Lucius may be able to take over from Nero Germanicus. Patience is in order – remember Quintus Fabius. He saved Rome by biding his time.'

'That's good, that's good. You're a friend, Callimachus. And when I insult you tomorrow by taking you to what we call "Games" here in Rome, we'll both grit our teeth and think about Quintus Fabius. You could stay away if you wanted.'

'It's better,' I said, 'to exhibit me publicly, which is Seneca's idea. So your mother doesn't get suspicious. As to the Games, I've seen death a good many more times than most soldiers.'

'Seneca,' said Nero, 'won't be there.'

'Seneca's doing his part,' I said. 'He writes, he doesn't rule. And even if you distrust him, and I don't blame you, he's the only person who ever wrote an Essay on Compassion in Latin. There has been progress. People treat their slaves decently nowadays. If you hold on and stay on the rails, in fifteen years Rome won't be recognizable.'

'I hope so,' said Nero, 'and you've restored my appetite.' (I hadn't noticed anything wrong with it.) 'Let's call for the entree.'

But we never got to it. One of the two gorillas came in.

'Hail, Caesar. A message from the Best of Mothers. She is

indisposed and requires your presence. Will you go now, or later?'

He went first white, then purple. He said, 'She requires? Requires? Will – I – go – now? WILL I GO NOW? May all the Furies damn her to everlasting Hell! It's a plot – she must have had a spy in your misbegotten College!'

And he smashed first the jug with the water in it, and then his lyre, which was on the side table, jumping up from the couch and battering it on the furniture. I gave the temper-tantrum a count of ten and said, 'Steady, Caesar. Remember Quintus Fabius!'

'What?' said Nero.

'If she dissembles, Caesar, we'd better dissemble. And she may really be ill.'

'Not her,' said Nero, 'she has the constitution of a Getulian elephant. Poison can't touch her – Locusta filled her with it by increasing doses to make her invulnerable. She must have heard I was alone, being Lucius, the name my bloody father gave me, so she requires me. Stilicho, will you cut her throat?'

'If you order it, Caesar,' said the gorilla, who was a centurion in mufti and damned uncomfortable at the whole performance. 'But permission to speak, Caesar.'

'All right,' said Nero, 'go on.'

'With respect, I think this gentleman is right.'

I was amazed how fast he came down. 'I agree, Stilicho. Of course he's right. I have to go. I was angry because I was upset to hear of my mother's indisposition, and like a child I broke my favourite lyre. I shall have to replace it – it can't be mended.'

And like a lamb, he went – no word to me. Nero Germanicus was back.

'She always takes him like that,' said the gorilla. 'If she doesn't kill him, he'll kill her. Are you his doctor?'

'Not really,' I said, 'a friend.'

'Yes,' said the gorilla, and left me to my own devices. I hoped Seneca's babysitter was around, and went to the door to check. There were two men outside – one of the Secret Service people, and another, so that was taken care of. I went back and ate the sucking-pig myself, but I also had plenty of food for thought. Nero, if he kept his head, could explain me – after all, I was there with the Best of Mothers' consent to treat his wife. But I had my hands full.

2

It had been arranged that I would meet Caesar officially next day, when he opened the Games, and that he wouldn't refer to our previous meeting: this one was going to be official. I bathed, ate, and was fetched by the same young man from Celsus' staff. We walked out to the nearest point where wheeled vehicles were permitted. I didn't see exactly where we went or how we got there. Finally, ostlers opened the doors, and we went up steps and through a good deal of marble and gilding. Then there was a longish wait in an ante-room full of fairly good copies of Greek statuary (the Romans leave the marble plain, not painted) with a few soldiers on duty and a good deal of coming and going. The nomenclator came round with his tablets and checked our names. Celsus wasn't there. Seneca came in, said good morning, and went in through the door where the guards stood – presumably into the Emperor's quarters. There were precious few guests, and none of us spoke to each other. The nomenclator checked our particulars and disappeared. I walked about, looking down at the mosaics, and feeling remarkably exposed to fire. It was quite a relief when I saw the nomenclator coming back with somebody else.

This somebody was a tall dark soldier, certainly no Roman. For a start he wore moustachios like a Kazak; his rich woollen cavalry cloak had a fine gold clasp, and he gave it to the slave, clasp and all, with a fine gesture of unconcern. Under it he wore a plain tunic, a baldric, and boots, and his curiously irregular shape when he came in, which attracted my orthopaedic eye (for a moment I thought he was misshapen) turned out to be due to a bow, which he carried in a leather half-case on his shoulder, with a cylindrical quiver on the other side to match. It struck me that quite apart from the oddity of marching into a social occasion armed, this bow was idiotically small for such a large man. It was about the size one gives to a child of seven or eight. I wasn't the only one to notice it. The guard Captain, one of

Burrus' men, was eyeing the bow as if it were a helmet full of snakes.

'The worshipful Tiridates, Lord of Armenia, Envoy of Parthia,' yelled the nomenclator. The guard Captain came to attention for the formality, then was in motion. Tiridates, seeing me the only other non-Roman in evidence, raised his hand to me, and I bowed to him.

'Beg pardon, your Excellency,' said the Captain, saluting.

'Yes, Captain?' said Tiridates, looking a bit bored, as if he knew what was coming, and dangerously genial.

'The bow, your Excellency. I have to take charge of it.'

'Charge of it? Why?' said Tiridates.

'Excellency, only we can bear weapons here.'

'Oh,' said Tiridates, 'but it's not a weapon. It comes under the title of insignia. Like the standard-bearer's lion skin. It is part of my religion to wear it.'

'Beg pardon, Excellency, you may not with respect wear it here,' said the Captain, very red in the face.

'Please, Captain,' said Tiridates, in mock alarm, 'don't try to take it from me, will you?'

'I have orders, your Excellency ...'

'Because in that case I might become angry,' said Tiridates, 'and knock you down. It is my custom to give orders, not argue with junior officers. Stand to attention, damn you, when you address an officer! That's better. Now dismiss.'

The Captain was at least persistent, and he kept his temper. The nomenclator, after dithering around, had gone for the Colonel.

'With respect, Sir, I'm not under your command, and I have my orders. Give up the bow, or leave.'

At which point the Colonel arrived.

'Sir. His Excellency Tiridates insists on keeping his bow.'

'I see. My regrets about the misunderstanding,' said the Colonel. 'This soldier is only following orders.'

'I commend him,' said Tiridates, genially. 'We have had this kind of trouble before. However, Caesar ...'

'Has given personal orders that your uniform shall be respected at all times, Excellency.'

Tiridates bowed and turned his back on the two of them.

'All right, Captain, all right,' said the Colonel, under his breath. 'Wish they'd told me in advance that armed foreigners were in order. Apparently it's happened before. See he isn't challenged. We'll settle his hash, the Gods willing, in Parthia one day. You can see it's a toy bow, and the string's tangled, so I think we can make an exception. It's insignia, not a weapon.'

'Like your breastplate,' said Tiridates, genially, and he planted himself on the mosaic, looking down at the doves and vines.

It was not long before the doors opened. Two buglers with wolfskins on their heads stationed themselves on each side, then a full imperial guard, then the nomenclator. The guard came to attention.

'Nero Claudius Caesar Drusus Germanicus!'

Crash went the salute.

Nero looked sleepy, I thought, and slightly hung over, probably on food, not drink. He embraced us, however, like a private citizen greeting total strangers and set on being affable.

'Greetings, Tiridates. Greetings, Callimachus. Let's refresh ourselves, and then we have public duties, but at least it's a festival. Tiridates, you'll take wine with us, iced water for me, and we have hydromel for you, Doctor – you see, I don't forget my guests' tastes. After that we can go to the show for a while. I have to make an appearance, they like that.'

'We will see warriors fight?' asked Tiridates.

'This afternoon – this morning there will be belly-dancers, clowns and ... contortionists: very good, I'm told. Actually it's due to begin now, but you won't want to see the start, and I certainly don't. They execute criminals then.'

'How?' asked Tiridates.

'Animals kill them. Callimachus, I know how you Greeks feel about Roman barbarism. I agree. It makes me nauseous. I suggest we wait until it's over.'

'What exactly will occur?' Tiridates asked.

'Five forgers – three men and two women – will be destroyed by a bear, and a woman who killed her husband by dogs. Don't tell me it's barbarous, I know. If any woman should be torn to pieces for killing her husband, it's my mother.'

'Caesar could pardon them?' said Tiridates, politely.

'I could, but I can't keep interfering with the criminal courts.'

'Caesar could have them punished with decency?' said Tiridates.

'He could, and will as soon as he can. That's my intention,' said Caesar, 'but Seneca says you can't change a people overnight. If I stopped these things now I'd have riots. The mob is scum. But I'm weaning them already. They will learn to listen to singing instead of screams, and watch athletes instead of ex-convicts killing each other. The swordfighters will be the last to go, but go they shall. I've stopped most of it in the Provinces on grounds of economy. But how much faster can I move than Rome will move? For the time being I show my disapproval – I stay away whenever I can.'

I couldn't tell whether Tiridates was naive, or insolent, or both. Caesar was taking him at face value. We gave the atrocities three-quarters of an hour to be completed, then the litters were brought – Caesar in one, we two in a second, larger, with eight large chairmen. I bowed to Tiridates, as became a civilian, and he mounted the litter. Waiting behind him I got a close look at his bow, because it was practically in my face. I could make nothing of it, and it puzzled me. The thing was far too small for a weapon, but far too elaborate for a badge or emblem. The string was enormously thick, and seemed tangled round the cheeks like a catscradle, and it had an odd bracket like a stirrup or pedal bolted to the side, close to the handgrip. The rest of it was hidden by the case. Tiridates flopped back at ease picking his teeth and smiling, and we lurched up and off.

'What are you doing here, physician?' asked Tiridates.

'I tend the Emperor's family,' I said, 'and you?'

'I have come,' said Tiridates, 'on an unofficial visit – scouting, if you like. At Caesar's invitation. And under safe conduct from Rome. You know we're at war?'

I told him I had heard something concerning war in Armenia, though the affairs of that quarter were rather remote from Cos.

'I could,' said Tiridates, 'talk sensibly to Caesar's general, as soldier to soldier. He's an honest man and a good commander. Unfortunately, there was a little disagreement between us as to how many troops should accompany us to the rendezvous. Corbulo brought rather too many with him, so we never came within speaking distance. In my profession one must be suspicious. But Caesar wrote to me himself, and in my own language, undertaking an oath which I thought it unlikely he would break himself, or permit his subordinates to break. I said to myself, this may be a sensible Roman. We in Parthia have suffered a good deal from Romans. I had to see for myself.'

I asked him why on earth, if he was too suspicious of ambush to parley with Corbulo, he would risk himself in Rome, on the strength of an oath.

'I didn't,' said Tiridates. 'I'm holding sufficient Roman hostages, or rather my sovereign brother, Volosges, is, to keep Rome's hands off me, or so it is hoped. But also, I'm a gambler, and I had to scrutinize this Caesar myself. It was my feeling we must meet eventually. And I wanted to see the wolf's lair.'

'You talk pretty freely to a stranger,' I said.

'Why not? You're a physician of Cos, aren't you?'

I told him that as such I certainly kept secrets, but avoided state secrets on principle.

'State secrets nothing. All that, I shall tell to Caesar himself. Odd that he wants us both beside him at the show. I don't know why he wants you there, but he wants me for my own protection – so that my presence is known. If I were not on business, wild horses wouldn't get me to this occasion – it's humiliating. Caesar himself apologized. Well, at least we shall have the sexual acrobats – spintriae kill nobody.'

This soldier, I thought, isn't the happy warrior he seems to be. He's the future King of Armenia, and a small-scale Caesar in his own right. Two affable monarchs in two days are quite a strange experience when one is a young provincial doctor. I wondered what the Hades I, Callimachus, was doing here.

I couldn't stop puzzling over Tiridates' ridiculous little bow. I was on the point of asking him about it when a memory clicked in my mind, and I suddenly saw what it really was, and how it worked. It was not too small, and the string was not tangled. What Tiridates had was a compound bow, made of steel springs – something I had read about but never seen. As to the odd-looking bracket, I figured that out too. Tiridates' bow could be held in one hand and drawn with the other – on horseback, for instance, at close range. But it could also be drawn with both hands and fired from the instep, lying down. In that configuration the archer becomes a large crossbow. He would have fantastic range and present almost zero profile for return fire. So, far from being a toy, Tiridates' bow was quite the nastiest piece of artillery I had ever seen, and the Romans hadn't spotted it. By my guess it would have an accurate range of over three hundred yards.

We arrived under an awning and went in through a plain arched passage like a whitewashed sewer, lined with guards and sprinkled with, of all things, rose petals. I could hear the place buzzing with the crowd inside as if it were full of bees, then up flights of steps and suddenly into the box. All round was a huge sea of faces tossing up in little breakers of white cloth, napkins probably, with the crawling movement of grass in a wind or big crowds generally, but still there were some spaces – chiefly the high-priced seats on our side, under the shades. The bleachers were jammed, as they always are. The crowd wasn't noisy, but its sheer sound at rest was enough to blot out the music which was being played under us to fill the intermission. Then there was bugling, a bit of a hush, and Caesar made his entry with his party.

In spite of the awning, there was September sunlight and the arena was dazzling. Its acoustics were incredible; one could hear all the murmurs and talk as if it were one voice. Caesar raised his hand and got a perfunctory cheer. On the bleachers, people were eating and drinking – forbidden after midday, for Augustus regarded swordfights as a sacrificial rite, but now they were picnicking. The sand was being cleansed – any bloodstains had gone, fortunately. It took a few seconds from our entry in file for the praetor to rise, and then the crowd roared, 'Caesar, Caesar!' I could see Nero beginning to expand, and that he liked audiences but feared crowds. I was embraced by a number of flashy young executives whom Caesar presented – 'This is Otho, whom I have destined for a Province; this is Tigellinus, who looks after the security of my person – breeds excellent racehorses, too. Please, be seated, guests.'

Three archers had come in. They saluted our box, then the stalls, then the bleachers. From the entrances leading to the dens, a cloud of white doves was suddenly released. The archers, firing at speed, managed to bring down all but a couple. There were white birds lying or flopping all over the arena.

'In Parthia,' said Tiridates, to nobody in particular, 'they throw lemons and split them. Each archer throws his own.'

When they had picked up the doves, there was a trumpet blast and the next event was signalled.

'Now for the belly-dancers,' said Caesar. 'Oh, no!'

They had wheeled in a cart-like structure bearing a wicker cage, and in the cage was a woman, incongruously adorned with a garland. Behind the cage stood an executioner, wearing a bronze Fury mask, and holding a heavy iron paddle studded with hooks, with which to dispatch the victim if the dogs did not do so. Out of the other entry came the dogs, three large Molossian hounds, running obediently together. They stood still. The executioner pulled a cord, and the valves of the cage fell open, leaving the woman exposed. She and the dogs looked at one another. The executioner raised his paddle, and she turned and ran. The dogs did not move – they were controlled, I think, by a silent whistle – until she was half-way across the arena, coming towards us.

Tiridates got up. 'Caesar, excuse me. It was something I ate.' And he sauntered out of the box, turning his back on the arena. The crowd, which had been remarkably quiet, began to shout, and then to chant. The dogs suddenly went off like three streaks of brown and surrounded the woman, staying away from her. Then one snarled, ran in, made a pass at her, and fell back. They were well trained, and they would not kill until ordered.

'Attack dogs from Mamurra's estate,' said Tigellinus. 'He trains them himself.'

There were three such passes. She had now simply covered her face with her arms. The crowd was getting noisier and noisier. It was they, not the dogs, who bayed. Nero, I noticed, looked quite unwell. 'Oh, for the Gods' sake, finish it,' he said. A dog fell back, turned obviously at a command, and I saw that this pass would be in earnest. He bristled, snarled, and then went in like an arrow. I did not want to see him catch her by the shoulder, and I would have closed my eyes, but as it was I blinked for another reason. The dog appeared to have been hit by a silent thunderbolt, for it was thrown backwards in a complete somersault, and fell stone dead. At the same moment the other two dogs charged, one from each side, and each, only fractions of a second apart, was blasted as if the pair of them had been hit by two leisurely fists. For a moment I thought they were trained to 'die', but then I saw blood and a protruding feather, and the bleachers straining to see where the shooting was coming from. They were pointing up at the only bow in sight, the golden bow on the statue of Artemis, whom the Romans call Diana, above us and to the right. She, with a smile on her face, was covering the whole arena with her drawn arrow. The woman still did not move. The executioner, who did not seem to have expected this, was coming in long strides, measuring his blow to tear open her back. He got to within three paces, with the silence turning to a growing hum, and then the paddle flew out of his hand and he went down clutching his shoulder. A colossal yell of 'Habet' went up, and Caesar joined in. The woman lowered her arms, and suddenly, with great presence of mind, I thought, prostrated herself first towards

Diana, and then, running to the foot of the imperial box, to Caesar. Everyone was clearly puzzled, some disappointed, some cheering the peripeteia as a clever bit of showmanship. But the ringmaster was running towards the praetor's box, shouting and pointing – there was quite evidently something wrong. He had his whip in his hand, and he was near the middle of the arena when a menacing puff of dust came up ahead of his feet. He took two more steps, then stopped, mouth open, inspecting an arrow which had pierced not the shaft but the thong of his whip – either a fluke, or an incredible piece of sharpshooting. When another cut a red line on his bald scalp, he threw down the whip and fled. The bleachers went mad – 'Habet! Habet! Coward,' Yells, refuse, catcalls, cheers – the guards completely forgetting themselves, were jumping and yelling like children at the display of musketry.

The woman stayed prudently face down in front of us. Two police were heading for her, and there appeared to be confusion of some kind backstage. Caesar stood up, applauding, and began to move towards the rostrum.

'Careful, Caesar!' said Tigellinus.

'Nonsense. It's my cue!' said Nero.

It would have been enough to point first to Diana, and then in a gesture of dismissal at the woman, but I didn't know Nero. He threw his cloak over his shoulder, struck a pose, and suddenly bawled, in Greek:

> 'The Queen and Huntress from before our eyes
> Caught up the maid and hid her in the skies –
> See, in her place a bleeding stag she yields'

(He pointed at the executioner, who was making his way offstage, nursing his arm; the Greek-speaking part of the audience laughed at the joke.)

> 'And all the assembled princes clash their shields.'

He went on for several more lines, among mounting uproar. Finally, he switched to Latin:

> 'Woman, you have the Goddess' mercy, accept Caesar's!'

And he bowed and returned to base.

The stalls, which might have understood Greek, was thin at this time of day, and the rest of the circus gave him a mixed reception – the woman had killed her husband, and I was not sure that the pardon was popular, even if the ham performance was. A policeman pulled her to her feet and told her to make herself scarce before Caesar changed his mind. She ran to the bleachers – hands reached down the wall and pulled her up, and she vanished in the crowd.

'Well,' said Nero, 'was I good?'

'The Iphigenia reference was witty, Caesar. May I ask whose Iphigenia it came from?' I asked.

'Mine, of course,' responded Nero.

I bowed appreciatively, glad I hadn't said it quite obviously wasn't Euripides.

Tiridates was sitting calmly in his place again.

'You missed,' said Caesar, 'marvellous shooting – the best stunt I ever saw here. They had an archer who cut down the dogs, and grazed the executioner – it was brilliant! You know, that was a compliment to me. They didn't kill her in front of me, they gave me the occasion to pardon her on behalf of the Gods. I like that.'

'At least, Caesar,' said Tiridates, 'I didn't miss your recitation.'

Everyone was arguing how it had been done, and the crowd was getting restive, because the next turn was not ready. Meanwhile, I could hear an altercation going on sotto voce behind us.

'Colonel!'

'Colonel?'

'Look, next time live rounds are going to be fired near the Caesar, could you possibly take the trouble to let me know? I was about to call a full alert when the shooting started.'

'Look, Marcellus, I was as surprised as you were. Didn't the ringmaster warn you?'

'The ringmaster didn't know. It was bloody murder – the executioner had an arrow through his arm – and those were pedigree dogs on loan. They cost ten thousand sesterces each. Caesar himself must have ordered it. Where was the shooting coming from?'

'Search me. And Caesar didn't order it. I saw his face.'

Tigellinus had slipped back.

'Did you say Caesar didn't place that marksman?'

'Yes, Sir. I'd swear to that.'

'And neither did the editor?'

'No, Sir. He's as mad as a buck about it.'

'And you didn't see where the firing came from?'

'Probably up there by the statue. He was behind the Goddess, I imagine.'

'Then that's a good two hundred yards,' said Tigellinus.

'Yes, Sir. More than that. Good Hercules!'

'Precisely. Wait here.'

He came round the back of Caesar's chair.

'Caesar, where did you get that fantastic marksman?' asked Tigellinus.

'I didn't, Tigellinus – I don't how they did it – brilliant, wasn't it?'

'Yes, brilliant, Caesar. I'll go and find out.'

'And get his name,' Caesar ordered.

Tigellinus passed the officers, still in earshot and trying not to raise his voice. 'For your information,' he said, 'there's now a maniac at large who's a dead shot, and he's got a weapon which is accurate up to four hundred yards. No, don't start a panic, you idiots – he'll be long gone by now. I'm going to talk to Security. And don't alarm Caesar – yet.'

The dancers had begun, among mounting noise. Police were converging on the standing room, which was the focus of the trouble, but when they cracked a few heads, the row spread rapidly to the bleachers – respectable citizens started to move towards the exists, coins and dirt were falling in the arena. Caesar, who had been chatting happily about his performance with a bunch of flatterers, suddenly jumped up.

'Scum!' he shouted. 'I can't take any more! Blood is all they want. They don't deserve culture. You gentlemen can keep them company if you like, I have work to do. Guard!'

Of course, we all followed him. His litter, I noticed, had a double guard, shields up. Tiridates lay back opposite me grinning like a wooden Indian.

'I salute you, Tiridates,' I said, when we were moving.

'You are thinking?' said Tiridates.

'That you're a better sharpshooter than diplomat,' I said under my breath.

'Those sons of bitches,' said Tiridates loudly, 'set dogs on a woman and invite me to watch. It was an insult.'

'But you didn't need ...'

'Nor did I intend. I went to find some clean air. But when between the Goddess's legs I saw an easy target, and the coast was clear, I couldn't resist it, and she said to me, "Shoot, Tiridates, shoot!" So I shot.'

'The guard might have killed you,' I said.

'Then I could have taken thirty Roman clowns and one emperor to hell with me.' He was still grinning. 'But I stood there quite openly, shooting through the Goddess's crotch, and nobody saw me. Nobody does see you, if they are looking elsewhere.'

'They are bound,' I said, 'to find out. And that will make Rome very unsafe for you, and for any future kings.'

'Think again, physician,' said Tiridates. 'Caesar enjoyed the shooting – it spared his cowardice and it gave him a chance to perform. He loves to perform. Also, he'll know, if he's sharp as I think he is, that he needn't fear me. If I meant to do him a mischief, I could have done it then. All his staff saw the shooting. Suppose they found out that I, Tiridates, did it? Well, there are thirty thousand archers in my own regiment alone – why do you think I brought my toy bow here? I am not such a bad diplomat, I am thinking, though as you say, I am a better archer.'

So we went back the way we had come, and in past the guards and the flunkeys. I wasn't looking forward to what would come next – lunch with Caesar and his unprepossessing cronies, who wouldn't have been out of place in a street affray or on a racecourse, and would probably get drunk. I despise drunken men.

But it didn't happen. Caesar assembled the bunch of us civilly, gave us drinks, and said, 'Now, gentlemen, with that foolery over, I have work to do while we lunch. Tiridates, Sir, and you, Doctor Callimachus, if you'll excuse my rudeness in reading while I'm your host, and sit with me, I'd welcome your company. Be so good as to commend me to your lady wife, Otho. Tigellinus, we'll all meet at dinner.'

'Caesar,' said Tigellinus, 'a word.'

He took Nero aside and whispered to him. 'I know, I know,' said Nero, 'I saw it all – do you take me for a fool? Tiridates, you shot those dogs, didn't you? Well, you've frightened poor Tigellinus. What do you want me to do, Tigellinus? Have my guest arrested? Cause an international incident? This imbecile thinks you are going to shoot me, Tiridates. No sense of humour. I appreciated what you did. Wish I could shoot like that myself.

Might pick off a few of the Families if I could. Now, gentlemen, this way.'

So we two ate in silence while Nero ate and read – legal opinions. Finally he grinned, threw one batch of tablets to me and the other to Tiridates. 'Read,' he said, 'but don't stop eating. I want an opinion. The sooner this is out of the way the sooner we can talk.'

'I'm not a lawyer, Caesar,' I said.

'No, but you've got a brain. You're a Reasonable Man. Tiridates is a foreigner and he'll have an original view of this typical Roman mess. It's about money, of course.'

So the Emperor munched and wrote while we two foreigners read the opinions. I'm not familiar with Roman law. What I got was a tiresome dispute over an intestacy. The dead man had expressed before witnesses what he intended to do with his money and had even named the slaves he meant to emancipate, but had failed to put it in writing. The three legal gnomes who had gone over the case chose one option each: go with the deceased's intentions, split the case down the middle, and suggest that as a patriotic citizen the intestate would have wished to cut the Emperor in.

'What is your verdict?' said Nero.

'I'd want,' I said, 'the evidence first. Who exactly are the witnesses?'

'Precisely. Beneficiaries of the daughter. And so, I suspect, is the referee who gave the first opinion. How about the third?'

'Well, he's clearly playing for office.'

'Which he won't get – split it with me, indeed! He's a holdover from Caligula. I'll put a mark against that man's name.'

'Which leaves number two.'

'Compromise. What it doesn't, however, say is why this came to me in the first place. Something is clearly going on here which doesn't appear in evidence. Want to see my judgment?'

Nero had written, 'In view of the complexity of the evidence and in the interests of equity, Caesar commends to the litigants that they agree themselves out of court. Failing which, let the case be decided according to the legal precedents.'

He sent for more food, wiped his mouth, and said to Tiridates, 'Now, my friend, about this crooked tax contractor. How would a Parthian court treat him?'

'If it were my decision,' said Tiridates, 'I'd put him up for my men as an archery target. Crooks like this, Caesar, are the people who are endangering Rome's relations with all the Provinces.'

'The first I can't do, much as he deserves it. With the second, I agree,' said Nero.

'Find some kind of pretext to hand him over to local justice, then,' said Tiridates, 'and raise yourself in the esteem of the people he has been cheating.'

'He's a Roman citizen. Why do you think he appealed to me?' said Nero. 'The real remedy is to abolish indirect tax collection altogether. It will be a fight, however. So we add Mr. Quintus Mamurranus to the tax file. Along with Vipsanius Laenas and about fifty other official crooks. Meanwhile we order him to disgorge with compound interest to every individual citizen who proves civil cause, fine him 200,000 sesterces, which isn't much, and condemn him to infamia. We also banish him to the Province he's been robbing. That should settle his hash. Moreover, it only confirms what the judge would have done if he hadn't appealed, plus the infamia and the exile for appealing a very reasonable sentence. Phaon, this is another for the tax file.'

The man who had come in with more papers took the file from Tiridates, plus Caesar's notes, bowed, and went out. Nero didn't introduce him – I only learned later he was the secretary a rationibus, who ran Treasury affairs. Nero finished his meal.

'So now,' he said, 'ask your question, gentlemen.'

'What question, Caesar?' said Tiridates.

'Why I invited two foreigners to a working lunch. It's been hanging out of your mouths, both of you, my friends. Answer – because I wanted you to *see* me working. You, Callimachus, because you think I'm a spoilt child – yes, you do, Doctor, and I don't hold it against you. Probably true anyway. You, Tiridates, because you're going to have to negotiate with me one day. Either when you come here officially, if you ever do, or unofficially, now, when you aren't really here. You're the man I have to deal with – I'm the man you're going to have to deal with. If we do it sensibly we can avoid a ridiculous war. You wouldn't talk to my general – I invited you to come here as a Parthian emissary on the quiet. You agreed to come. So I take it you want to talk to me.'

'Caesar is quite right,' said Tiridates.

'And to take a good look at me. And frighten me into fits with some swashbuckling. Well, you've had a look. Can we talk, or will you talk to Corbulo as I suggested?'

'I respect Corbulo,' said Tiridates, 'but there were logistical problems. He turned up at our parley in arms – with a battalion, in fact. I'd told him he could bring the entire army if he wished, but in parade order, without weapons. So I greeted him from out of range, and we went our respective ways. A most unfortunate misunderstanding.'

'Most,' said Caesar. 'Corbulo informed me. He also told me that infantry in parade order could be cut down by a handful of your bowmen.'

'I see his point,' said Tiridates.

'So I thought,' said Caesar, 'that I should approach you directly. *I* took the risk Corbulo wouldn't, very properly, take as commander. I'm unarmed – you have that very effective bow. In fact, I gave strict orders it wasn't to be taken from you.'

Tiridates was grinning. 'I like that,' he said, 'Caesar has a sense of humour.'

'Caesar also agrees with what General Corbulo told you – that you can have the throne of Armenia without bloodshed if you drop your military plans and talk sensibly to me.'

'Do I have reason to trust Rome, Caesar?' said the Parthian.

'No, you don't and neither do I.'

'How do I know that this is not a plot to get me out of the field while Corbulo ...'

'Sacks your fortresses? Because I ordered him to hold his fire until you return to Armenia. Either you have to believe me or fight me, Tiridates. The second would cost us both men and money. I'm holding Rome off as long as I can, so do we talk, or don't we?'

'We can talk, unofficially,' said Tiridates.

'That,' said Nero, 'we'll do in private. I wanted this doctor to see that I conduct my own diplomacy. It's all right, Callimachus. I lost my temper in front of him the other night, Tiridates. If he's to be one of my medical advisers and treat my family I wanted him to see how I live, officially as well as privately. That disgusting performance this morning would have given you both the wrong idea of Romans, and of Caesar. Now, if you'll excuse me, Seneca, Phaon, Doryphorus and I have a meeting. Good day to you both.'

And he rose himself to show us out. He'd made his point.

'So there are two Caesars,' said Tiridates, as we left. 'Caesar, and Caesar. I'm going to deal with the one we just left. I hope to our good God that he survives. The other one had me fooled.'

The next professional invitation I had was to meet, in his own house, our archiatros, Stertinius Xenophon: something I had not expected or hoped for, for he kept himself pretty much in the background. I was immensely pleased, suspecting that I was meeting him only through Celsus' good report of me. Of course, Herondas, none of us admits early in our professional career that *we* hope to be archiatros one day, and every one of us does – you do, if you're worth your salt. When one is archiatros, however, it feels less impressive – but let that pass.

Xenophon was tall, lean, and distinguished – a big-nosed man like a benevolent raven, with a deep, quiet voice (caw, I was about to say, for the bird resemblance was quite striking). He was kindly and avuncular but a bit crushing at times – you recall the story of the Syrian officer in whom Xenophon diagnosed jaundice. The Syrian said, 'Stuff and nonsense – you never saw Middle East sunburn.' Xenophon went out, came back with the man's urine in a glass and said, 'I suppose this is sunburned, too?'

'I'm glad you came, Callimachus,' he said. 'Celsus tells me you are doing well, and I wanted to meet you. What is your impression of Caesar? You saw him privately, I believe. You may speak frankly.'

'He's immature and troubled, Archiatros,' I said, 'and he has massive problems. He's also an extremely competent administrator, or will be if there is no interference.'

'Did that surprise you?' asked Xenophon.

'It did, Archiatros,' I replied. 'There are two Caesars.'

'There are, indeed,' said Xenophon. 'We have to fuse them, eh, or extinguish one and further the other. There are also some new developments which are rather threatening to what we all have at heart. I've invited Celsus and Seneca to join us. I would have invited Gershom ben Eleazer, whom you must meet as soon as you can, but he cannot eat in my house. The fourth guest will be Tiridates of Parthia, who is known to you.'

'Why Tiridates?' I asked. 'Are the Parthians in on this?'

'Tiridates will be here in his own right. He has a better understanding than Celsus or Seneca of another matter, which is known to you. He isn't only the Parthian nominee for the throne of Armenia, with a strong interest in keeping Caesar out of mischief. He's also a distinguished magus. His people, as you may know, are initiated through the agency of soma. It is lawful to speak with them as brothers. And he has a great deal of sense – more, I think, than Lucius Annaeus.'

'Do you want me to report what I've seen, before they come?'

'Only if you want to. I sent for you, and I'm quite happy to leave Caesar in your hands.'

When the others came we exchanged small talk, and listened to Tiridates on the subject of Parthian riding and horse-training (their horses are trained to fall flat on command, so that an archer can shoot over them, using the horse as a parapet, as well as firing backwards from the saddle and under a moving horse's belly). We ate rather moodily, had the meal and the servants removed, and settled to business. I'd have loved to hear Xenophon on the subject of Claudius and Claudians, but it wouldn't have been a tactful matter to raise: it had nearly cost him his life, and had made him retire from practice.

'This little conference,' said Xenophon, 'is about the mother. I wanted you here, Callimachus, because you are going to have to see her – get past her, in fact. But events are taking a turn which I didn't expect, and I don't want my man in the middle. How well do you get on with Caesar? Privately, I mean, of course?'

I told him I thought I got on extremely well, and had his confidence, and I'd have got further if his mother hadn't sent for him and set off a tantrum, but it was early days yet, and I was going to play it by ear.

'Did Caesar make any suggestion to you? About his mother, I mean?'

'No – none at all. Though the pair of them seem pretty destructive of one another.'

'Good,' said Xenophon. 'I was afraid he might.'

'What kind of suggestion, Sir?'

'A pretty unethical one. As he didn't make it, I won't. And I don't want to spoil your transference, Callimachus, but look out.'

'It's bad as that, is it?' said Tiridates.

'As bad as that,' said Celsus. 'Tigellinus has been sounding out Chaerea, he's the mother's physician and one of my ex-residents. He came straight to me.'

'Pardon me, physicians,' said Seneca, 'but what exactly are you talking about? Say it in plain, will you?'

'He means,' said Tiridates, 'that the mother is being prepared for surgery. Of a summary kind.'

'And I,' said Xenophon, 'am not going to have anyone from Cos mixed up with it.'

'Good Gods, you don't mean it?' said Seneca. 'I thought we'd laid that to rest.'

'Well, it's been fairly obvious to the entire world, outside and inside Rome, that one of them would eventually destroy the other,' said Tiridates. 'It's a subject of bets in every guardroom which of them will strike the blow. Don't shake your head, Seneca. Some medicine is stronger than your philosophy. Incest is one such medicine, an ambitious unscrupulous woman is another, a young man who wants to choose his own wife and his own way is another.'

'Nero hates bloodshed,' said Seneca. 'You all know that.'

'Nero hates watching bloodshed,' said Xenophon. 'If the lady were an ordinarily interfering mother, he'd retire her firmly.'

'He is doing,' said Seneca, 'he's stopped her putting her head on the coinage as if she were Empress ... he even snubs her in public.'

'But if, when he tries to handle her, she simply takes him to bed...'

'Something has to give, I agree,' said Celsus. 'Who is putting it into his head? He's too ambivalent to do it himself except in a tantrum, and mother knows how to handle tantrums.'

'Well, Tigellinus for one. From saying "if she were my mother I'd slit the old witch's throat" he's moved on to saying "be a man, Caesar, or if you can't, leave the arrangements to me," ' said Xenophon.

'The mother can handle Tigellinus,' said Seneca. 'She has dealt with much harder people in her time. He's as scared of her as I am.'

'Yes,' said Celsus, 'she calls you the Expatriate Professor – sorry, Seneca, but it's true. She might kill Tigellinus, though. She won't kill you. If she'd intended that, she'd have done it on – er – an earlier occasion.' That struck me as a bit below the belt, but Seneca was wince-proof. His tutorials with Caesar were too old a story to bother him now.

'If Caesar does this,' said Seneca, 'I'm finished with him.'

'It's the last emperor-philosopher you'll educate?' said Tiridates.

'Perhaps he won't. Perhaps she'll kill him – it's possible, and she is the more operationally effective of the two. What we ought to be doing is some contingency planning.'

'Precisely,' said Xenophon, 'that is what I had in mind. Now, gentlemen, in a sense the outcome is none of our business. Should the worst occur – and as a matter of fact it may not be the worst, because in spite of your squeamishness, Lucius Annaeus, people have died in the Palace before, as I should know, without bringing the world to an end; and without his mother, Caesar might go on governing as well as he is now letting you and Burrus govern – *should* the worst occur, I say, it has one consequence of merit. Your inquiries won't be necessary any longer, Callimachus, because Caesar will become ineligible as an initiate, and he knows it. So I don't think it will compromise the Project. Also he will marry Poppaea, and our information is that that would be a positive step.'

'Personally,' said Tiridates, 'I can't for the life of me see why we're all being so mealy-mouthed. One would think Posterity was listening. What you doctors really mean is that if he kills the old gorgon it will be a good riddance and Caesar will be able to grow up – at last. I want to deal with the man, not the mother-fucking baby. For two pins I'd lend him an archer or shoot her myself.'

'How about Poppaea? I said. 'I haven't had a chance to size her up. What is she like?'

'You can size her up thoroughly when you examine her,' said Celsus.

'Not an easy lady to sum up – pretty, intelligent, educated, funny; also she's recently discovered sex, and she likes it.'

'Without reservations,' said Seneca, 'though to look at her you wouldn't know it.'

'In that respect,' said Celsus, 'Caesar, she, and Otho make a trio. Seneca walked in on them the other night – he's been saying ever since that he won't talk about it, haven't you, Lucius?'

'It wasn't,' said Seneca, 'particularly edifying.'

'Well,' said Tiridates, 'they're young. I imagine it was the usual thing.'

'Well, not exactly. Nero is nothing if not original,' said Celsus. 'Tell them, Lucius.'

'Otho,' said Seneca, 'had been ribbing Caesar about his hatred of the Games – which is one of the traits I like most in him. Caesar took it for a while, I gather. Finally he said that if they so enjoyed seeing people eaten by beasts he'd put on his own private Games for them to show them how it should be done, and that would be really amusing. When I came in, Caesar had tied the two of them to a column, as victims, and put a hearthrug on his back – I, like an unsuspecting square, came to see what the noise was about, because Poppaea was screaming her head off. And Nero was...'

'Eating them?' suggested Tiridates.

'In a manner of speaking, yes. Moreover all three of them were quite sober. It's easy for you to laugh, gentlemen. This isn't a foolish undergraduate with a misplaced sense of humour. Caesar and his friends, Caesar and his wife, won't be running a whelk stall or a bawdy house, they'll be running the civilized world.'

'The what?' said Tiridates.

'This entire machine. And its operations extend into your country too, Tiridates.'

'I think,' said Tiridates, 'that you're losing your nerve. Rome frightens me, Caesar doesn't. He isn't another Caligula. She isn't another Messalina. If she were, we wouldn't be engaged in furthering her canonization as the future Augusta. The lady reads Zendavestan and Hebrew. She sent for one of my people to explain our religion to her. She has a Jewish guru. She meditates. In my view she's an intelligent, spirited, sensual bored woman who is living in the wrong place, at the wrong time, with the wrong company. I have as great an interest in the future of your Machine as you have – it isn't only Romans that the Roman machine crushes. There might be something to be said for seeing it guided by a Caesar who has a sense of humour and dislikes gratuitous bloodshed, together with a fullblooded educated articulate woman who can satisfy him and stand up to him. Agreed?'

'That's precisely what I still hope,' said Seneca, 'and why I carry on. Caesar is bound to move away from me, but I hope it won't be in the direction of more wild oats, or worse. Which is why this mother business is so worrying.'

I was still trying to make sense of Poppaea. On the whole I guessed that Tiridates was right. I was beginning to admire Seneca's stamina – he'd stuck by his pupil, trying to make a philosopher-prince out of a frightened, ill-parented young man who wanted to be a musician, had an incestuous mother, put on a hearthrug and ate people, and sent me a spoiled, infibulated small boy as a personal present – a young man who was going to have somehow to master the Machine, its goons, its warehouses, its professional armies, its brainless Tradition, and its vast size: or be killed or assimilated by it. He'd made a start. Caesar had let me see him taking his own decisions. His civil service was cleaning up graft, getting the corn market organized, undertaking some sensible public works. Meanwhile, back at the Palace ... it was insane, risky, and tottering on the verge of another Claudian-type disaster, but Seneca – and Caesar – might just possibly bring it off. If it wasn't for the mother. If Caesar killed her, he'd probably regress and go to pieces. If she killed him, we were back to Messalina and mad Empresses, with nothing gained. It was probably going to be worth the gamble, but I couldn't get over the size and ponderousness of the apple and the pathetic rottenness of the core.

3

By and by I got this letter from home. It had come on the next ship, and had been written the day after I left Cos.

> 'Acte commends her love to her Callimachus. It has been a long time for me already, and I wanted this to reach you soon. To keep myself content I went out early to get herbs and your dispensary will be fully stocked. I will keep it replenished however long you are away. So that I may not have to sleep alone, not knowing for how long, I will go to Arbaces ...'

(He was a very decent young merchant-captain who owned his own line of business. He would treat her considerately, I knew, and was anyhow a good friend of mine: he bought all the drugs and books for me on his ventures. The only bad part of the arrangement would be that he'd be likely to be away as much as I was.)

> '... since I may need help when the child is born, and before. But he means nothing permanent to me except as your friend. Today I was called to the College – to supply drugs, they said – but blind Diodorus greets you, and he gave me assurances as to my son, for which I thank you, Callimachus, and told me I could call on him for help. But I need none now, with my weaving and the sale of drugs, which is good. If it is possible that you write me, to tell me you are safe, do so. And use all care, for both the sea and the land may be dangerous places, with storms on one and robbers on the other. But you will do your office well. My love and greetings to you.'

Obviously, in her condition, there was going to be no chance of her joining me. I had to hope Arbaces would do my job for me.

Away from Caesar and my troubles, I was getting used to Rome. Among such people one forgets that outside their circle there are ordinary folk who work and bring up children. A surprising number of these started coming in as patients –

because I was new, because I didn't know the Roman fee scale and charged the first few rather honestly, so word began to get round. I could stay here and practise, I said to myself, without the periodical bag of money from on high, though I didn't expect I would get the chance. It wasn't a bad prospect. For all I have said about Romans, I liked these folk.

Then I got a different kind of call. A young man put his head round the door, and said, 'Anyone there?'

'I'm there,' I said. I was sitting at the desk, as usual, working out how much it would cost to bring Acte and her child out if I stayed long enough.

'Are you the doctor?'

'I am.'

'Look, nobody's in today – would you mind very much taking a look at my cook?'

'What's the trouble,' I asked, 'is your cook infertile?'

'That I wouldn't know, but he's damned ill. Even if you're a women's doctor, you'd be better than nobody. And I can pay.'

When he saw me picking up my case of jars, he said, 'I'm sorry, that was inelegant. Most of 'em won't turn out to see a cook.'

I told him I'd see anyone in an emergency.

'This is one,' said the young man, 'if we aren't too late already. My chairman can go at a trot. Got what you need?'

So at a trot we went. My companion was young. He didn't sound Roman to me. I asked him where he came from.

'I'm from Provence. But don't talk about me, talk about him. The poor devil's dying, if he isn't dead.'

It was a story of increasing abdominal pain and vomiting without flux, which could mean any number of different diseases – I told my companion I was going to have to wait until I could examine the man. I asked about illness in the household, particularly those who ate the food the patient cooked, then about the precise order of the symptoms. By that time we were pounding uphill, past the front walls of fashionable villas, round the back, and into the court of the servants' quarters. The man from Provence was out before we stopped, shouting, 'This way.'

They'd put the cook in a comfortable bed, with two women tending him – wife and daughter, I thought. His eyes were shut, but I noticed his knees were not drawn up. His belly was as hard as a board.

'Any pain?' I asked him.

'Not now,' he managed to say. One of the women spoke to the master.

'He's had a motion,' said the young man. 'Is that good?'

'I hope you kept it,' I said. What they had kept was not a motion – it was mostly pus. I felt the pulse again and thought – I'd seen three cases like this. I told them to put hot towels on the man's belly and beckoned the master outside.

'Well?' he said.

'Touch and go,' I told him. 'Evidently an abscess has formed and evacuated itself. His pulse is too slow for a progressive mortification, and his pain stopped suddenly when the abscess burst.'

'So?'

'He's got about once chance in three. If his wife and daughter nurse him well and he's of a good constitution.'

'He's not married,' said the young man. 'Those two women are my own nurse and one of my servants.'

'Well, he's got a better chance still, with a master who looks after him properly,' I said, 'and puts him in a decent bed.'

'It's my bed,' said the young man – 'couldn't leave him on his own mattress. Dammit, he's a friend of mine, as well as a damned good cook. Medicine?'

'Poppy and henbane – it's made up,' I said. You, Herondas, are probably laughing at my poppy and henbane. No, I don't give it to everyone, regardless – yes, I do make use of other medications. But it so happens that to resolve the pain and colic after the evacuation of such an imposthume, what relaxes my tense infertile ladies is also appropriate. Yes, if his fever subsided I would move him on to honey, lac Veneris, which is china clay, and gentian. But I do not need to justify my prescribing to you.

'Food?'

'Iced water only by mouth until his pulse settles. Take it every half hour – I'll leave the minute-glass with the nurse – and don't wake him to give him medication.'

'I'll see to it. My thanks, Doctor. My bearers shall take you home.'

'They won't,' I said, 'I'm staying. He's not out of the wood yet.'

'You,' said the young man, 'are a doctor of a new sort. A sort that leaves a good practice downtown to sit up with my slave.'

'He's also my patient. I take it you've a spare bed.'

'Certainly. I'm also aware that in my concern – and, to be quite honest, in my dislike of doctors – we haven't been introduced. I'm Titus Petronius Druentinus. I know your name from your shingle. Never again will I be rude to a physician.' And he embraced me warmly there and then.

It's funny how when one is called to a patient one sees everyone under forty as 'young' – I have been writing about a 'young' man, but Petronius was actually a little older than I was – probably about twenty-five. I stopped feeling like a greybeard, now the work was over, and started seeing him as a contemporary. I embraced him in return.

'You don't think much of doctors, Petronius?'

'Not the ones I've seen. They all order duck soup when I'm ill, and I hate duck soup.'

'I never order duck soup,' I said, 'at least not when the cook's out of action. I take it we can still eat?'

'We can eat, but not as well as I would like, with a guest. It'll be Roman food, not from Provence. If Carbo gets over this, I'll have you back and show you what eating is really about. Come and drink wine at least, while they get something ready. All my people are in uproar.'

'Hydromel,' I said, 'if you've got it. And don't you drink much wine either – we may still have to make a night of it.'

Petronius' atrium took some getting used to – it was not very large, and the whole villa was not very large, but he had some extremely expensive stuff: genuine Greek marbles, not the usual copies of copies, some truly beautiful glass, books everywhere. When we reclined, to wait for the meal, he was watching me closely.

'You think I live like a physician?' he said.

'No comment. But you live pretty well.'

'That,' said Petronius, 'is thanks to the old man. He had a good province-milking franchise, and my brothers were sickly. There'd be more if I hadn't spent the rest. But if you come back in five years it may look rather different.'

'You're either an entrepreneur or an administrator,' I said. 'Let me guess.'

'Both. I have entered the Caesar's new Trade Office to regulate grain. How did you know?'

'Well,' I said, 'those are either bills of lading or official papers.'

'Right. Actually they're camouflage, because I'm not either, except in order to eat. I'm one of the rare Romans who has to work to do that, at least in the sense in which *I* like to eat. I'm a writer.'

'Poetry?'

'Gods, no – nobody pays for poetry. When I know what I want to write, I'll tell you what sort of writer I am. At the moment I know what sort I'm not – no essays and tragedies like old Seneca.'

'Histories?'

'I'd love it. But if I was honest they'd have my balls. How do you put up with this place, Callimachus?'

'How do you mean?'

'Well, you're a Greek – how do you think Homer would have liked writing here? Or Euripides? You have to write for an audience: how do you write for rogues and Romans?'

'Well,' I said, 'I suppose you could write *about* rogues and Romans. If you're fast enough on your feet they'll love it, because they won't recognize themselves.'

'That,' said Petronius, 'is exactly what I'm going to do. You, Callimachus, are a man after my own heart. I've only told that idea to two men, and they've both said the same thing. The other man was Caesar.'

'You know Caesar?'

'Luckily, yes. Still more luckily, he likes me. You know he's a writer, too?'

'I've heard he writes poetry,' I said.

'He does – damn good poetry: with a bit of help from his friends, but all poets need that. He wants me to write an epic about rogues. Then we can both say what we really think of this society.'

'You're going to write it together?'

'If Caesar doesn't lose interest – or get too busy building new meatmarkets and outsmarting the Parthians. Caesar needs someone like me to give him a bit of recreation. Caesar wants us to write a Roman epic.'

'About Romulus?'

'Up my ass with Romulus. About Romans. We'll do a Roman Odyssey in modern dress. The hero's going to be a corner-boy who incurs the curse of Priapus and can't get it up. There were a couple of fellow-students of mine who shared a nasty little boy. They hitched all round southern Italy swindling people. I've got one of them lined up for my Odysseus.'

'It sounds pretty edifying,' I said.

'It'll be edifying all right. It might also be a bestseller. Caesar says I'll have to give them all Greek names if I'm anxious to stay out of trouble. Rome will love it, and I can hold up the mirror. My father will be in it, too. He used to give ridiculous dinner parties to impress his fellow freedmen. I'm going to put one of those in. So I can satisfy all my grudges in one work.'

'Well,' I said, 'you're in good company. Aristophanes would have enjoyed it. I never read anything Roman which was funny.'

'Neither,' said Petronius, 'did I. You didn't have a Roman education. In our schools you don't learn about life in the street, you learn to give declamations on subjects out of a penny dreadful – tyrants making sons execute their fathers, pirates abducting heiresses, the lot. It's idiotic, but when you think about it, it's a real picture of how we live, or with suitable alterations it could be. We don't live tragedy or comedy, we try to live comic-books.'

'Are you putting a doctor in it?' I asked.

'It's an idea,' said Petronius. 'Probably would have done it, and made him a rogue, if I hadn't met you. Do you want to join the syndicate? You'd be damn useful – you're the expert on Priapus, aren't you? To tell you the truth, I nearly came to see you in any case for some local colour.'

I said that I thought he and Caesar, plus a few others around, probably knew more about that deity than I did, and I told him about the juvenile pathic Caesar had sent me. 'You could try asking him,' I suggested, 'he seems to have experience beyond his years.'

'I know Pythagoras,' said Petronius. 'Caesar too wants me to put him in. You and Caesar read each other's minds. And don't underrate him – he really is a child virtuoso, and I should know. You missed a very interesting experience.'

In the end, so far from going to bed, we slept in our clothes on two of the dinner couches. I got a call around dawn – Carbo had awakened, without pain; his pulse was settling and he had had a normal stool. I let him have broth, ordered the lac Veneris and gentian, told them to continue the poultices for two days, and call me if he showed any major change. Then I went home without waking Petronius.

Two days later he came round in person to pay me. 'You shouldn't have left like that,' he said. 'You should have stayed to breakfast.'

'I didn't want to disturb you,' I said, 'and I wasn't needed any longer.'

'Well, you could have awakened me,' he said. 'I usually sit up all night and sleep all day. When's Carbo likely to be fit again?'

'He should cook in a month, with luck. Light cooking, perhaps – no roast boars.'

'I don't serve roast boars,' said Petronius. 'That was my exorbitant father. When Carbo's operational, I'll give you aioli, or bouillabaisse – real food.'

In fact, I got to know Petronius rather well. He was angry, and he had nobody to tell about it, though possibly the book would purge that, if he ever wrote it. He'd apparently joined Otho and Tigellinus as one of Caesar's set. I'd had to be careful what I said about that, but he was the least unprepossessing of the trio, and at least he was encouraging Caesar's taste for literature.

As you know, Herondas, I don't trust Romans – but I did develop quite a high degree of confidence in Petronius. I let him into no secrets, and he made no inquiries. You may think him an odd friend for a physician: most Romans regarded him as a rake.

'Obviously,' he said, at one of our meetings, 'you're as concerned occupationally with the Art of Love as I am. But you don't have a woman here.'

'I don't, Petronius,' I said, 'nor do I have a bed-boy. Caesar sent me one, but I gave him his marching orders.'

'You told me – very wise,' said Petronius. 'I know that little blighter – intimately. A pity – you missed an experience, but you were dead right. But may I ask you your reasons – woman at home, professional etiquette, or vow of chastity?'

'None of them. Acte's always telling me to find some company here. Rome's just too bloody dangerous.'

'Yes,' he said, 'you might get someone planted by the old lady: she'd both spy on you and poison you if instructed. But I could find you someone who wouldn't.'

I told him it would hardly be fair to the woman. I might have to run for it, like our archiatros, and she'd be made to talk.

'I think,' said Petronius, 'you underrate other professionals' professional standards. A real professional would die under torture before she'd reveal a confidence. Quite a few have. And you've got more sense than to blab in bed. Let me send you Pyrrha: all her clients are physicians – she likes them. One can only masturbate for so long!'

I had some doubts about this offer, Herondas: not professionally, for doctors are human and share human needs: there is no disgrace in having a sex life, provided it doesn't involve patients, and we practise the better for it. I was simply scared of Rome in general.

Pyrrha did come to my office (whether Pyrrha was a name or a nickname I never asked her). We liked each other immediately. She was gentle, discreet, skilful and businesslike, and she enjoyed her sexuality unfeignedly. Also she was as unlike Acte as she could be, although she was Greek, having red hair and tiny freckled breasts, and she didn't shave like the Coan girls – neither her sex nor her armpits. She also said, 'You need have no anxiety: I am barren.' My conditioned reflex went off, of course, and I told her that if she minded that we might be able to do something for her – not thinking of the consequences.

'I mind,' she said, 'but in my way of living it's a clear advantage. And I don't want to become your patient, Callimachus.' I didn't want her to, either.

I wrote to my Acte, and she, sweet girl, was delighted. She sent 'her sister Pyrrha' a charm to wear, and besought her to take good care of me for so long as I should be absent in Rome.

Pyrrha wouldn't accept gifts, or appear with me in company, or talk about herself or her other lovers, except to confirm that she would sleep only with physicians, 'because they are men who do good.' A nice idea. I came, beside being fond of her, to respect her enormously. She was a true professional and a very sweet person. If I say little about her, it is in keeping with her own discretion.

Petronius once told me he had had an odd oracle from the Sybil, which said, 'You shall be consul and no consul, and lose your name, shall be childless but have more children than Caesar, and being torn to pieces, men will assemble your fragments.' I think, in the light of events, that the first part of this prophecy came true, since Titus Petronius Druentinus was never consul: he has been persistently confused with Gaius Petronius Afer, who did indeed hold that office, and with another man, too – Gaius Petronius Turpillianus, who was also consul.

And he did in fact 'lose his name', for Caesar nicknamed him The Critic: it stuck as a cognomen, and everyone who has since written the history of the times refers to him as Titus Petronius Arbiter – never Druentinus. The remark about children may possibly refer to his works, for all Menippean satirists he has had the most literary children, and they continue to be born, whereas Nero had only one child, and she died young. What the last part of the Sybil's oracle means I do not know – perhaps his works will reach posterity only in a fragmentary form, and scholars will be exercised trying to make sense of them – though they are hardly works which would appeal to professors, unless, like this professor, they find them funny.

I also touched bases with one of Bar Cochba's Jewish friends, Gershom ben Eleazer, and went to a very different house, to eat meat without milk, and talk to some civilized people for once, with Gershom's wife and daughters present, and heavy bars on the windows. I felt that this family lived perpetually packed and ready to run for its life, never knowing what Rome would do next. Gershom was a doctor, and a very good one, who doubled as a religious scholar after his own faith. The reason I hadn't met him at Xenophon's wasn't that he wouldn't enter a non-kosher house – it was really, he told me, that Seneca couldn't abide Jews. His brother Gallio had become sick of settling theological disputes and dealing with riots, which broke out every time Rome fell foul of a religion it didn't understand and didn't want to understand. According to Seneca, the Jews are a bunch of bigots and terrorists, and an enemy of philosophy because they know the answers from God. So the archiatros, who had a less Roman view, kept Gershom and Lucius Annaeus out of each other's way.

Gershom's concern was simpler than the Project. He saw no chance of an independent Judaea, simply a need to save lives. It was essential that the Jews should somehow convey to Caesar what he could and could not do in Jerusalem. They had managed to establish some kind of contacts in Claudius' lifetime, but the Best of Mothers wanted her son's image erected in all the Provinces, as a patriotic object. She saw the Jews as the trigger for nationalist uprisings everywhere, and she read her son some Jewish oracular predictions about Rome which detailed with grim satisfaction exactly what God would visit on Caesar in His good time. Gershom didn't like Romans, any more than I did, and was even more moralistic about them than I was, but his main aim was damage control.

He hadn't been able to get to Caesar, because he couldn't get past Seneca. Then quite unexpectedly, no doubt inspired by the Jewish God, Poppaea had sent for him and asked him to tell her about his tradition. Gershom didn't know who Poppaea was, and didn't listen to pagan court gossip, but his co-religionists did. If she were to marry Caesar, perhaps she might be a new Esther. His community's attempts to win over Seneca had gone badly wrong – they had persuaded him to answer a philosophical letter from a rabbi in Roman custody, offering to dispute with him, because they assumed the rabbi must be in trouble with the Roman governor for asserting the Mosaic Law. It had turned out badly, however, for the rabbi Saul was a heretic, in trouble with the Jews for maintaining that another teacher, Joshua ben Joseph, whom the Romans had executed, was the Jewish Messiah and had risen from the dead – and Seneca had wanted to talk with him precisely because of his unorthodoxy, which chimed with his own Oriental interest in avatars. So there were going to be two pieces of potential damage to control. Poppaea could be the key to both.

I couldn't help much, but at least I could make sure I didn't say the wrong thing, from the Jews' point of view, and I promised Gershom I'd do what I could. Agrippina was right, in a sense – Greek independence and Jewish independence were one cause but the Greeks are too lazy to fight for it, and the Jews run the risk of being destroyed when they fight. I was sorry for Gershom – he was humane, sincere, and immensely kind: he was also in a bind. His religion gave him great strength (I never saw a Greek family pray naturally at table and obviously enjoy it), but a lot of worry, because beside punishing Rome he was afraid his God might also punish the backsliding of Israel, in which case the righteous, like Gershom and his family, would bleed as well. In fact, he felt safer in Rome than in Judaea, where bloody war might break out at any moment. Now, to his horror, the most visible Jews in Rome were the same sect of Messianists who were recruiting non-Jewish converts and reading some of the more bloodthirsty oracles aloud in public, together with a few predictions of their own about fire from heaven and impending judgment. Worst of all, a lot of their converts were slaves, and cults among slaves scare the Roman owners worse than the devil himself. 'The Romans,' said Gershom, 'can't tell one Jew from another. These misguided people,' (he meant the Messianists), 'will destroy us all. They say the new kingdom they are preaching is a heavenly kingdom, but the Romans know only one kind of kingship. Do what you can for us, and speak to Caesar if the occasion comes.'

I told him that I would, said goodbye to my colleague and his nice family, and prayed that Asklepios would look after them and put in a good word with their jealous God, who seemed to be another more righteous Caesar, and with whom also they needed an advocate.

The exchange of letters between Rabbi Saul (who took the Roman name of Paulus) and Seneca is interesting, and some of it has been preserved. For example, Paulus appears to have been trying to get Seneca to communicate his teaching to the Imperial household: 'The fact that you take these subjects seriously,' Paulus writes to him, 'has been rewarded with some insights which Providence only vouchsafes to a few. I am certain that I am planting strong seed in a good soil … I strongly advise you to avoid all superstitions, both Jewish and pagan. As to the partial insights you have reached, pass them on by all means to Caesar, his family, and any discreet friends, but use judgment in doing so. They may find such ideas unpleasant, or miss the point, and take little notice of what you say. But the divine Message, once the seed is planted, will ultimately change their character and set them in search of God.'

In another letter Seneca is telling Paulus to stop attempting rhetoric, because he is weakening the impact of his writings, and concentrate instead on mastering correct Latin. Paulus luckily was out of Rome on the occasion when most of his sect were killed in a pogrom; we know that because Seneca wrote to console him for what had happened.

4

So finally, Herondas, at the end of my third week in Rome, the Best of Mothers sent for me, in extraordinarily courteous terms, and I met her in person.

I want to emphasize 'in person'. Such figures, whether it be Caesar, or Paris the actor, or the archiatros, or the Best of Mothers, inhabit our heads as if it were a stage, and their names wear masks and buskins. That one can meet them 'in person' is of itself something of a surprise, for how does one part one from the other, the historical mask or the public reputation from what lives inside it?

Everyone had spoken of Agrippina in such alarming terms that I would not have been surprised to meet Medusa herself. What I met, and kissed the hand of, was a middle-aged lady, reclining, though if she stood she would have been stately – the statue of Rhea Mater grown a little old. Her jewels were those of a temple image, her hair was built up with horsehair, or perhaps gold wire, into one of those strange Roman coiffures. On each cheekbone she had a patch of rouge. What she said was, 'Doctor Callimachus, we are all deeply in your debt. You have come very far to gratify the dearest wish of an old woman. You are welcome. It is doubly good of you, because you will have heard a great deal of ill concerning me.'

I told her that I set no store by gossip, and had come to meet her myself. Narses, her secretary-factotum, who had brought me, looked a little doubtful at this, as if he expected lightning to strike, but Agrippina smiled as if it pleased her. I could see why she could charm people.

'Well, you see a great criminal,' said Agrippina. 'My crime is quite unforgivable – I love my son more than I should. Roman women today, Callimachus, are mothers only by accident. I think they care more for their fishponds and their houses than they care for their children. You see, I am unfashionable. And one cannot explain to a man how it feels to bear a child within one's body.'

She looked at me hard, to see if I had the proper empathy for motherhood, and I tried to convey comprehension.

'I made my son Caesar, you know?'

'I have heard so, Madam.'

'And you met Caesar.'

'Madam, I have.'

'And you saw, no doubt, that he is young, thoughtless, easily led, and surrounded by dangerous and designing people.'

'Caesar is Caesar,' I said, 'and I had the privilege of seeing him at work on affairs of state. As to being young, so am I, but I am not called to be Caesar.'

'But you also exercise powers of life and death,' said Agrippina.

I told her that I didn't, I simply practised medicine, which was by no means the same thing, but I'd do my best for her.

'Thank you, Callimachus,' she said, 'I'm sure you will. You know what Caesar desires – his wife, whom he has shamefully neglected, has no child. I have had to be her champion. And Caesar is going to give me my wish. They are to be reconciled. Or rather they are now to be married as I understand marriage. They were both too young to undertake it when the formal marriage occurred. A child will set a great many things right, in my opinion. It won't, however, be easy. You know that?'

'I have been told,' I said, 'that the lady Octavia had a very difficult childhood.'

'Difficult? You know her mother was insane? You know she was stabbed for her misdeeds in front of her daughter? Of course you know. She ensnared my late husband by sorcery. It was my privilege, at the very end of his life, to give him some of the consolation he lacked from her.'

I swallowed hard – but Xenophon swore that it was not Agrippina who had fed Claudius the mushroom, and Agrippina was wiping an invisible tear from each eye.

'If there is one thing harder than being the mother of a Caesar, it is being the widow of a Caesar. One is called whore and murderess, and there is nobody, not even one's own son, to whom one can turn for protection.'

'I cannot promise, Madam,' I said, 'to make Octavia bear a child. You know that?'

'Of course I know it. But you will do what you can. You will see her, and you will tell me your frank opinion. If she cannot, that is a punishment I must bear for loving my own son too much, and I shall know that the Gods are jealous of me. But I wanted to see you first. Octavia cannot be turned over to some doctor who learned his skills on the fertility of cattle – I told Caesar, I won't have her suffer any more. I often wish there were women physicians – then we might have gentler care. There was absolutely nobody in Rome whom I would allow to touch her. They'd have made matters worse by their probings and pawings. Then I was given your name. I told Caesar, very well, but I want to see the young man myself – I am a judge of men when it comes to women's matters.'

'I hope, Madam, that you will have confidence in me,' I said. 'If not, please tell me. I agree that the wrong physician might well make matters worse.'

She looked me over as if she meant to buy me. 'Oh yes,' she said, 'you'll do. You aren't scared of me, you didn't flatter me, and you don't look at me lasciviously to see what sort of a woman took Claudius from Messalina. I will tell Octavia that you will be seeing her.'

'I suggest, Madam, that when I do, you yourself should be there, rather than some attendant,' I said.

'If you think that wise.'

'I do, Madam.'

'Very well, that's arranged. I will send for you. By the way, you aren't just a woman's doctor, are you?'

'No, Madam. I have a general training,' I replied.

'Splendid. Then there's something else you can do for me. You can call it a test of your medical skill. I'll call it doing a service to an old woman who can't get sense out of Roman doctors. An old swordfighter on whom I have often won money is dying. He's my luck, and nobody can cure him. They say his case is hopeless. I want you to see him for me. If you say there's hope, I will take your word for it.'

'What is he dying of?'

'A suppurating wound. He who has survived for so long in the arena is dying of an accident.'

'I'm not a surgeon, Ma'am. He would do better with Celsus.'

'But I want *you* to see him. Go immediately,' said Agrippina. 'He may be dead tomorrow. Goodbye, Doctor. Narses will show you the way.'

'You bought it, physician,' said Narses, when we got in the litter. 'I don't envy you your patient. If you've any sense, you'll watch it, Greek.'

'Trouble?'

'You could call it that. Sporus was the hardest man in the swordfighting game.'

'What's wrong with him? Not swordcuts?'

'No, he got drunk and a cart went over his leg. You can smell it down the street – the bone's sticking out.'

'And,' I said, 'your lady mistress thinks he's a hopeless case, and I shall finish him off.'

'My mistress thinks he's a hopeless case and he'll finish you off,' said Narses. 'She should have been a man. She wants to see whether you're one. He's lying on a pallet holding a sword, and he swears by Hercules that he'll kill any physician who comes near him.'

'Why?'

'Well, for a start he's delirious, but the duty surgeon tried to stun him with a mallet – to operate, you know. One doesn't stun Sporus – he saw the mallet coming. There's a pair of nature-cure doctors trying the efficacy of prayer from a safe distance. Here's the barrack. Good luck to you, Greek – and don't go too close. Sporus had a four cubit reach in the arena.'

It was a forbidding place, the swordfighters' school, more like a prison – which in fact it is – with an armed guard chained to the doorpost. The trainer was waiting for us – the biggest black man I had ever seen.

'You're the doctor-man,' said the lanista. 'Come in, Doc. You'd better look through the door, but he won't last the night.'

I followed him past the guard into the gallery of cells, and I could smell suppuration already.

'He's in there,' said the lanista. 'Take a look.'

I opened the Judas and looked in. The two quacks, with pointed masks to keep out the miasma, and looking appropriately like a pair of ducks, were busy making medicine over a portable altar. Sporus was half-lying, half-sitting on the pallet, holding the sword, as Narses had said. And he was certainly no Roman – around his neck was a golden torque.

'What's his real name, coach?' I asked. I'd seen all I needed.

'Real?'

'Yes – he's a Briton, isn't he?'

'Welsh. His name is Caradoc – same as that terrorist man out there, you know?'

'And what was his biggest fight?'

The African scratched his head. 'With Musca, I'd say. Went

ten bouts. Sporus got his missio that time, but he signed up again like a fool. He cut Musca in half – never saw anything like it, before or since.'

'Thanks,' I said, 'that helps. We'll go in now.'

The coach wasn't enthusiastic. 'I suppose,' he said, 'you know what you're doing.'

Personally I'd never felt better. If anyone could handle Caradoc I could. As I told you, mother was half-Welsh.

Caradoc had tousled iron-grey hair, drooping moustaches, and he was desperately sick. His face seemed on fire, part-anger, part-delirium. I could see his chest heaving. He heard the door open and looked at me as if I'd entered the ring with him, looking for the place to strike. There was a clean pallet ready, but they hadn't been able to put him on it.

'Nos da, Caradoc,' I said.

'Ye Gods,' exclaimed Caradoc, in Welsh, 'who are you, man? Or aren't you there?'

'I'm there,' I said, 'sick as you are, Caradoc.'

'You're not another bloody Roman, come to hit me on the head?'

'No, man. I'm a Greek. My mother was Welsh, however. Sorry I am to see you in this state. May we talk, then?'

'In Welsh?' said Caradoc.

'Yes, in Welsh. Let me get rid of these, though.'

The two quacks were staring – I couldn't see their faces because of the masks, but I gather Cos wasn't popular. I could pull rank, however.

I turned back the covers. Caradoc groaned – anticipation, chiefly, because I did not disturb the limb. It looked like a stinking ham. Sure enough, there was a piece of broken femur in the middle of the mess. The bed looked as if it hadn't been changed in weeks.

'So, gentlemen,' I said to the quacks, 'what is the teaching?'

They looked at one another. Then one said, 'Instruct us, sir.' – the usual consultation-disputation formula. I admired their cheek.

'When there is pus ....' I began.

No reply. So much for them and their medicine.

'When there is pus,' I said, '*you must let it out*. We will do that. Now colleagues, which of you will assist?'

They didn't answer. Instead, they packed up their altar and split, as if the devil were after them, which I hope he was, and I hope he choked them.

'Good riddance,' I said in Welsh, 'to bad rubbish.' And I sat down by the patient, who hadn't let go of his sword.

'Good riddance,' said Caradoc, 'but Doctor bach, can you ease my pain, and send the others away?'

'What others, man? I see no others,' I said, 'only us two, and the coach here.'

'Those others,' said Caradoc. 'I don't know their names. Men I killed, mostly. They keep at me. I daren't sleep if I could.'

'You were the man that beat Musca, weren't you?' I asked him.

Caradoc raised the ghost of a grin. 'In ten rounds – you know that? But he's been here, both the halves of him, taunting me, and I can't kill him, Doctor, I can't kill him.'

'No,' I said, 'but I'm afraid you're going to have to fight.'

'To fight. I'll fight.'

'You're going to win this one, too.'

'With Musca?'

'No,' I said, 'with old Death. But you'll have to take a wound. That's how it goes. I don't need to tell you.'

'I've got my wound. My leg's rotted,' said Caradoc.

'Another wound. A clean one.'

'I had to let Musca's thrust in,' said Caradoc, 'so I could get inside his guard.'

'That,' I said, 'is how you'll win this one.'

'I can't take more pain, Doctor. Let me die in peace.'

Nepenthe would have finished him off. 'Caradoc,' I said, 'have it your own way. But you're in the final round, Caesar is watching you. His mother sent me to you. If you give up in front of these Roman pillocks you'll shame me, man.'

Caradoc sighed deeply and took a tighter grip on his sword. I turned to the lanista.

'You know his lingo,' said the African. 'What are you going to do?'

'Give him his shield,' I said.

'What the hell for?'

'Give it to him and look sharp.'

'Yes, Sir!'

'Don't throw it, fool. Give it to him.'

Carodoc took it.

'Now,' I said, 'you're on. When you feel his thrust, not sooner, cut him in half!'

'Who, Musca?'

'No, Death. Not me, Death – do you understand me?'

'*He's* Death,' said Caradoc, pointing his sword at the African, who beat a hasty retreat.

'No, he isn't. He's your coach. Here's Death. He's pale, and you can smell him.'

And I hung one of the filthy towels over a chair, within swordlength, feeling in my lap-pocket for the bone forceps and praying to Asklepios that the splinter wasn't joined on.

'Now – on guard!'

His shield came up like lightning.

'Lanista, this man is fighting Death,' I said, 'which is that towel. Now coach him.'

'What? Are you crazy?' said the coach, 'Oh, you mean humour him. All right. I get it. Now, you keep that shield up, man, and watch your guard. Keep your eye on his swordpoint, not yours, or you're a dead man. Left parry!'

And Caradoc, covered by his shield, so he couldn't see me getting out the instrument, did so like a lamb.

'When you feel his steel, Caradoc,' I said, and I grabbed the splinter. It didn't budge. Then half his femur seemed to come out in a torrent of pus and gas-bubbles. Caradoc's stroke bisected chair and towel, and he fainted, which was the best thing that could have happened. The sword fell with a clatter, narrowly missing my feet.

'Faugh!' said the coach, 'I'm feeling very sick.'

'Later,' I said. 'Pick him up and put him on a clean mattress. Get this mess out of here. And I want five mouldy loaves, sharpish. Really mouldy, d'you understand? Jump to it!'

The lanista picked up Caradoc like a sack. 'So where do I get five mouldy loaves?' he asked.

'That's your problem,' I said, 'get them and look sharp about it.'

'Sir!'

'And get that bed out of here. Burn it.'

'Sir!'

'And thanks very much. You saved that man's life.'

'Yeah,' said the coach, 'me and you. That was neat.'

Later, when that was over, and the other swordfighters came out of hiding, I got hay and incense in, and washed out the wound with salt water and vinegar. Caradoc was stirring, but he gave no trouble. I gave him poppy in wine and he passed out again – this time, sleeping, which was a good sign. Providentially, the mouldy bread arrived from the commissary, not very mouldy, but mouldy enough. I had more set up for next day's poultice, sent for resin and bandages, and between us we set the leg. In the end, I got through about midnight and the chairmen took me home. Caradoc, of course, never fought again, which was as well, but his fever was down next day, and he was up on crutches in a month, thanks to Asklepios and my Welsh mother. The cosmetic result was shocking, but at least he kept the leg. I never asked Agrippina if I passed muster, but she sent me a gold ring with a lionhead on it, and before Caradoc was out of bed, I was summoned to do what I came to Rome to do.

And it was, in every respect, a near-impossible case. Octavia was a quiet, polite young girl with very little to say for herself. She was actually then eighteen, but by Greek standards she looked about fifteen. I saw her alone with Agrippina. She was able to say a little about herself: yes, she wanted a child, because she wanted to be reconciled with Caesar, and it was her duty as a wife to bear one.

'You have tried to have one?' I asked.

'Not very often.' It was said mechanically, without looking at me.

'You find it difficult?'

No answer.

Agrippina said, 'Dear child, we talked about this, didn't we? You know that the doctor must ask you some unpleasant questions. You must speak to him as frankly as you do to me. Try to imagine you are speaking to me, not to him.'

'Yes, Mother.'

'How difficult?' I asked her. 'Is it painful?'

She nodded.

'How about the first time?'

She nodded, and clutched her kerchief in her fingers – still not looking.

'My son was a mere boy,' said Agrippina. 'He wanted to prove he was manly. He was horribly rough with her.'

'Has it ever been easier than that?' I asked.

'It was, for a little while. When I healed,' said Octavia.

I noticed that at each question she not only clenched her fingers but drew her knees together. I'd stopped, however, worrying about her fertility. I asked her what she weighed.

'I don't know,' said Octavia.

'Do you eat well?'

'Enough. I try not to get fat.'

'Why?' I asked.

'I don't want to be ugly. Caesar wouldn't ever love me if I were fat.'

'And are your periods regular?'

Octavia shook her head.

'Since Caesar stopped treating her as a wife, she hasn't had one,' said Agrippina.

'I have, Mother, once.'

What would you have done, Herondas? Asked her about Messalina? About what she'd seen as a child, and heard since, and tried to do some psychotherapy there with the Best of Mothers as chorus? I was taught never to ask the question on the tip of your tongue, which is probably an obvious one, unless you can close there and then any can of worms you open. So I asked her nothing else. I didn't ask Agrippina, either, if there had been any fights over food, because she'd told me Octavia preferred to eat by herself and read while she did so. If I could have talked to the servants, I'd have asked if they ever found uneaten food hidden.

As it was, I had to examine her. That was a disaster. In fact, it was impossible. She could no more tolerate a pelvic examination than a ticklish person, however cooperative, can hold still for tickling. At one point she went into complete tetanic rigidity, such as one sees with poison or after a poisoned wound. Agrippina soothed her, shouted at her, and finally offered to hold her down. I told her it wouldn't be necessary, and spoke exclusively to my patient.

'All right, Octavia. I won't examine you further like that.'

She lay quite still and relaxed while I examined her head and neck, her hands, her pulse. As I examined the abdomen she began to tighten again.

'Heavens,' said Agrippina, 'I didn't realize how thin ...'

'You're getting tight again,' I said. 'You can't let me touch you, even though you want me to examine you. Is that what happens with your husband?'

She nodded vigorously.

'It's all right,' I said, 'I think I understand. You'd like me to help you?'

'Yes, doctor.'

'Very well. I'll try. That's enough for now. I'll talk to your mother.'

And Octavia dressed and left us, very composed, thanking me for having come so far.

'You see?' said Agrippina, 'the child's terrified of men. Or else she's bewitched. Why is she so thin, doctor?'

'I'll come to that in a minute,' I said.

'If she could come gradually to relax ...'

'Madam,' I said, 'I came here to look into Octavia's barrenness. That's the least of our worries. If it was a simple case of vaginal spasm, it could be overcome with patience.'

'How?' said Agrippina.

'With a healthy girl I'd try to accustom her gradually. I would tell you to get the olisboi that men use to break in boy concubines, and let her learn that she can dilate herself. With patience, and with an extremely patient and gentle husband ...'

'My son is both gentle and patient. I'll get them – never mind if that is a strange prescription for a married woman in my position to fill. You've spoken bluntly, so I mustn't be prudish ...' said Agrippina. 'I will have some made.'

'But this is not a healthy girl,' I said. 'I don't think I want to worry about her fertility, because at the moment I'm worried for her life.'

'Her life?' said Agrippina, looking really shocked. 'Is she sick?'

'Not physically, except that she's starving herself,' I said.

'Then she must eat,' said Agrippina. 'But she does eat – how can she be...?'

'She eats alone?' I said.

'Yes,' said Agrippina, 'she prefers it.'

'And hides the food,' I said. 'She doesn't eat it.'

'Then she'll have to eat at my table in the future. She must be made to eat. I'll see she does.'

'That would be about the worst thing you could do, Madam,' I said. 'If you make her eat, she'll go outside and vomit.'

Agrippina stared at me in total incomprehension. 'But why?' she asked.

'Nobody knows. It is a mental sickness, and it may be mortal. I think perhaps she does not want to become a woman.'

'I understand,' said Agrippina. 'A woman like her mother!'

'For whom womanhood was fatal. Precisely.'

'Then, Callimachus, what do I do?'

'It would be best if she were cared for in a hospital,' I said, 'away from her family. There, it's possible they could get her to eat. And I would try to get her to talk about her mother.'

'And where in Rome, apart from my house, do you imagine she would be safe, Callimachus? This isn't Cos. You aren't a child. I've had to defend my own life once on trumpery charges. They said, on a wicked woman's testimony, that I was plotting to dethrone my own son. That woman was my friend, doctor.'

'Of whom are you afraid, Madam?' I asked her.

'Of my many enemies,' said Agrippina.

'But not of your own son?'

'Yes!' she said. 'Of my own son!'

I saw why they were afraid of the Best of Mothers, why Caesar was afraid of her. I wasn't doing any psychotherapy with this family.

'I think,' said Agrippina, 'that you are letting your clinical mind run away with you. She does not eat because Caesar does not treat her as a wife. Change that and you change all our fortunes. I'll order the olisboi. It's a repugnant idea – I hate my son's slave-boys, they've stolen my daughter's bridal bed from her – but I'll make sure she uses them, if I have to see it done myself. Then we shall see how things fare.'

'It is your decision,' I said, 'or rather it's Octavia's. I'm only here to tell you what my opinion is.'

Agrippina looked me over as she'd done once before – as if she intended to buy me. 'I took a risk, bringing you here, Callimachus. You wouldn't play an old woman false, would you?'

The implication was menacing. I assured her that I would not.

'I think,' said Agrippina, 'I believe you. You've done your best. This is a harder thing than Sporus' leg.'

'Much harder. Call on me again if you want me to help.'

'That,' said Agrippina, 'won't be necessary. I know as much now of the teaching of Cos about Octavia as you do. I'll be her physician. That is what I intended, and you must accept a mother's gratitude.'

I did accept it, and my fee, which was handsome and befitted the Best of Mothers, and got out of the house as fast as my legs would carry me.

'Well?' said Caesar, expecting a full report.

I told him that I had examined his wife and advised his mother, but I couldn't discuss a patient even with Caesar himself.

'Your mother,' I said, 'has had my advice and says she will act as Octavia's physician.'

'Gods,' said Caesar, 'I'll bet she will. Well, you saw her, my wife. It's like trying to put on a shoe which is all sole.'

'If you do lie with her again, Caesar, try to be gentle. As gentle as you probably are with a boy.'

'I will, I will. I'll probably have to lie with her. But it'll be a duty, not a pleasure. Well, you've got past Medusa. Did she suspect anything?'

'Probably,' I said.

'She'd do that in any case. Now, as soon as I can arrange it, Otho will send for you to see *his* wife. That'll be a very different matter.'

I did not tell Caesar about Octavia's self-starvation. I saw trouble for her if he knew.

You may feel, Herondas, that I didn't do the best I could for my patient and am worthy of censure. I ought to have taken up residence in the Best of Mothers' household and worked with Octavia, incurring the suspicion of the entire town and giving Caesar, if he lost his nerve, a handle to accuse Octavia and myself of adultery and his mother of complicity (I had seen enough of Tigellinus to know what *he* would advise if he got half a chance). I ought not to have been party to what amounted to a deception. Very well – you would have done better, and lost your own head and several other folks' heads in the process. I decided to play it by the book. I had given the right advice, the milieu was hopeless for any kind of psychotherapy, and if Poppaea wished to ascertain the cause of her barrenness I would not be responsible for the use she might make of the advice. In such circumstances, if you are unfortunate enough to *be* in such circumstances, I suggest you do as I did. I also suggest that you probably would do so.

The lady Poppaea was indeed 'a very different matter.' She was a striking young woman with light-brown hair (her own), a fine clear skin with one tiny crater from the small-pox in childhood, which actually served as a dimple. She was attractive rather than pretty – articulate, modest, and quite unembarrassed.

'I hope this isn't difficult for you, doctor – but I expect you are well used to nervous women. I'm not nervous.'

'Good,' I said, 'it's only difficult for me if it's difficult for you.'

'I'll treat you,' said Poppaea, 'as if you were the midwife.' She answered my questions frankly and quickly. When I examined her, she held the waiting-woman's hand. There weren't any problems. The uterus was rather small but mobile, the adnexa normal. She had had a child who was living. After that there was a history of two early miscarriages. I saw no reason why she shouldn't conceive again. Her husband, Otho, the plump fellow, sat in the next room with the door open while I made my examination. Poppaea thanked me, called him in, and told him to make me welcome. 'I expect you'll want to talk,' she said. 'We're most grateful to you, Callimachus, for coming so far.' No questions on her behalf – I was to talk to her husband. Correctness, by Roman standards, couldn't go futher.

'Well, doctor,' said Otho, 'what's the verdict?'

'Nothing wrong that I can find. Certainly nothing gross. Her womb is rather small. That's probably something we can correct, and the remedy will be to hand about now if we were quick.'

'Oh,' said Otho, 'that's good – she wants another baby. What's the remedy, doctor?'

I told him that the only medication which I thought really effective for a small womb was young spring grass infused, and then only if it was quite fresh, so we'd better get to work, or we would have to wait until next March or April, '... but it's quite likely she'll conceive in any case by then,' I said, 'so it may not be needed. If she does, she should avoid exertion, at least for the first three months.'

'Isn't she marvellous?' said Otho. 'I'm incredibly lucky.'

I didn't know what to make of this pair. Otho was a fat, genial, easy-going character who would get a lot fatter, I felt, if he didn't exercise more and eat less. The house was expensive, full of Roman rococo; Otho had a lot of wall paintings of nymphs and chariot races which would have looked better in an inn, or a sporting club. I fended off first perfume, when a slave tried to pour it over me, then very good Falernian in a very expensive cup, and asked for my usual, and got it.

'I'm ready for you, doctor,' said Otho. 'Poppaea said you only drink hydromel – I said, he's Greek and he'll drink my Falernian. She wins her bet.'

We drank to one another, to the lady, and to Caesar, and I pointed out to Otho that it takes two to make a baby.

'You mean, there's something wrong with me?' he said.

'I have to exclude it.'

'Wrong horse,' said Otho, and, sotto voce, because the door was still open, 'I've fathered one child by her – and children by other women.'

'Recently?'

'Not very. Two years ago. With Poppaea around, I've cut out the others. No need.'

'You like the baths?' I asked him.

'Love them. Spend hours there – or I did, before I built my own. Trying to get my weight down – Poppaea thinks I'm getting fat.'

'Hot baths, or cold?'

'Hot. I'm not a Scythian.'

'Then cut down on them. The combination of hot and moist distempers the seed.'

'I'm glad you told me,' said Otho.

'And your Falernian,' I said, 'partakes also of hot and moist. So cut down on that.'

'It's still,' said Otho, 'the wrong horse.' And he grinned.

I had to play the charade – I couldn't say, 'You mean, she sleeps with Caesar, and we can't both of us be unlucky.'

'You get my meaning,' said Otho. 'Isn't she marvellous? Butter wouldn't melt.' He motioned the slave to shut the door.

'You know, that girl was a virgin when I married her. Butter wouldn't melt then – I was expecting a very dull life. But she might have been in bed with me all her life. After ten days she asked if there was anything she could read that would make her better still, and I gave her the book by Elephantis. She's perfection – they don't make Roman wives like her any more.'

'You're very fortunate,' I said.

'She's bright, too. Much brighter than I am – reads philosophy like one of your Greek ladies, talks four or five languages. You can't keep a woman like that in a cage. Not that we don't love each other – we do. But Poppaea is a law to herself. Will you be around for a while? I'd like you to keep an eye on the local quacks – and, of course, if she gets pregnant, I'd be happier if you were on hand.'

'Probably not,' I said, 'but Celsus will look after her for you. I'm at Caesar's disposal.'

'Aren't we all?' said Otho. 'Celsus is too stiff for me. He reminds me of old man Seneca, except that Celsus is real, and stiff all the way through. I wish you'd stay – you could set up here and enjoy the good life. Come and stay with us if you want.'

We parted on excellent terms. Otho insisted on giving me the cup I'd used, and he sent my fee to my office instead of handing it to me, or letting his head man hand it to me, as Agrippina had done.

As to Poppaea, I saw his point – she was perfectly respectable, sexually proficient, and the ideal two-way bet: wife and mistress for now, meal-ticket in the future. Pandarus was taking his turn with Cressida as well as being her manager. That was Otho's point of view. But it wasn't Poppaea's. She was far too intelligent to take Otho seriously and I didn't blame her. Meanwhile he gave her everything she wanted and she gave him everything he wanted. Whether she could handle Caesar I had no way of knowing, but from her coolness and her brains I thought it extremely likely. She wrote me a letter of thanks in which she intelligently gave me a release of confidentiality. 'Otho asks me to tell you to convey our good news to Caesar, who wishes us both well, and desires that we should have the child we desire.' A clever, clever lady.

All the time, while I was answering Caesar's questions, I was thinking that I'd done rather well, fulfilled the College's mandate, kept out of trouble, and I was working out how soon I could leave and get bact to Acte. That I did not was the work of some God other than Asklepios.

'Excellent,' said Caesar. 'Will you report to me in writing that Octavia is incapable of marital relations?'

I considered that a bit. In the circumstances, I thought, she isn't capable. I'm reporting what is, not what might be the result of treatment. A court would probably agree with me.

'I think I can truthfully say that, Caesar,' I said.

'Then we can go ahead. You have the combined thanks of Nero Germanicus and of Lucius Ahenobarbus. You're a real friend.'

I thanked him, and privately agreed with him.

'Callimachus, I want you to become my personal physician.'

'I have to return to my duties, Caesar. And I have family responsibilities,' I blurted out.

'Of course you have. But we'll see to those.'

'It's not possible, Caesar.'

'Oh,' said Caesar, 'I'm not trying to make you spend your life here. For a month or two – I have reasons for asking you. Then you can go home a very rich man.'

Financial considerations were the last thing in my mind just then. I was wondering what Caesar's reasons were.

'Give me two days, Caesar,' I said, 'and I will answer.'

I intended to ask Xenophon, but I knew what he would say and he did. I was fairly caught.

Seneca said that if I was to be Caesar's physician, I had to be fully aware of what was going on, and the structure of the pecking order. At the centre was Caesar himself. Around what one might call the recreational side of Caesar stood a collection of playmates and boon-companions: Otho, Tigellinus, lately Petronius, and, of course, less ostentatiously, Poppaea. This bunch, who called themselves the Illuminates, met regularly and went to sporting events together, all except Poppaea, who had to be more discreet than the men. Their time in Caesar's company was devoted to eating, talking, writing poetry, organizing sophomoric pranks, and enacting a heavy programme of sexual fantasies, most of them suggested by Caesar himself, which were, I think, the main order of business, and were certainly the main attraction. Other people drifted in and out of this circle – ranging from scions of the great houses to actors and charioteers: Caesar was highly democratic in his choice of associates for these recreational activities. The Illuminates were a typical schoolboy secret society, complete with rituals and initiations. Caesar never tried to involve me in its meetings, probably because in declining the offer from Pythagoras I flunked the entrance test.

In complete contrast, the non-recreational Caesar had a small cabinet of advisers, headed by Seneca himself, Burrus, the commander of the Praetorian Guard, who was responsible for Nero's safety, and the senior civil servants: Phaon (Treasury), Doryphorus (Home and Provincial Affairs) and Archiatros Xenophon (Communications and Greek Affairs). Burrus was a Gaul, a tough military officer who had made a career of protecting Emperors. When Claudius died, he put himself, as a matter of military duty, under the orders of the First Lady – Agrippina – and the Pretorians proclaimed Nero, not Britannicus, the next Caesar. It was he who had had to preside when Agrippina was charged, by an erstwhile lady-friend whom she had insulted, with treason. The charge misfired, but Burrus' link with the Best of Mothers was always a problem to the others – even though she referred to him publicly as the Military Cripple (he had a hand which was paralysed by an old wound).

Seneca had long since given up trying to interfere with the Illuminates. They were at least reasonably discreet, and their activities took place in private. They were, in his view, preferable to what had happened before, when Caesar had gone on nocturnal excursions in the town, picking up assorted street people as companions, and getting involved in all manner of hooliganism. He had had to be protected constantly on these forays by police in mufti, or by a goon squad of boxers and swordfighters, and even so, things commonly got out of hand. For example, when fans of rival pop dancers rioted at a concert, Caesar offered a prize to whichever side won: as a result, troops had to be called out, and the Senate proscribed pop concerts and banished all the performers.

Faced with the Illuminates, Seneca's chief concern was to keep them out of the life of Caesar the administrator. This dam was beginning to leak. It did not matter too much that Doryphorus, who was a minister, also had a sexual affair going with Caesar. That was a separate operation, and in any case Doryphorus was a first-rate administrator. He was definitely not one of the Illuminates. They had, in fact, decided to haze him on one occasion – they grabbed him and put him through an elaborate burlesque wedding with Caesar as the bride, complete with torches and a ceremonial defloration. Caesar, always the actor, entered into the spirit of this and gave a very funny (and noisy) performance as the reluctant virgin. Doryphorus said nothing – he was physically scared of Tigellinus, who had a considerable reputation as a ruffian – but he was furious at being humiliated by the Emperor's cronies. From then on, he tried to phase out Caesar, who was the pursuer, not the pursued, by encouraging him to concentrate on Acte and leave him, Doryphorus, alone. Caesar persisted, however, Acte or no Acte – chiefly, Seneca thought, to annoy the Best of Mothers – and showered Doryphorus with money.

A far more serious problem was Tigellinus, because Caesar had made him his security adviser, over the head of Burrus, who was the proper officer. Burrus, of course, had the loyalty of troops, while Tigellinus recruited his own unofficial police force, much of it highly undesirable. This bunch, in a showdown, would be no match for soldiers, but there were the makings of trouble – the Illuminates were leaking out of the bar and the bedchamber into serious affairs. So Seneca, realizing that he could not put his thumb in the dyke without getting it chewed off, had changed strategy. If Poppaea were no longer joint mascot of the Illuminates with that precocious child Pythagoras, but were married to Caesar, she might be able to exercise a restraining influence without spoiling the fun, and Caesar might grow out of fraternity capers into the arms of a woman who was as sexually creative as he was, but sensible with it. I had seen the shape of most of this already, but Seneca put it in plain. He reckoned I could help, because I was the first friend of his own age that Caesar had accepted without bringing him into the club.

On the non-recreational side, as I have indicated, Seneca himself was the key man. Most people, Herondas, can be described in psychiatric-history terms: anyone reading the summary can make some sense of them – Caesar, for example. Seneca completely defies this sort of dehydration. In consequence nearly everyone around him got him entirely wrong. When I first met him, so did I. He was transparently the talented immigrant Professor of Rhetoric and Literature, who enjoyed the Good Life, provided it wasn't too scandalous, enjoyed being a don and hearing the sound of his own voice, was a closet yogi at the cheese-and-wine party level, and had struck it unbelievably rich when he landed a future Caesar as pupil: just about then he was finding the ride a little alarming but was scared to get off. A good many Romans thought the same, and looked on, rather as one watches a bull-riding acrobat, betting on how big a tumble he would finally take. The other mythology about him is that he was an austere philosopher, trying to shape an embryo tyrant into a decent ruler, and quitting with dignity when the young oaf disappointed him. That was a fantasy, too.

Seneca, as I've said, was a Spaniard from Cordoba. The whole family was talented. His father was an administrator and an academician, his brothers were a provincial administrator and a successful banker: the banker-brother's son was the poet Lucan. Seneca started in legal practice, became quaestor, had a near escape under Caligula when a mistress he shared with the Emperor saved his life by telling Caligula that Seneca's cough was due to terminal consumption, so that he would die soon in any event. Claudius threw him out of Rome, for sleeping with the celebrated Julia Livilla, Agrippina's sister, which was a national pastime then. The row and the ensuing banishments when Claudius found out what his aunt had been up to depopulated smart society. In fact, not having slept with Julia would have been evidence of sheepishness rather than virtue. The Gods turned this affair to good. Seneca travelled widely, took his doctorate in Alexandria, and came back, finally, in time to catch the eye of Agrippina as a tutor for her promising son. Messalina was behind Julia's conviction, and Agrippina was a natural friend of any enemy of Messalina.

The first thing which punctured my tidy picture of a rather scared academician sitting on a fortune in his swimming pool and wishing he was in the Library at Alexandria was Seneca's immense industry. For the first three years of Nero, when the recreational side was very much to the fore, Seneca was virtually Emperor, and no Emperor since Augustus had worked so hard. Seneca put in full office hours seven days a week. On 'blank' or ill-omened days, when official business stops, he worked at home. The amount of administrative planning he got through is staggering – tax collection policy, foreign affairs, currency, and a great deal of minor matters as well. There were eighteen shelves of reports, working papers and policy outlines, every word of which Seneca wrote. I suppose it is possible that as soon as he knew his pupil would be Caesar, he started stockpiling memoranda over years, but the fact is that when Nero came down out of orbit and began to tackle administration himself, everything was in place, except his signature.

That would have been a fair stint for any one man. But Seneca, at the same time, was running a banking and loan business, a string of estates, and a wine factory.

Typically, though he himself was a lifelong teetotaller, the wine was some of the best in Italy. The most interesting thing to me – and it may surprise you, Herondas – was that Seneca had all this time no official position. He was not a secretary or a palace officer, he held some largely honorific magistracies simply because, like the chairmanship of the Chamber of Commerce, they were expected of him. It was only shortly before my visit that he reluctantly took a consulship. He was as rich as Croesus already on the capital he'd got from Agrippina, so he had no need of Caesar's munificence. His only apparent motive was love of administration and concern to see Rome decently governed. On top of all the rest, he wrote steadily – plays, letters, essays, an enormous literary programme. He had a family, a social life (two, in fact, because beside entertaining his own friends he had to entertain on a vast scale ex-officio, and at his own expense), a large establishment in Rome, and constant interruptions to service Caesar. He even found time for a very discreet extracurricular sex life which I never penetrated, as well as being twice married, to two exceptionally nice women. This programme of living would have taxed an athlete, but on top of it all Seneca was an asthmatic, who virtually never felt brimming with health. It was a pretty striking performance.

Performance, of course, is the word. Caesar was a natural actor. So, in his way, was Seneca. But the cases were entirely different. Caesar was like one of those unfortunate criminals in the plays staged by Domitian, who found himself playing Herakles in the arena in the knowledge that he would be burned alive for real at the end of the last act.

It was plain to me, and it must I think be plain to you, Herondas, that Seneca had at some time seen – by what means, and with what assistance I do not know, though I suspect it was when he was working with Kausalika – in fact, he virtually told me as much. Now seeing as we know has different effects on difficult people – some of them lose all interest in serial reality and become contemplatives. Or it can be seriously disturbing – the scenery the Mother has constructed has to be solid, or we would come to a standstill: when some people get a look at the back of the set they decompensate, or consider themselves adepts and develop an unpuncturable elitism, like the Pythagoreans: they know the answers and can manipulate others. Or once they stop regarding life as a thread and realize that the Sisters are weaving in three dimensions, not one, they lose motivation in a different way – if all such games are a superposition, why bother with this one? They resign and wait for the board to be set up again in some other component of the superposition.

Seneca did none of these, because somebody (probably not Kausalika, who was a Saiva guru) told him about Krishna's sermon to Arjuna at the Battle of Kurukshetra: being involved in the play, perform your role! So being a Roman administrator, administer Rome. Knowing it is a play, still treat your role as real, or you will be simply a bad actor. The trouble with Seneca was that he was the entire cast in himself, so he had many Kurukshetras – as professor, as writer, as administrator.

When Caesar gave public performances later in his reign, he suffered from disabling stage fright and was scared of his adjudicators, hostile to fellow performers. I think he was reliving his childhood attempts to satisfy Cnaeus Ahenobarbus, who was a thug, and a violently abusive father, and his adhesive mother Agrippina. He saw them sitting up there with the adjudicators, and was terrified that he wouldn't succeed. Seneca was his own judge. Both realized that the performance was a performance, and both wanted to do it perfectly, but the reasons were different. Seneca virtually told me his position at our first interview, but I had to study him to see how it worked in practice. From Kausalika he got the skill of rejecting asceticism. As a result, half of Rome saw him as a philosopher who managed to be a millionaire, and in consequence a humbug. The other half saw him as a philosopher who was also a sensualist, and in consequence a humbug: a humbug, moreover, who flattered Agrippina, was well-rewarded by her, then presided over her murder. Seneca had his own standards, however, and didn't give a row of beans. He never tried to convey the experience of seeing to Romans – Romans have tunnel vision about 'reality' which is either superstitious, or super-Democritean, or both. He'd have wasted his time. He gave up trying to communicate it to Caesar, because Caesar was so disturbed he'd have been thrown by it. The attempt to communicate with him Tantrik-style, through sensuality, was a bad error and Seneca knew that now. But he was emphatically one of us. We had precisely one discussion on such matters – our first. He then sat back and let me find out about him for myself. Moreover, even if the play is not 'real', in Rome it had a way of becoming a horror story, and the Mother's effects can include real fire and real blood: 'It is a valuable exercise,' Seneca wrote, 'to run through in your mind such things as exile, torture, war, shipwreck. They are unpleasant, but survivable, and less of a shock if you are ready.' Domitian's plays were drama, of a sort, but it is still painful to be burned alive. Accordingly Seneca was scared, yoga or no yoga, but it never stopped him getting on with the Battle of Kurukshetra as a kshatriya must.

It was a tough row to hoe. Seneca came back from his guru a vegetarian (which is another reason for believing that he'd sat under a Vaishnava teacher as well – Tantriks eat meat as a sacrament) but dropped it when Tiberius banned 'foreign cults' – try explaining to the Romans that meat-eating sits ill with transmigrationism, because one might eat one's father! Later on he took it up again because it improved his asthma – he was probably sensitive to animal matter – but by then he had his ideas a little straighter, and a clearer picture of the way in which human life-lines fit into nature generally. Quite a character, in other words. One wondered what a man like that was doing in such a situation, and what kind of a doctor he would have made – probably a good one.

My official duties turned out to be limited to putting in a daily appearance at Caesar's levee, transport provided, and being perpetually on call. I would have, I found, to move into the Imperial household and live in the quarters formerly occupied by the archiatros, when he looked after Claudius, but there was no hurry for this: for the time being I stayed at my office, which became remarkably fashionable overnight. I was a little scared that my proximity to Caesar would make the Best of Mothers suspicious, but evidently she misread me as part of Caesar's impending reconciliation with, and penitence over, Octavia, and sent me occasional messages to the effect that my patient was gaining weight, overcoming her fear of penetration, and so on. Some of these were accompanied by gifts – the non-edible ones I kept, the edible I avoided, and all of them I reported to Caesar.

'She makes me almost sorry for my wife,' he said. 'You know, I gave Mother a diamond once, and her reply was "I gave that ungrateful boy the Empire, and this is all he returns to me." Oh well, we're on course. Patiently does it. So long as she doesn't find out that you saw Poppaea.'

I pointed out that it hardly mattered, since all the Roman society ladies either had reproductive problems or wanted contraceptives, and I'd have been bound to see Poppaea eventually. Caesar should get Otho to announce I'd seen her, and he'd called me as soon as he heard of my official appointment. He might also talk a lot about his disappointment at not having an heir. The Best of Mothers must know about the Illuminates' antics – it was the threat of a marriage which hadn't yet been unmasked. I could help Caesar put off a trial of consortium with Octavia on medical grounds, though not indefinitely. When the Best of Mothers reckoned my patient was ready, he was going to have to try, or call Agrippina's hand.

Being the official Caesarian medical attendant gave me free access almost any time of the day or night. I had only to show my seal. I avoided evenings, except when invited, because I didn't want to walk in on an Illuminate session. In fact, most of the time was needed for seeing patients, but I mentioned to Caesar that unless he sent for me I had difficulty in finding transport.

'You mean,' said Caesar, 'you don't have a horse? Or a litter?'

I told him they hadn't been issued, and forthwith got both. This meant that at slack times, provided I left word of my route, I could now see Rome. One cannot deny it was impressive, even though they still had scaffolding up in the Circus Maximus and on the Aventine, repairing the damage from the fire which took place there. Caesar's predecessor had got a lot of public credit by paying for the rebuilding, and compensating the victims, out of his own pocket. Nero, who was still trying to get the urban Prefect to enforce the fire regulations, reckoned it would happen again. 'And I will have,' he said, 'a similar opportunity, sooner or later. It might make it possible to clean up this warren of shoddy apartment blocks. One seems to fall down or catch fire every week. If they all burn down, we can step in and replan Rome like a Greek city. Might be no bad thing from the health point of view – eh, doctor?'

Although Caesar treated me as a personal friend (he was far more approachable than most professors of medicine – too approachable, in fact, by the wrong people, such as Tigellinus), there was no point in dropping in on him. I would be looked after by servants and left to contemplate the fixtures, because Caesar was perpetually in conference – with Phaon, on tax policy or inflation: gold was flowing out of Rome at an alarming rate to pay for imports – with his secretaries *a literis* and *a libellis*, dealing with papers – or with Tiridates, who was doing some hard bargaining to end the Armenian crisis. Caesar was determined to get a settlement which he could put to the Senate before producing Tiridates as an official emissary.

But after about a week I did go, to inspect my new quarters, and met a very agitated Tiridates coming out. He stopped only long enough to say that he had been recalled, and to wish me better fortune in Rome than he had had.

I learned what had gone wrong from Seneca, not from Caesar. They were close to signing an agreement, but when Tiridates arrived it was obvious that things had gone wrong.

'My work was vain, Caesar,' he had said, 'the truce has been broken. My men ride faster than yours.'

'I'll recall Corbulo!' yelled Caesar, 'What does he mean by ignoring my orders? He has disgraced Rome!'

'He hasn't, Caesar. My royal brother has disgraced Parthia. He attacked Corbulo.'

'So Corbulo reopened hostilities?'

'As he must, Caesar.'

'Damnation!' said Caesar. 'We had reached an understanding. Go back, Tiridates. See what you can salvage.'

So Tiridates took his bow back to Armenia, to fight a war Caesar had hoped to avoid. The visit, however, was not wasted – much later, and after a great deal of pointless fighting, he came back to Rome officially. But Caesar, who had just missed a major diplomatic coup through Vologses' belligerency, stopped work for the day, sent for the Illuminates, and retired to his quarters.

Seneca, who favoured diplomacy, was disappointed. He was also furious with Burrus, who took the line that Parthians were treacherous savages, and that Caesar had got what he might have expected, a stab in the back. 'He should leave Tiridates to Corbulo and stop meddling in Armenia, and so should you. The Army can handle this. It has no need of philosphers. And on top of it, you let the fellow go. Dammit, the truce was broken, so the safe conduct should have been abrogated. If you ask me, you should have let us arrest Tiridates and nip the whole kingship business in the bud.'

Seneca said nothing, but I had to listen afterwards to his opinion of Chiefs of Staff – an odd assignment for a very young physician. But I was getting used to this kind of psychotherapy.

Much to my astonishment, on my first official visit as physician-in-waiting, Caesar had handed me an unopened letter from Acte – *his* Acte, not mine. 'She wants to ask a favour of you,' he said.

Acte's passage with Caesar was ending, as she knew it must, and much as she would have liked it to continue. Caesar was not, and never had been, about to marry her – that was a story designed to provoke the Best of Mothers (Agrippina had first of all stormed about Greek sluts, then offered Caesar her own bedroom for 'the recreations normal to his age and station'). It was decided to use the threat of Acte to make Poppaea Sabina, who was a Roman and of good family, more palatable as a successor to Octavia when the time came for a showdown. Knowing how matters stood, and having been very generously treated by Caesar, Acte had decided shrewdly to go back into business, but not a business which would attract obloquy and which might prove dangerous. She knew Caesar's concern with the future of the grain supply and of communications, so, with her Rhodian background, she had decided to go into shipping. Cos, since the decree of Claudius, had been made a tax haven (largely as a compliment to our College). Acte asked if I knew any Coan captains who had fast vessels and would agree to sail for her. Obviously, I did, and I sent letters to Arbaces, telling him that I could get him a prime backer who had influence with Caesar, as a small token of appreciation for looking after *my* Acte, though having her available was reward enough in itself. Moreover Arbaces' ship *Bronte* ('Thunderbolt') was unusual. It was, in fact, an old smuggler of the kind known in the islands as a flying caique, not the usual tugbottomed merchantman. It was built for small cargoes, but it could outsail anything else afloat. I explained this to Acte, because it would affect the use she might make of it, and she'd need to trade in silk, or in medical herbs (both of them areas where I had contacts), not coal or marble. Don't, I said, be put off by the look of her. In harbour she could pass for a rather rangy fishing boat. Part of her awkward appearance comes from the fact that her mainmast rakes forward, not back, and the yard of her sail sticks out aft when it is stowed. No Roman or Adriatic captain would give her a second look – until they see her under way, doing an easy gallop when anything but a rowing galley is becalmed. As far as I know, she's unique, but if she pays off it might pay you to have a fleet of them built. For one thing, she can outsail any ordinary pirate, or revenue cutter. I didn't mention that because she was carvel-built and had a specially-flared counter she was also absolutely silent. I didn't want to put ideas into Acte's head. I did, however, say that *Thunderbolt* had double bargeboards instead of a fixed keel and one could bring her over any harbour bar at any tide, or, in fact, float her in the village pond. But her main selling-point was her sailing – we've all seen Roman merchantmen, with a main squaresail, topsail and spritsail – the kind we call 'artemon' – tacking and tacking to wear into the harbour at Cos. *Thunderbolt*, with her fore-and-aft felucca rig, could sail a good forty-five degrees into the wind.

The member of Caesar's cabinet who surprised me most was my archiatros, Xenophon. His official, nonmedical, post as the civil servant responsible for Greek relations turned out to be secondary to a far more time-consuming study on communications. It was this, not medicine, that he talked about when I dined with him on several occasions.

The Roman postal service was good, but the chief crimp in good policy-making was still the impossibility of getting real-time information in Rome. The Tiridates episode clearly illustrated this – Parthian couriers had ridden faster than the Imperial mail, and in another situation Rome could have been taken short by information reaching an emissary before it reached Caesar's policy makers. Ships might in some cases be faster than land-based couriers (I put him in touch with Acte, and her projected fleet of fast Greek packets, which made her a richer woman than Caesar had done, did in fact work for Caesar's overseas intelligence when she built it up a few years later.)

What Xenophon wanted was a scientific conference on communications technology. What he never got was any Roman commitment to fundamental science as such. This blind spot is in fact a consequence of the power of naive patriotic Fundamentalism in Rome – as Xenophon said, to be a scientist one must first proclaim one's impiety, and risk charges of necromancy or treason. What Rome did have, however, was excellent technology – engineering in particular. Provided someone else, usually a Greek, had a fundamental idea, the Romans could execute it, and well – whereas we in Greece devise things and then argue about them instead of putting them into production. Xenophon's point was that it was idiotic to limit the rate at which news could be sent to the speed of a horse. The army had a chain of beacons running the length of Italy one way, and over the Alps the other way, which could be used to signal some pre-specified event, but there was no way a complex piece of information could be coded. What Xenophon proposed to use was the device long since developed by Archimedes in Syracuse, the heliographic mirror. He persuaded Caesar to have six large bronze mirrors made, and a military detachment was given the task of testing them. At the time we talked, he was working on a code which would enable the letters of a message to be sent in flashes of varying length. Ultimately, because Caesar lost interest and Xenophon could not convince Burrus, the project never became operational – Xenophon had a small version of it under test, however, between Rome and his house in Baiae, worked by his own servants. It had the drawback that it was necessary to send a message to each station when a test was to be run, but Xenophon overcame this by running one on the fifth day of each month and having the relay teams in place by prearrangement. I suspect that he had a business use for it – possibly in anticipating grain and other commodity prices – but I didn't question him about it. So far as I know, the only other official observer of these experiments was a naval officer called Anicetus. This Greek sailor had been Nero's tutor in naval tactics and was now fleet commander in Baiae. He used to stay with Xenophon whenever he came to Rome for staff meetings. I used to see him arriving with rolls of plans for warships under his arm. He spent a good deal of time with Caesar at that time. If Xenophon and I had known what they were discussing we would probably both have left town.

Xenophon was also badly worried about inflation, and the way that Caesar, like his predecessors, was expanding the money supply. He measured the specific gravity of the silver used in the coinage, and grimly drew a chart of its declining purity. Now the same thing was starting to happen to gold. Caesar's idea was that by tying coins to the intrinsic value of the metal, Rome was deprived of a valuable way of increasing revenue – according to him, if the coins were better designed and looked more authoritative, the Romans wouldn't worry about how much base metal was in them. The Germans or the Jews might, but they could be moved out of coinage into nonmonetary bullion if necessary.

'So,' said Xenophon, 'if you take my advice, you'll change all your earnings into the oldest coin of current weight you can get – otherwise you'll end up holding brass as a reward for your very considerable labours.' It is a piece of advice for which I am still grateful to him. I was indeed earning more coin than I had ever seen before, and I hung on to the Tiberian and Claudian pieces which came my way, and which today are worth many times their face. The other piece of advice came from Gershom ben Eleazer – 'Make sure your money is portable,' he said. 'Expensive glass and pedigree horses are of no value if you have to run for your life. Invest in real estate if you like, but get the proceeds into coin and have a chest with a false bottom – and remember, gold is heavy.' In fact, little by little, mine sailed back to Cos, in boxes of ointment or books addressed to Diodorus, and found its way into the College strong room. It now supports my retirement.

Rome had come to seem almost friendly. The spell cast on me by my new position had to be broken, and it was.

The first cloud was a letter from my own Acte. 'All goes well with me and our child,' she wrote, 'and Arbaces greets you. He is a good companion, though I wish that you were here in his place. For myself, I am not sure where I am going, for my dreams are preparing me for some change. If you are able soon to leave Caesar, I would wish to see you, but do not compromise your new appointment which brings to me, and to Diodorus, both joy and anxiety. In a dream last night I was in labour and gave birth to a male serpent. He who tended me – I think it was Asklepios – took the serpent and said, "Well done, daughter. Now you shall have a new assignment." And at once I was five years old, the daughter of a physician in Sicily, speaking not Greek but Latin. I knew my father's name – it was Lucius Geminianus, and my mother, his wife, was called Hippolyta, a Greek. You may tell as well as I what the god means. So much is clear, I will bear you a physician. Your Acte greets you from the house of Arbaces.'

I did indeed know what the god was saying, as you will know, Herondas, and it greatly disquieted me; so much so that I prepared to ask Caesar for leave to go back to Cos and see her. But what our patron resolves is not to be defeated, and in any case I had other things on my mind for the next few weeks, because I was dragged out of my bed by Sosibius, shouting that Caesar had sent for me. It must have been about three hours before dawn, and the messengers were a detachment of Praetorians.

'What's wrong?' I asked the sergeant.

'I think Caesar needs you as a physician,' said the man. 'They told me to see that you bring remedies.'

'Remedies for what? Fever? Sword wounds? Childbirth? They are different, you know, Sergeant.'

'I've no information about that, Sir. But Caesar was well when the guard changed. In your place, Sir, I'd think of injury or poison.'

So I grabbed a surgical bag and the medical emergency bag, mounted, and rode off with a police escort at top speed to the Palatine. We sounded like a fire brigade and woke the entire neighbourhood.

I was passed in so fast from room to room that I arrived out of breath. Caesar was sitting up in bed, looking not ill but badly scared. Seneca and Tigellinus were with him.

'Good,' said Tigellinus, 'you're here. I've sent for Xenophon, too, to make sure.' He looked disgusted rather than alarmed – Seneca looked cross and worried. Not a death-bed but a panic, I concluded.

'Callimachus,' said Caesar, 'thank the Gods that you've come. I'm probably poisoned.'

'What have you taken, Caesar?'

'The Gods know that. It's in capsules. In my food.'

'We don't know,' said Tigellinus, 'that Caesar took anything except pastry. However ...'

'Do you feel anything, Caesar?'

'Yes, bloody frightened. I wouldn't feel anything, would I, until I drop dead.'

Vital signs were normal, and compatible with anxiety alone.

'You think an attempt may have been made on your life?'

'I think it *was* made on my life,' said Caesar.

'Then we'd better make sure,' I said. 'Luckily I possess the universal antidote and you can take it at once.' It was actually charcoal, lac Veneris and some ground bezoar. I gave him salted wine, stood to attention while he regurgitated a very interesting dinner, mixed the powder with water, and made him drink it. It is, in fact, quite a good antidote for a great many simple poisons, and an excellent one for panic. Caesar's spirits improved at once.

'Now you can sleep without anxiety,' I told him. 'I'll stay here until morning.'

They settled him down. Tigellinus motioned with his head. Seneca and I followed him into the anteroom.

'What was that about?' I asked. 'This,' said Tigellinus. He held up what looked like a dirty pearl.

Seneca explained. 'Caesar heard there was a lady who makes baklava with honey. She worked for Aulus Furius, but Caesar insisted on hiring her as pastrycook.'

'And I ran a check on her,' said Tigellinus, 'as nobody else had bothered to do so. She's Locusta's freedwoman. You know about Locusta?'

I did. She was the poisoner by royal appointment to a long series of homicidal Claudians, including, according to rumour, Agrippina the Best of Mothers. 'Bad,' I said.

'So I had a check made of her personal effects. We found these.'

Xenophon came in, in a great hurry. 'Is he all right, Callimachus?'

'Yes, Archiatros – mostly scared. I emptied the stomach.'

'I heard what happened,' said Xenophon. 'Tigellinus, I hope to the Gods you didn't arrest the lady.'

'Do you take me for a fool?' said Tigellinus. 'If Agrippina sent her, there's sure to be a baby-sitter.'

'Right,' said Xenophon, 'you're learning. You've arranged for Caesar to go where?'

'To Baiae, for a rest by the seaside.'

'The staff there haven't been penetrated?' said Xenophon.

'Not likely, but I'll change them to make sure. What next?'

'Where does the suspect live?' asked Xenophon.

'She's been living in. She's sleeping here now. But she has a flat in town, near the Circus Maximus.'

'Good,' said Xenophon. 'Are your men ready?'

Evidently they were. Somebody medical had to go with them. I expected it to be Xenophon, as I had to stay with Caesar, but Xenophon said rather shortly, 'I can't go with them, and I can't stay with Caesar. I'm not in practice. Call Celsus to stay with Caesar and take Callimachus and Sosibius. We need a drug expert who can recognize raw materials. In Cos we don't deal in poisons.'

He was pardonably sensitive about this type of situation.

It took an hour to get Celsus. We briefed him and I handed over my charge with the authority of the archiatros.

'Don't grab your suspect before we know what is in that flat,' said Xenophon. 'And when you do grab her, see she doesn't swallow anything. Look in her mouth, look in her hair for pins and hairbeads – better strip her naked to make quite sure. Otherwise you'll have a corpse, not a witness.'

'You should have been a police officer, Doctor,' said Tigellinus. 'Let's go.'

'One minute,' said Xenophon. 'Give me that pill. It may be for the pastrycook's period pains.'

He cut it in half. There was a resinous material inside it. 'Nothing I'm familiar with. It's no use giving it to the dog – it may be a slow poison, if it's poison at all. All right, you can make your search.'

Police raids are not to my taste. It was, however, up to me to find out what if anything Caesar had been given. Tigellinus' men grabbed the concierge and kicked in the door. It was a rather ordinary apartment, very appropriate to a middle-aged lady who worked as a pastrycook. 'What did you think you'd find?' said Tigellinus. 'Drums of snake venom? Turn it out. We're looking for Locusta's stock in trade, not a few pills.'

They did, and found nothing. Sosibius pottered around in the uproar, while Tigellinus' police turned out the cupboards. I had the impression he'd done this kind of thing before. The man who had arrested the concierge came in and whispered to Tigellinus. 'Quiet!' he said. 'The two girls next door worked for Phryne, the porter says – if we haven't scared them away. You, you and you, follow me.'

We froze as directed. There was a crash followed by screams. 'Right!' shouted Tigellinus. 'We've got both the birds. Search this place, too.'

So we searched that flat, too. The two girls whom they'd dragged out of bed were on the floor, tied back to back. One was weeping. The other was twitching her head, as if she were trying to get at something with her teeth. 'Hairbeads!' I said to Tigellinus. 'Hercules, yes, I'd forgotten.' He dived for the prisoner, but she had the bead in her mouth. There was a tussle, Tigellinus was bitten and slapped her face, but she laughed at him, gave a little sigh, and quite quietly died.

'At least,' said Tigellinus, 'we've come to the right address.' There was nothing suspicious either. We stood and looked round.

'What,' said Tigellinus, 'is out of place?'

We all looked at the same object. It was a domestic shrine of Isis. It was rather too big for the room. Tigellinus stuck a swordtip behind the thing and pried. It opened. Inside was a neat cupboard with about fifty numbered packets and jars. Sosibius came forward and looked at them, took off lids, smelled a few. 'Well, Sir, it's a nasty collection. This one's probably aconite. I don't know what all the others are. But there are some books in there as well, so perhaps Dr. Callimachus and I can identify them. It's Locusta's store all right.'

I had to think quickly. 'Those things can't go to my office,' I said. I didn't say, 'There's probably enough chemical warfare ammunition here to make a clean sweep of all Romans whom Tigellinus doesn't appreciate, including some here present.' Instead I directed that they be taken to the College of Medicine under guard and handed over to Aulus Celsus for scientific analysis.

Caesar was not only unpoisoned next day, but left in ostentatious high spirits for an impromptu holiday. Tigellinus quietly grabbed the pastrycook Phryne, conveyed her out to the house in a blanket, and took her away to make her talk. Word was put out that she'd gone home for cooking utensils. Sosibius and I set to work on Locusta's pots.

I filed the following report:

'Callimachus to Caesar, greetings. I examined the materials comprising forty-seven jars, eighteen packages, four books and account books seized in my presence on the premises at the Casa Faboniana, apartment 12, on the Kalends of April, in this year, the fifth year of your reign, which have been marked in evidence with my seal and with the seal of the Urban Prefect.

'There is in my opinion no doubt that this collection represents the stock in trade of a professional poisoner. Although not all the contents of the containers have been positively identifiable, (1) all those identified were poisonous; (2) none of the materials identified has any recognized use in medicine; and (3) of the unidentified materials, approximately half were rapidly fatal when administered to animals (edible dormice) in doses comparable to those which would be contained in a capsule.

'Packages IV and IX contained respectively waxed silk capsule shells and small pieces of animal membrane (probably sheep bladder) prepared for the manufacture of capsules. Package XII contained thicker membrane of the same type which appeared to have been partially tanned. Investment in this membrane might delay the acute effects of any drug contained in it.

'It was established by me and by the pharmacist Sosibius that jars I, III, V, and VII contained respectively aconite, hemlock, a preparation of an unidentified dried fungus, probably fool's morel, and unidentified grey crystals with an odour of almonds which caused the death of an experimental animal in approximately 1 minute from ingestion. Jars II, IV, and VI contained crystalline mineral materials. That in jar II appeared to be white arsenic; the material in jar IV is identical with the white powder produced by repeatedly boiling lead turnings in vinegar. Jar VI is an unidentified mineral resembling realgar. The fact that of the remaining vegetable materials identified, all those bearing even numbers are slow poisons, and all those bearing odd numbers are acute poisons, supports the hypothesis that this classification was adopted consistently. In my opinion the only legitimate pretext for the possession of these materials, either by a lay person or by a physician or pharmacist, would be their use in the manufacture of antidotes. The books are apparently pharmacological works in oriental languages, which are now being translated. The accounts contain no names, but record the receipt of sums totalling five million sesterces. The earliest date is placeable during the lifetime of divine Augustus, the latest early this month.

'The cause of death of the woman apprehended in the adjacent apartment 11, was in my opinion ingestion of the crystalline material contained in jar VII and concealed in a hair-bead. Other hairbeads worn by her, by her companion, and removed from the suspect Phryne contained a similar material.

Callimachus, Iatros of Cos
Physician in Attendance.'

The rest of the story wasn't in the report. 'You can save yourself time,' said Tigellinus, 'the best authority on this stuff is Phryne. At the moment she's hanging out to dry. You ask the questions and I'll persuade her to answer them.'

'Nothing doing,' I said. 'Quote: "any member of our College who participates in the interrogation, execution or punishment of any person, whether convicted or not, or who attends at, directs or moderates any such interrogation, execution, or punishment, or otherwise acts in a professional capacity in any way regarding the same (other than by tending injuries received by such interrogated or punished persons, such attendance being strictly after the event), shall be guilty of infamous conduct in a professional respect ..." '

Tigellinus started bowing to me as if I were a priest, or a Vestal Virgin.

' "... And shall forfeit his membership of this College. Any person soliciting a member of the College so to act shall incur a curse," ' I went on.

'Oh well,' said Tigellinus, 'please yourself. Do I get the curse?'

I told him he did, and I hoped his piles would come down, and he could do his own dirty work.

Unfortunately Sosibius came in next day and said, 'That's saved us some time, Sir. Phryne's come clean on jars III and VII. Doesn't know what's in the others, because she was given them by Locusta. You were right about the number code.'

I was furious, but I could do nothing about Sosibius – he was, as I suspected, an old military corpsman who was now in Tigellinus' police. Phryne's confession did, however, put us onto the sugar of lead. As to the grey stuff in jar VII, it was made by heating soda, potash and charcoal to redness in a sealed iron cylinder. I don't know what it was, but it was the fastest poison I had heard of. Even the vapour killed flies. According to Phryne one could get the same stuff out of laurel or bitter almonds.

My real concern was what else Phryne had said. If she'd named accomplices, there might be a general massacre. Romans in general, and Caesar in particular, were likely to lose their heads if anyone mentioned conspiracy. I asked Caesar, in Tigellinus' presence, what if anything had come out.

'Be your age, Callimachus,' said Tigellinus. 'There has never been more than one suspect, Caesar.'

'My mother,' said Caesar, glumly.

'Phryne admits that?'

'She admits it. My mother didn't hire her in person, but she got a verbal message and a down payment.'

'That,' I said, 'could be a plant.'

'It could,' said Caesar, 'but it isn't. Somebody's told her about Poppaea. She wrote to felicitate me on my lucky escape when I was down at Baiae – how did she know? And she hoped that since the Gods had spared me I wouldn't disgrace her further by marrying a luxurious wanton who was another man's wife. You'd be wise to move out of that office into the palace – it'll be easier to guard you there. Never mind the practice – I'll pay your losses.'

'How about Poppaea?' I said.

'In hiding,' said Tigellinus. 'Agrippina thinks she's gone to Antium. We sent one of her girls, wearing her veil and clothes. She's in a safe house.'

'So what next?' I asked.

'That,' said Caesar, 'we intend to discuss. You can sit in.'

Tigellinus, who had done very well with his spying, kept quiet and deferred to Burrus, which was well taken. 'As I see it, Caesar,' said Burrus, 'this can't possibly go on.'

'I agree,' said Seneca, 'but let's keep a level head. You do have some civilized options. You could banish her.'

'To somewhere I can't keep an eye on her,' said Caesar.

'To an island, under guard, Caesar.'

'I can't banish her network,' said Caesar, 'and Burrus hasn't got the manpower to keep an eye on *it*.'

'With the evidence to hand, you could put her on trial.'

'And have her weep and harangue her way out of it as she did last time, when Burrus let her off,' said Caesar. 'We can't prove she hired Phryne. Or she'd admit it and plead I drove her mad with worry by my hardheartedness to her and to my damned wife. That woman has to go. Burrus, I order you to send an officer and see she opens her veins – or takes the whole of jar VII. If she won't, he's to ram it down her throat.'

'Caesar,' said Burrus, 'with respect, I can't.'

'You what?' said Caesar, 'You finished my wife's whore of a mother, didn't you?'

'This woman, Caesar, is the daughter of Germanicus,' said Burrus. 'Do you want a mutiny?'

'Then bloody well obey orders and do it yourself,' yelled Caesar.

'With respect, Caesar, if I lose control of my men, you can kiss your life goodbye,' said Burrus. 'Tigellinus here is not commander of the Praetorians. If you want this done, you must do it yourself. My men can't be involved.'

'Nor I, Caesar,' said Seneca, 'nor I.'

Tigellinus and I saw one of Caesar's tantrums building. I was about to try Quintus Fabius. Tigellinus got in first. 'Burrus is perfectly right, Caesar,' he said. 'It would be wrong to involve soldiers and philosophers – or physicians. This is a family matter. Agrippina is in your potestas as head of the house. It is proper to resolve such shameful matters privately, not in the sight of Rome.'

The spectacle of Tigellinus in the role of Cato had me flummoxed – I'd underrated him. In Rome the paterfamilias is the tribal chief, and he could theoretically execute an erring wife, daughter, mother, slave, or even son, but I didn't see that sitting well in a modern court. It was five hundred years out of date.

'I apologize to you, gentlemen,' said Caesar. 'In my anger I made a suggestion which should not have been made; a man must confront his own mother, however unnatural she has shown herself. Our private griefs and scandals mustn't be paraded. I am ashamed they have come to your notice. I will speak to her.'

We looked at each other. Seneca opened his mouth and shut it again. He was terribly unhappy but was scared to tackle Tigellinus.

'Now, Caesar,' said Tigellinus, 'will you see Anicetus?'

'Not a word ouside this room,' said Caesar, and we left.

To everyone's surprise and Seneca's relief, Caesar went to see his mother that evening and they spent two hours alone. He gave no details of what had passed, but he said, 'I don't think the old witch will try that again,' and appeared to put the whole affair out of his mind.

What surprised me was the treatment of Phryne and her surviving assistant. I'd expected them to be strangled at least, or more probably fed publicly to a crocodile. Instead they were jailed, or rather filed in custody. That was precisely what had happened to Locusta. Underground operators of that quality may get tortured, when information is needed, but they don't get killed. Moreover Poppaea came out of purdah, and Tigellinus assured me I could go back to my office, because he'd got men there and my cook was one of ours. Later that week, on Xenophon's instructions, Celsus and your former professor, with the Urban Perfect, who had taken an oath of secrecy, threw all Phryne's materia medica in the Tiber after removing the caps. It might get into the wrong hands. Jar 46 had been particularly worrying. It contained aira, or spurred lolium, and jar 47 contained dried fly agaric. These I certainly did recognize, and Xenophon took charge of them. The two numbered jars we dumped contained powdered bryony as a replacement – it seemed wiser to omit them from my report. Such things are not to be entrusted to Claudians, or even named to them. As to jar VII, Xenophon said, 'Well, at least we know now what killed Britannicus – and who. What an unpleasant and dangerous lot of people!'

Xenophon, of course, was absolutely right. Burrus had the nerve to suggest to Caesar that he should take charge of Locusta's arsenal, with a view of settling the Parthian question once and for all. Caesar was furious. He told him, with some original military oaths, that if Burrus was a fool, he, Caesar, wasn't and neither was Tiridates. 'Any food you send him, he'll try on his dog, and we'll lose any credit we ever had,' said Caesar, 'and in any case it's all been destroyed on my orders, to keep ideas out of the heads of idiotic officers. Dismiss, damn you, Burrus, and don't come here with that kind of operation again!'

Apart from that, Caesar came back from his awkward session with the mother not merely affable but positively hilarious. He told Seneca, 'She's been caught red-handed, and she knows when she's beaten. In fact, we parted good friends. Agrippina always respected a strong hand. Not only did I make her swear on the memory of the divine Augustus never to try another trick like that – I told her to her face she'd married me off when I was a boy, to a neurotic, and now I am a man I intend to choose my own wife, as a man should, not let his mother do it for him. So Mother said, "I implore you, Caesar, anyone but Acte! I couldn't bear the shame of a whore as First Lady." I asked her why in that case she married me to a whore's daughter. Not a squeak, only a couple of large tears – she did it for the best. Then stay out of my affairs for the best, I told her. No, I am not going to marry Acte. But I will marry as, when, and whom I choose. And you can convey my regrets to Octavia, tell her it was a mistake – yours, Mother, not mine – and if she ever becomes a normal woman she can marry whomever she likes with my Imperial blessing. Now we can proceed. I feel years younger, and older.'

Seneca still did not like it. I told him that if it were true, we seemed to be home and clear. 'Caesar,' said Seneca, 'is an extremely talented ... actor. As to us, we can only keep our heads down. Caesar is out of my hands. I hope he hasn't transferred himself into the hands of Tigellinus.'

If he was right, Caesar's acting ability appeared to be inherited, because Agrippina wrote to me saying that she owed me an apology. She had, she said, been driven insane by worry, but a dream from Asklepios had restored her. It was plain that Caesar and Octavia were not destined by Fate for one another, but she hoped that by following my advice Octavia's health would be restored, and she was eternally in my debt, etc. She would be still further in it if I could exercise my influence on her son to postpone any rash choice, and watch over him to ensure that he was not the victim of a sorceress as his step-father had been.

'Never gives up, does she?' said Caesar. 'Give me that – I want to show it to Poppaea.'

Caesar seemed to be redesigning the navy – he was as diligently working with Anicetus as he had done with Tiridates on the Parthian quesion.

Caesar told me, about this time, apropos of nothing, that he'd asked Poppaea if having first a Magian, then a Jewish instructor didn't confuse her.

'Certainly not,' she had said, 'the Jews worship the One with no fellow, the Magians say that the One casts also a shadow. You seem to see One as Many, like the Greeks. Well, the God of the Jews told them, "I the One am the Elohim, the Many, and I am One." I see no difficulty over that.'

If it had been safe or prudent I'd have liked to talk more with this future First Lady. I wondered what her influence would be on Caesar. She also told him that the Jews in Babylon had been more influenced by the Magians than they liked to admit, which to my mind is true. I could not tell whether such topics would prove salutary or dangerous.

I always regretted that I couldn't, for reasons of common prudence, talk to Poppaea about knowledge: from what I've said of her, Herondas, I imagine you are grinning, but I was serious. Seneca – who was there – thought as you probably do, and opined, out of Caesar's hearing, that the only knowledge on which Poppaea was likely to be an authority was carnal knowledge: I had a suspicion that the two Poppaeas fitted better together than the two, or multiple, Senecas, but I kept extremely quiet on the subject.

Arbaces made his first run into Ostia about this time, also, and Acte found out both how fast *Thunderbolt* was (he made it from Cos to Ostia in ten days) and that Arbaces needed some handling. When he had taken on cargo, he slipped his moorings and left without paying port dues, so the coastguard cutter gave chase. When Arbaces saw her, he dawdled while the Roman came up, steadily increasing speed and steering nearer and nearer the wind, until the Roman, on *Thunderbolt*'s tail and not watching his own pennant, went aback and was brought up standing. When that didn't deter the cutter, Arbaces proceeded to give its master a sailing lesson, finishing by running *Thunderbolt* over a sandbar, bargeboards up, and leaving the Roman aground. Then he went back to Ostia, told the harbourmaster he had been at sea overhauling the new tackle, paid his dues, and set sail in earnest. The coastguard was still stuck fast when he went by, hailing for a rowing tug to warp him off the sandbar.

Arbaces came to my office while he was in port, and I asked him about my Acte. 'Sweet as ever,' said Arbaces, 'but distant. I thought she was thinking about you, or the child, but I think the God is in her. She dreams all night.'

I told him I still hoped to get back to her.

'Don't take this ill,' said Arbaces, 'but I don't think she needs you – or me, for that matter. She looks through me – like a helmsman looking for a landfall. You're the doctor: is it all right for me to make love to her? I wouldn't want to harm your child.' I sent Acte my love, told Arbaces that he wouldn't harm the child, but should be careful in the last trimester, and gave him three of Nero's new gold coins for her, mounted as a necklace.

'What's it like here, in the wolf's lair?' asked Arbaces.

'Slippery,' I said.

'I guessed as much. If you ever need a quick return passage, get hold of me. I'll be here at full speed if my crew have to fight their way back to the ship.'

I asked him if by any chance he knew anything about Anicetus.

'Only,' said Arbaces, 'that he used to be a pirate. Or so they say. He joined the Roman navy under Tiberius when Tiberius used to come to Rhodes. He was a wanted man down in Egypt, I gather. What's he up to with Caesar?'

'Designing a new fleet, I gather.'

'It makes sense,' said Arbaces. 'He's a fine seaman, and a finer hand with a cutlass. I'd avoid crossing his bow, if I were you.'

This information I took seriously, because piracy and smuggling were matters to which Arbaces referred rarely, with the same horizon-watching expression he'd seen in Acte. I wondered when, and if, she and I would see each other again, and left her in the hands of Arbaces, and of Asklepios.

5

Historians have put forward the influence of Poppaea, Nero's desire to be rid of his wife, and the dangers which might follow if Agrippina remarried, as having been the considerations which made up his mind to get rid of her. Having been with him at the time, I am satisfied that the main factor was the threat to his life, and I think the actual decision was taken, not when the Phryne plot was discovered (Caesar was in too big a panic over the poison he thought he had taken to decide anything), but when the options were put to him and he realized that in any power struggle with his mother the loyalty of the Praetorians might be doubtful. Caesar could have divorced Octavia at any time, though Agrippina would have raised the Furies. When Agrippina was dead, however, he did nothing for three whole years, and then only when his hand was forced by others. There were, of course, deeper reasons – she probably signed her own death warrant when she seduced her own son, but I am inclined to distrust psychiatric history. Caesar and the Best of Mothers could not coexist because no area was big enough to hold both of them without a spectacular explosion.

The Phryne plot was supposed to be secret, but of course the palace leaked like a sieve. Nobody in Rome who keeps large numbers of servants, least of all Caesar, has the slightest privacy, even in his bedchamber. Petronius stopped me on his way in to the Illuminates' session (I was on my way to the office) and asked me if he could have some of the material in jar VII.

'I'm not at liberty to discuss that,' I said.

'Why not?' said Petronius, 'You'll be the only person in Rome, including Caesar, who doesn't. Phryne is a public benefactor.'

'Why?'

'Well,' said Petronius, 'think what you could do with it. Disinfest yourself of relatives and debt collectors, increase the turnover of property, make executions less messy ...'

'What would you do with it, Petronius?' I asked. 'You can't

have any, because it's been destroyed by order of Caesar, but I'm curious to know.'

'Well,' said Petronius, 'I'm bound eventually to need some. Every civilized man gets disgusted in the end, with old age if not with society, though I don't see myself as likely to survive into my dotage on the present form. I thought of setting a fashion in hairbeads. Take care, Callimachus!'

I thought, if he and Caesar get that book written, both of them might be less at risk. Anger is a very poor prognostic sign, in my view, and Petronius was full of it, at his father, at Rome, and, of course, at himself.

The panic and the air of menace we'd had when the plot came to light were over. Caesar was to go to Baiae, with Otho, but not Poppaea, and I was to go with him ex-officio, but I caught cold. Caesar made a great fuss, called Xenophon over my protests, and Xenophon declared me unfit to travel. Caesar said, 'Of course he mustn't travel. I don't need a physician constantly at my elbow – if I break a leg there are army surgeons in Baiae. I managed very well before Callimachus came, and I can manage now – I'm not made of glass.'

I asked Xenophon what he thought he was doing.

'I don't want you in Baiae. I want you at my house three days from now. You'll be officially cured by then, cold or no cold,' he said. Quite obviously Caesar didn't want me there either.

'I'm going to see Mother while I'm taking the waters,' he said. 'Now the old lady's bitten the bullet she's become quite good company. We'll all have dinner in Bauli at Otho's expense – no, don't look worried: Otho and I have arranged to swap plates! And Otho's got some Syrian girls laid on for the rest of the stay – I might take a couple of them and introduce them to Mother. She'll end by beseeching Poppaea to marry me before we get a belly dancer for First Lady. I'm going to enjoy this thoroughly.'

When we met at Xenophon's house – Caesar left, if you please, at midnight, so that he could have a torch-light procession to his first stopping-place – it was very late. Seneca was there, and we sat around, yawning and waiting for something or somebody. What arrived, in the end, was the Infant Prodigy, Pythagoras, dressed rather appropriately as a woman, and he came in by the back way. I thought for an unworthy minute that Seneca and my archiatros wanted to borrow him in Caesar's absence, but he was a changed urchin – no camp, no insolence, very much to the point.

'Well?' said Seneca.

'It's going ahead,' said the boy. 'I'm sorry to come so late, but it wasn't safe sooner. Otho and Caesar both wanted me before I left. I had to get cleaned up.'

'How is it going to be done?' said Seneca.

'Anicetus is fixing it. He's got a trick ship ready.'

'I might have guessed it,' said Xenophon. 'Do you know how it works?'

'Not clearly. Caesar and Otho were killing themselves laughing about it. But the trick ship is definite.'

'You know, boy, that we rely on you? Try to remember exactly what was said.'

'I can't. You wouldn't hear clearly if you were working on that fat Otho at one end with Caesar working on your other end, and both of them laughing like demons. Caesar calls that a Pythagoras sandwich.'

'Quite!' said Seneca.

'And they'd put a cocktie on me which was hurting a lot.'

'That's enough of that,' said Seneca. 'I understand you couldn't be seen to be listening. But what exactly did they say?'

It sounded from what he heard as if on a given signal one of two things, or both, would happen – the bottom would fall out of the boat, or a boom, with lead ballast weights fixed to it, would fetch away and go through the roof of the cabin onto the heads of Agrippina and her party.

'Right, Pythagoras,' said Seneca, 'you've done very well. Now get back before they miss you. If they miss you, say you went out as a joke to see if anyone would pick you up dressed as a whore. With Caesar and Otho out of town you should get a few days' peace.'

'There's still Tigellinus,' said Pythagorus. 'They work me like a mule.' And he left.

'That's the kind of thing I was afraid it would be,' said Xenophon.

'Messy?' I said.

'Not only messy, but it'll probably miscarry.'

'Just how serious,' I said, 'is the outlook?'

'The outlook,' said Seneca, 'is that Agrippina is going to be killed in one way or another. Whether that is serious depends on whether Burrus is right in thinking that he can hold the Guards. If not, Caesar, and probably all here present, are likely to be killed.'

Xenophon said, 'Send now, Lucius, and wake Burrus. He'd better know.'

'If she does drown,' said Seneca, 'there should be enough confusion over what happened to obscure the issue and let the officers get things in hand. If Agrippina comes ashore yelling "Murder!" and Caesar panics, he'll have her finished off messily, and anything might happen.'

We had an unpleasant spell of waiting. It was nearly dawn when Burrus arrived and heard the particulars.

'Well,' he said, 'we're ready. Thanks to you we don't have the element of surprise. As to the contingency plan, I think we can leave that to Anicetus. The sand has run out for Agrippina with my men. If Caesar had ordered the Guard to kill her, that would have meant trouble. If someone else does, and my officers aren't implicated, the men couldn't care less. Gods, it'll be a load off all our minds. Do you know they're making a book in the guardroom on which will kill which, Caesar or the Mother?'

'I'm glad to hear it,' said Seneca. 'Men don't mutiny over something they have wagers on. What are the odds – do you know?'

'Six to two on Caesar killing his mother,' said Burrus.

'So winners will outnumber losers,' said Seneca. 'I think we can relax. Go and get some sleep, Callimachus. Take things quietly. We have a day to wait. We shall hear before Rome does, thanks to the ingenuity of the archiatros here. Lucius and Sextus Afranius, make yourselves comfortable. The servants will look after you. I'm going to bed if you'll excuse me.'

'Shouldn't wonder,' said Burrus, 'if the old skinflint places a bet himself. He's never missed a market if he could rig it.'

In Greece, Herondas, sitting around waiting for the commission of matricide would, at least since the fall of the Atreidae, be an unusual occupation for a philosopher, two physicians, and a senior officer. In Rome, it seemed perfectly natural. Ever since that period of waiting I have viewed the Chorus in Sophocles as realistic bystanders. I thought about the distinctions between foreknowledge and complicity. One is not an accomplice of something one cannot stop. Warning Agrippina, and she might possibly have heeded a warning from me, would not have stopped Caesar from having her killed with even wider repercussions, and would have certainly, unless I made myself scarce, have cost me my head. Nevertheless, I spent that day thinking about medical ethics. You might care to consider, Herondas, precisely what you yourself would have done. I for my part took a tip from Gershom ben Eleazer and made sure my effects were portable. By an ill dispensation of Fortune, since Arbaces had only recently sailed back southwards, there would be no chance of getting hold of him. I settled for a horse to the Adriatic and ship from there.

The committee reconvened at Xenophon's house on the evening of the fatal day. Burrus had brought an officer from the signals party. We waited around uneasily for dusk, had a brief welcome from Seneca's wife Paulina, who came to bring him his cloak, and apparently thought, or affected to think, that he was there to witness a test of Xenophon's equipment: it had turned cold, and she was anxious about his chest. She may have had other grounds for anxiety: Seneca and she were very close, and he must have talked to somebody. When that was over, he settled down – to write the address Caesar would give to the Senate in reply to their felicitations on his remarkable deliverance from his own mother.

'Time,' said Xenophon, and we followed him to the roof. The stairway came out under a low porch with stone benches. The equipment was there, a round concave bronze dish set on legs – how were we going to use a heliograph at night, I wondered? The signals officer took the torch, lit a fishing lantern, of the kind our people use to bring the squid for spearing, and hung it from a hook at the highest point of the dish, swinging the thing round to point at us under the porch.

'It's a long shot,' said Xenophon. 'If there's mist anywhere, or one link doesn't operate, we'll have to wait until sunup. But it's worth trying. Signals, do you have the bearing?'

'Yes, Sir.' He was squinting through two perforated slats set on a circle at the edge of the flat roof.

'Right,' said Xenophon, 'lights out and eyes open. Keep that beam pointed behind us or you'll see nothing.'

Waiting, the lights of Rome, children, dogs, firesmoke.

'There's going to be too much light from the city,' said Xenophon.

'Compared with the sun,' said Seneca, exactly as if we were students, 'you don't have much light intensity to play with.' And he started coughing.

Quiet again, in which beside the city I could hear Seneca beginning to wheeze. Finally he said, 'I have to go down,' and left us.

'There she goes, Sir,' said Signals. High on one of the hills, where there were two smoky lights from country houses, a series of short flashes.

'Turn the lantern,' said Xenophon. Signals lined it up and swung it on and off bearing. 'Tablets,' he said, and started to write down what the distant light-spot was saying.

'He's sending B R, B R, Baiae Roma. We're through,' said Signals. 'Nice work, Sir.'

'I didn't see a damned thing, Signals,' said Burrus, 'but I suppose you know what you're doing. What's the plan?'

'You go down and wait. Baiae will send B R at intervals to tell us they're there. Signals will send R B. As soon as anything comes through I'll bring it down. May be a long job, or nothing. I'll settle down here – I'm used to night calls, or I used to be. Take them down, Callimachus.'

So we relit the torch and went down, back to the interminable waiting. Seneca, wrapped in the cloak, was still wheezing, but writing steadily, mouthing the phrases unvoiced to get the weight of them. Burrus took wine. I dozed off.

NAUF MATER NATDO SALVA

Xenophon had the tablet, Seneca was spelling out the signal, Burrus was trying to figure what the devil it meant, and I was waking up – it was just about dawn.

'Naufragium – mater natando salva. Ship wrecked, mother swam ashore,' said Seneca. 'She would. Rather what we expected. Burrus, how long before word reaches Rome?'

'Not before midday, probably later. How is it rumours travel faster than horses?'

'Do you need to take any measures?' said Seneca.

'No, and if I spread the word what happened, my officers will think I organized it.'

'What do we do?'

'Wait,' said Xenophon, 'till the whole hand is played. The first thing to arrive in Rome may be the Best of Mothers, dripping wet and vowing vengeance.'

'I doubt,' said Seneca, 'if Tigellinus will let that happen.'

Later on, Xenophon, Seneca and I went to the bathhouse, saying little. We ate breakfast, and then lunch. Rome, seen from the roof, was in its normal condition – no riots, no fires, no avenging furies, but business as usual. I had cancelled patients, luckily, for the day.

Two hours past midday we decided to break up the watch and meet again by summons if and when there was news. Signals was still at his post. He had taken down the lantern, and polished the sun mirror. He was still scanning the hilltop to southward, now clearly visible over the rising dust and haze. Seneca was anxious to get home, so as to avoid worrying Paulina, but there was a holdup while Burrus and he argued who, if anyone, should be told, and how much. Then the matter was moot, because Signals himself came down shouting, 'They're coming through again, Sir,' and vanished with us in pursuit, Burrus shouting, 'Don't leave your post, imbecile! Get that signal down!'

'Yes, Sir. I have the signal. They're sending it in repetition.'

Xenophon took the tablet.

MAT GLAD DOMI INTERF

'Signals, is that DOMI or DEMUM?'

'DOMI, Sir. They're now sending B R and dashes. They're signing off.'

'Mater gladio domi interfecta. Mother killed by the sword at her home. That, gentlemen, is that. Anicetus kept his head if Caesar didn't.'

'I'll go,' said Seneca, 'and ensure that Caesar receives an address of loyalty on his deliverance from his enemies. Word will be here by the time I've rounded up the Senators.'

It was over. Burrus went back to his quarters. When he came out a few hours later, there was singing in the guardroom. The words of the song ran:

'Caesar and his mother went out to take a swim:
Caesar took the boathook, and did the old cow in.'

I question whether that gem was composed in advance by Seneca. Apparently it reassured Burrus. He convoked his officers, and told them that although he and they owed traditional affection to the daughter of Germanicus, this unfortunate affair was a domestic matter between Caesar and his family. If anyone had any questions regarding the duty of the Guards in such a situation, he would be prepared to answer them. Nobody had. The Senate, without any prompting from Seneca, were sincerely relieved in private, still more relieved when they were told that there would be no accusations of conspiracy (many of them had been fulsome on many occasions to the Best of Mothers) and fulsome publicly and in the extreme to Caesar. I went back to my office, and was frightened out of my skin when a military courier, with a spare mount, battered on the door. But all was well. Caesar needed his physician, it seemed. So I set out on an unpleasant and uncomfortable night ride, getting to Baiae early next day.

What had in fact happened was straight out of one of Petronius' yellow rhetoricians, or a popular version of Seneca's own tragedies. The dinner party had been not merely correct (Caesar did not bring any Syrian girls), but convivial and even affectionate. Caesar and his mother exchanged gifts, there was no mention of Poppaea, they embraced one another at parting, and lunch was arranged next day in Baiae. Caesar, who couldn't take his statutory guard in a boat, was to ride back with Otho, while Agrippina returned as she had come, by water. The booby-trapped boat was manned by some of Anicetus' men, including some old shipmates from his Egyptian escapades. Anicetus himself kept the whole operation under observation. It was, of course, dark, but the boat carried lights. Agrippina, together with her lady-in-waiting, Acerronia, and young neighbour, Crepereius Gallus, who happened to be in the wrong place at the wrong time, went into the cuddy, but Crepereius came out again to talk to the helmsman. When they were a few cables out, in deep water, and clear of observers on the beach, Anicetus' boatswain, who was in charge of the operation, went forward to inspect the rigging – the boat was being pulled with sweeps, not sailed. While dinner was in progress, he had triced up a boom along the mast, loaded with ballast weights, and held up by a halliard. The whole thing weighed several hundred pounds – it was an old smuggler's trick to deal with a boarding party. He now aimed it as well as he could to come down immediately over Agrippina's head, and cut the halliard. It went through the cuddy roof, struck Agrippina a glancing blow on the shoulder, and stove in the floor of the cabin, which had been hinged and caulked, dumping both women in the water below the keel. Acerronia had the misfortune to surface alongside the gunwhale. She screamed, 'Save Agrippina! Save the Emperor's mother!'

The boatswain, Cetus, thinking she meant that *she* was Agrippina, hit her with a belaying pin. Agrippina, in a good deal of pain, came up further away, heard the uproar on board (half the rowers were hired hands and knew nothing about the conspiracy), and prudently swam ashore. Or rather, she swam almost ashore, where a fishing boat picked her up – in consequence the whole of Bauli turned out and surrounded her to take her to her house.

Anicetus, meanwhile, waited for the boat, questioned the boatswain, satisfied himself that Agrippina was missing, believed dead, and went to tell Caesar. Caesar was in a terrible state already. He collapsed into a mixture of tears and laughter bordering on acute mania, which was made still worse when, first, word came from Bauli that Agrippina was on dry land and alive, and, second, when a messenger arrived from her to inform Caesar of her fortunate escape. Agrippina knew very well what had been behind the accident, and who: by sending this message she overplayed her hand, because one of Anicetus' shore party with great presence of mind put a dagger in the unfortunate man's hand and arrested him as an assassin sent by Agrippina to kill Caesar. Meanwhile Anicetus, the boatswain, and a member of the boat's crew, posted back to Bauli. The servants, who could read the signs of the times, had most of them bolted. Anicetus and his men broke into the villa, cut Agrippina's throat, carried her body out on a couch, and set the couch on fire. He then reported back to Caesar that the job was done, sent for the Imperial physician to give Caesar a stiff sedative, and was rowed out to his ship, towing the doctored yacht behind him and scuttling it in deep water. The Imperial physician was of course sweating it out in Rome, but the literal-minded guard on duty obeyed orders, and sent a courier.

Short of giving Caesar my entire stock of nepenthe, which might have had fatal results for both of us, no amount of medication was going to cure his condition. He was suffering from utter relief, abject guilt, and panic in case he should be punished. I think he expected his father to return from Hades and thrash him. I had no medications suitable for such symptoms. In the end I sat with him for several hours and listened. What cured him was the arrival of two Praetorian colonels sent by Burrus, who rode in covered with dust, in full uniform, and brought him the compliments of the regiment at having escaped a dastardly assassination attempt. They attributed the fact that when he heard them coming, Caesar hid in a closet, to shock at his recent brush with death, prudent security-mindedness, or both. The recovery was immediate and spectacular. Caesar stopped playing the guilt-stricken Orestes and invited them both civilly to dine with him. When he came out, he was cheered by his guard. But it was several months before he went back to Rome to receive the felicitations of the Senate and deliver Seneca's set speech, which he did extremely well. It was on the tip of my tongue to suggest that Burrus should have got Seneca to order Caesar a triumph, but I thought better of it. It was a triumph of a kind, though a lefthanded one. At least we were rid of the mother. On many occasions in psychotherapy one wishes one could destroy the patient's relatives in the patient's interest, but it is rarely possible to hope for such an outcome.

Diodorus has expressed the opinion that Caesar's withdrawal at this time reflects an acute depression. I was with him during most of it, and I do not entirely agree. It probably coincided with the 'work of mourning' which was necessary even after the death of a mother like Agrippina (the duration is approximately typical), but Caesar was initially quiet rather than depressed. He stopped carousing, and the only 'Illuminates' who spent much time with him at first were Petronius and Poppaea. Otho moved for the summer to his villa at Baiae and naturally brought her with him.

When one has been so long overshadowed by an Agrippina, time is necessary to accept independence. It is interesting that Caesar's main activities were artistic. He brought down Terpnus, the lyre virtuoso, to give him lessons, intensified his practice of singing and playing, and seemed for the first time lately to be quite uninterested in administration. Before long, too, Petronius was spending almost every evening with him, sometimes with a few of the other Illuminates, sometimes by themselves. Caesar had bought him a villa close to his own. I had the impression that even when the others were there, there was more literary activity and less horseplay going on: Pythagoras was not even sent for. Caesar was also even more reserved towards me than usual. I tried to draw him out and see whether he needed to talk about what had happened, and was happening. He grinned, and said, 'I have no need, Callimachus, of a confessor. If you want to know, Lucius Domitius is being merged into Nero Germanicus.' This struck me as insightful, and I did not press it – only time would tell what the merger would look like.

When Baiae caused Caesar to gain weight he started to worry about his voice. For exercise he took to riding – long distances, in company with Tigellinus, who owned thoroughbreds. Tigellinus had a stableman who had been, until he had a bad spill, a professional charioteer, and this man, at Tigellinus' suggestion, started teaching Caesar to drive. The long-term result of this proved to be unfortunate, for not only did Caesar turn out to be a daring and a natural driver, but he got it into his head that here at last he had found a sport at which he could excel, and which was both dangerous and, compared with swordfighting, civilized. 'It's the sport of gods, heroes and kings,' he said, 'and there's enough accidental injury to satisfy the Romans. I mean to cultivate it by example.' Meanwhile Seneca got on with business, sweating in Rome – he hated the frequent journeys down to Baiae, and pressed me to get Caesar operational. There was, in fact, the real danger that he would bring on himself the disaffection he had feared after Agrippina's murder. In fact, nearly everyone had taken Caesar's side, especially in in view of the fake assassination attempt which Anicetus had arranged, but by staying out of Rome his popularity was slipping. The Romans like to see the Caesar. Derogatory slogans started to appear on walls. But there was no budging him – all he would say to Seneca was, 'Later – if you can't manage together with Burrus, I'll send Tigellinus back to help you,' – which was the last thing either Burrus or Seneca wanted.

I saw the only evidence that Caesar was not rid of his mother yet, if ever he would be. He suffered from constant nightmares. I told him that these were natural, and that they represent the class of dreams which addresses things past, not things present or to come. Luckily, although my medications did not stop them, at the end of each sequence of anxiety-dreams he would dream of Asklepios and be able to sleep soundly for a few nights, until the next sequence. My guess was that these dreams would moderate, but perhaps never die out completely.

The weeks passed, I had very little to do, and I was reconciled to kicking my heels by the seaside pending Caesar's pleasure. I thought about asking for leave and making a flying visit to Cos and Acte, but I put if off several times. Before I could reopen the matter, Xenophon took pity on me, arranged to come temporarily out of retirement to provide Caesar with medical cover, and recalled me to Rome. I think he was anxious to form his own opinion of Caesar so that he could brief Seneca – and that with the hot weather due, he would rather I was in Rome and he himself at Baiae. Most of my fashionable practice was there too, I later realized, and I should have stayed where I was and asked Caesar to let me open an office, but probably Seneca and the archiatros had their own reasons. When I demurred, Xenophon said, 'Well, you can always commute.'

I spent May and June attending grand rounds at Celsus' clinic, and seeing patients. The Caesar set might have left town, but they were replaced by merchants' wives, so I was never idle. I wrote a guarded dispatch to Diodorus and sent it in plain – there was no way I could brief him completely in code made up of Homeric quotations, and I knew Rome enough by now to avoid sending suspicious-looking signals when a frank letter would serve. I also wrote several times to Acte, whose time must be near. When the child was born, I knew she or Diodorus would send me word. I regretted only that Xenophon's telegraph, which had been taken over to keep the administration in touch with Caesar at Baiae, did not reach as far as Cos. Xenophon was pleased. He'd managed to convince Burrus of the value of modern communications.

Another matter on my mind was Octavia – she, after all, was my patient, and now Agrippina was gone she must make her own decisions. It would have been impolitic, however, to write. I took the step of contacting her personal physician Andromachus, who was later Caesar's physician, for a consultation. From him I learned that after a period of terror following Agrippina's murder, in which she feared for her life, she had become a new woman – adult, discreet, a little devious, quite reconciled to the unlikelihood of any reunion with Caesar, and willing it appeared to wait with patience until the whole affair died down and she could plan her own life. 'If Caesar had intended to kill me,' she said, 'I think he would have done it then. Invisibility seems my best course for the moment.' This was unexpected – it had been Agrippina, not Caesar, who had been the focus of the problem, and I ought to have seen it, for Agrippina was the Mother: not another Messalina, but like enough to produce the regression I had seen, and she too had been stabbed. Octavia refused to hear any details of the murder. She also spoke of me to Andromachus with appreciation, which pleased me. Andromachus was anxious to meet me. He wondered who had prescribed the olisboi.

I was, as I said, busy enough with patients. One day in June I was sitting in my office, with Sosibius busy in the pharmacy. I was reading a book by Thessalus on his new Method in medicine, when I thought I heard the door open. I looked up, and there was Acte – my Acte. She was wearing my pendant, she was no longer pregnant, and there was no child in her arms. Nor did she address me when I spoke to her. Instead she smiled and waved, gravely, as she had always done when I set out on one of my journeys – and was no longer there. The door had never opened.

I was profoundly sad, though she, very considerately, had prepared me. Obviously she had done all that Asklepios intended, and must now pursue his intentions in another place. Since the child was not in her arms, I knew that he, being under the God's protection, must be safe. Knowledge, Herondas, makes us more able to view such things in place, but being human it is impossible to take them lightly, as Seneca rightly said. It took several more weeks for the letter to come from Diodorus. He expressed his deep sorrow. The College had had Acte in antenatal care, and sent Metrodorus, the chief of obstetrics, in person to deliver her. All had appeared well, but my son, with the bloodymindedness of our family, changed his mind hours before labour began, and presented as a breech, then as a prolapsed leg. Metrodorus, thoroughly alarmed, had done an internal version and extraction and delivered the child, but Acte was exhausted and impatient, I think, to be on her way. Infection set in, and she died quietly on the third day. 'Your infant son, Callimachus, whom, since you gave no instruction, his mother named Telesphoriades, is in the care of your resident Artemidorus and his wife. Though until you return he will be reared with Artemidorus' children, as own brother with his son Herondas, know that he has as additional fathers all the Faculty of this College, including myself.'

I was sorry Acte had so hard a labour, and glad she had named him after Asklepios' first assistant. There is no point in telling more of this to you, because you know the boy's history better than I. But I do not think we have ever spoken of how and when his birth, and Acte's death, were told to me. There is a sequel, which I will tell in its place.

Apart from Caesar himself, I decided not to share my grief, except with Pyrrha, whom Acte had called her sister.

'There is nothing to fear for her,' Pyrrha said. 'You and she will be linked at every turn. Some people are linked. Not you and I, Callimachus, but certainly you and she.'

'You think so?' I said.

'Of course. Though the games may be different. Sometimes she'll be the man and you the woman. I have been a man.'

'Who told you that?' I said, 'The Priest of Isis?'

'Silly!' said Pyrrha. 'I have drunk from the cymbal – like yourself. You didn't guess?'

I might have known it, Herondas: I knew we had more things in common than our genitalia. So instead of putting on mourning, I and Acte's sister gave thanks for her, both to her on her journey and to the Goddess. Word of my loss did eventually get around, and the bloody Romans praised my manly attitude: no decent Roman should be seen regretting a woman – other than his mother. They thought I bore myself well, for a Greek, and I wanted to kick their stupid behinds.

There was another consequence of all this – something I had feared but not actually anticipated in the form it took: on my visits to Baiae to consult with Xenophon, Caesar started to ask questions about religion. These, in turn, came dangerously close to being questions concerning knowledge.

On the first occasion, the subject started with some lighthearted remarks which had been made about the deification of Emperors. 'You won't like that will you, Doctor, being a Greek?' said Caesar. 'I can't say it bothers me much. Some eastern Emperors are supposed to be descended from the Gods: I'm not. I'm not even descended from Divine Augustus, and they only deified *him* because he was an outstanding Emperor. My late mother wanted to be deified, you know?'

I didn't answer.

'She's as deified now as she'll ever be,' said Nero. 'But with a plural society it makes a sort of sense – it isn't the man they're treating as numinous, it's the office. Caligula took it literally, but he was crazy. Look, supposing I was a musician, not a Caesar, and they deified me as Music, I'd say, they're worshipping Music in me – as they worship Jove in an image. The image isn't Jove. It's a focus, simply.'

'We take the point, Caesar,' I said, 'but you're quite right that we Greeks prefer not to deify men.'

'Not even athletes?'

'Not even athletes.'

'How about Asklepios, Callimachus?'

I told him Asklepios is the Ideal Physician, and good physicians approach him asymptotically, as it were. Moreover, if he ever lived as a man, he is not now with us to be spoiled by deification. Anyone who thinks himself the Ideal Physician has lost the chance to approach his goal, because (like a great many colleagues we could name) he thinks he has attained it, and stops learning. 'Asklepios is not one,' I told him, 'even Hippocrates, who was indubitably human, was not one. They represent the accumulated efforts of many. Asklepios represents the accumulated work of us all.'

'And I don't represent the accumulated wisdom of all previous Romans: *touché*,' said Caesar. 'I see the dangers, Callimachus. Overconfidence isn't one of my vices. However, nor do I see great harm in deifying mere men – Are not Gods in all of us?'

This didn't sound like Nero, I thought. Still less like him was what came next. 'Mirrors,' said Caesar, 'are not lamps. But lamps are reflected in mirrors. If the mirrors are very clear, it is hard to tell the difference.'

'Who told you that, Caesar?' I asked. 'Was it Seneca?'

'As a matter of fact,' said Nero, 'it was Poppaea.'

'You speak truly, Caesar,' I said. 'Which deity does your mirror reflect?'

'If I knew,' said Nero, 'I'd probably cease to be Caesar, or Lucius, and be merged with that deity. Callimachus, my friend, you are a great deal deeper in these matters than I, or Seneca, or Poppaea. If I joke about them it's because I can't grasp them. Forget the nonsense I've been talking. I need instruction. As a human being, not as Caesar. The place I hoped to get it is closed to me by the Fates. When I return to Rome, will you be my instructor?'

'In what way, Caesar?' I said.

'Like Poppaea's guru. She's a changed woman from what she has learned. But she can't impart it to me. Can you?'

'Poppaea's guru is of the Jews,' I said, 'and of their teaching I know little, except that it deifies neither men nor images. Will this guru not take you as a disciple?'

'He would,' said Nero, 'but it's politically impossible. Enough people think I'm manipulated by Greece. I don't want them to think I am manipulated by Judaea.'

You can see, Herondas, why this was so distressing. Caesar's need was evident: if it wasn't wisely satisfied he would try to be his own instructor. If he were well instructed, he might still attain knowledge. But I could not open it to him. There are times when I think that the secrecy enjoined on us is a mistake – the sages of India do not labour under this difficulty: they can instruct anyone they see to be ready, imposing their own tests on him, but there were no such teachers in Rome. Seneca, who had had such a teacher, had taken Caesar as far as his own weaknesses would permit, in the hope of training a philosopher-king. I didn't at that moment see the king, simply a human being ready for help, who, without it, would fall into the hands of some exotic theosophy he didn't understand, or worse, lose touch with reality and think himself Dionysus incarnate. I told him I would try to find him an instructor. I did, but I failed. Poppaea might in time be ready to instruct him – I couldn't be sure. I found the need to withhold matters from him sad.

'What makes you think, Caesar,' I said, 'that I could instruct you?'

He looked at me with real inner hunger.

'The woman's death,' he said. 'You knew, and you know what will become of her.'

He changed the subject, but I grieved, I think more for him than for her. Her journey was clear, his was not.

I dined with Burrus and Seneca and told them which way the wind was blowing in Baiae. Caesar was involved in something he had to finish.

'My fear,' said Seneca, 'is that he may go to pieces, and leave us without a viable Emperor, while he practises music and drives chariots, or seeks Enlightenment.'

'I don't think so, Lucius,' I said. 'He's quite clear what he must do. He'll be back when he's ready.'

'Any time on that?' said Burrus.

'Yes, Caesar is talking of autumn.'

'Well,' said Seneca, 'I hope you're right, for everyone's sake. I don't like the way Tigellinus is taking over. That man is capable of a putsch, and Caesar would be no match for him. Try to get him back, Callimachus. None of us are getting younger – Xenophon and I both aim to retire as soon as Caesar is clearly in charge. The mother's gone, and a man shouldn't have tutors nursing him for life. While Burrus is around, Tigellinus won't try anything, but Burrus is not immortal ...'

'And,' said Burrus, 'has had nearly enough soldiering for any man's taste. I had hoped one day to breed cattle.'

'So Caesar must be recalled to duty. With all deliberate speed,' said Seneca. 'Xenophon will represent to him very strongly that we understand his wish to compose himself, but he has a command to carry, which may slip away from him if he isn't careful.'

I had told Caesar of Acte's death on my first visit to Baiae. First he had wanted me to leave at once to supervise Acte's obsequies, for which there was no need: then he told me that he had sent gold to Cos to pay for a marble stele, to be inscribed 'Dear friend of the friend of Caesar', which I accepted on Acte's behalf – it was a kind gesture, and I appreciated it. I heard afterwards that he sent my son a gold rattle in the form of a horse's head, in care of Diodorus.

Finally he said, 'You'll want to return in any case, Callimachus, to see the child.'

I saw my chance and said, 'I will, Caesar, but when you return to Rome. We both have responsibilities. My boy will grow, and Asklepios is looking after him, to say nothing of Artemidorus and the College – but your chair will get cold if it is not sat in. Caesar should not leave it too long – he runs a good chance of finding another man sitting in it.'

'I take your point, Callimachus,' said Caesar. I had expected a possible panic reaction – Who? Why? Is there a conspiracy? But no. 'It takes time, Callimachus,' said Caesar, 'to grow both older and younger at once. Seneca sent you – it's obvious. Tell him I intend to return to Rome in September, that I am not sick or demoralized, and that I intend to take up exactly where I left off. His first task will be to help me organize a Festival of Youth. This time, whether the Catos like it or not, we are going to have gymnastics, not bloodshed. If the public insists something must be killed, it will be elephants, or tigers, or whales, or some other expensive monster. My mother would have done admirably, but that's over. After that, you can either take furlough and come back, if you want to stay in Rome, or go back to Cos, which is what in your place I think I would do. You know Xenophon means to retire – and old Seneca with him as soon as they've satisfied themselves I don't need dry-nursing and holding out to stool.'

And in September he did return to Rome, and got a rousing reception as I have said. I now had riches and nobody save a baby and the College to share them with, and I was in no haste to return to Cos and find my office empty of all but Acte's herbs. On the other hand, it was the right decision.

I went accordingly to Caesar's Acte, to book my passage. She could not detach Arbaces or *Thunderbolt*, so I would have to go in a regular merchantman. Acte refused absolutely to take any fare money. I asked her if she, too, meant to leave Rome.

'I think not,' she said. 'Caesar may need friends.'

I told her what had happened to her name-sister. 'It is no good telling you not to miss her,' she said, 'but consider: this is the wisdom of Asklepios. Very probably he had other work for her, and did not want her to fall into my situation. If Caesar had married me, I couldn't be First Lady among these toffee-nosed Roman matrons – I'd have caused trouble, and he'd have blamed me. If you'd married Acte, would the College have made you archiatros?'

I told her they wouldn't in any event, but no doubt she was right.

'Asklepios was kinder to her,' said Caesar's Acte, 'He will arrange matters in his own good time. All I can do is wait.'

So I sailed from Ostia on the last day of September, and this time I was escorted to the ship by Caesar, Seneca, Burrus, and all the Illuminates, except Poppaea. It was only when I got to sea that I found Caesar had filled the entire cargo space with books, engraved glass and other gifts, some of which have been broken in use, but most of which I still have. Leaving Ostia we made course for the Symplegades, passed between Sicily and the Cape in fair weather, and came safely, though in rather slow time by Arbaces' standards, to Cos.

6

What I did in the seven years following Acte's death and my return to Cos is another story, Herondas. I shall be brief about it here, because the medical aspects have been largely published already, and I shall confine myself to personal matters. In that time I had only one direct contact with Caesar, when he sent me a brief note together with a book which I will describe in its place. You should bear in mind, accordingly, that when I write what was happening to Caesar, or going on in Rome, during those seven years, the account I give is not what was reported at the time. Our intelligence at the College was good, but not that good. Nearly always what we heard was a series of versions, depending on what story was current in Rome itself. Information was more authoritative as long as Xenophon was himself in the administration, but he could not take too many risks with state secrets unless they affected the College directly, and in any case neither he nor, for that matter, Caesar himself, always knew the true version of some event until later. What I write here, covering the years when I was not there to see for myself, is what I now think happened, not necessarily what one heard at the time. Much of it I was able to check with witnesses later. Clearly this part of Caesar's history, which I didn't see, is a necessary part of his case notes – much as I dislike taking other observers' notes at face value: the outcome would make no sense to you without it.

I found Cos hard to bear at first, having expected a different homecoming. I went to my office on arrival. It was in beautiful order. The smell of the dispensary herbs still filled the place. On my table was a package – I was sure Acte would have left me something, probably a long letter, composed during her pregnancy, and telling me more concerning her dreams and the will of Asklepios, and that would be hard to read, seeing her handwriting and not her. But when I picked up the packet, it was light – too light for tablets. I opened it: inside was one of my round medicine-boxes, and inside that was a pendant – not the one I had given her from Rome (that one she had bequeathed to our son, for *his* eventual wife, or for some other woman whom he might love), but a little gold medal of Asklepios with serpents, the border of which was another serpent having its tail in its own jaws. The front said, 'iatros hieros' – whether that meant 'the physician is dedicated' or 'the dedicated physician' one could obviously take one's pick, for such medal-inscriptions leave out the definite article. Whether the compliment, or the exhortation was to me, to our Patron, or both, Acte left equally open. The gift was of herself and as subtle as she always was, in spite of her matter-of-factness. The ambiguity she'd have taken for granted.

Then I turned the medal over, and found she had had it inscribed. The inscription consisted of three words: 'We have loved, we love, we shall love.' Dear Acte, I thought, taking the message to be simply, 'I shall love you always, don't forget me.' Acte would have smiled gravely at my sentimentality – that wasn't in fact what she meant at all, and she had put the snake, the ouroboros, round the edge of the message to make her point, but just then I was too homesick for her to notice it.

The baby was a splendid specimen. At his tender age I could see that, and I hoped Caesar's gift would prove robust – in fact, Herondas, when I came to your father's house, *you* were playing with it, to make sure on the baby's behalf, you told me, that it worked. You may possibly recall the horse's head that rolled its eyes and rang bells when it was shaken.

Everyone, of course, was remarkably kind. The remedy for grief, however, is work – as it is for most other evils which lie within us. I had had some time already, too, to order my feelings. I went to Diodorus, who convened the Faculty, and the best part of a week was spent in debriefing me. Our original anxiety, that Caesar would demand initiation, and that a Claudian – even an adopted half-Claudian – who acquired spiritual knowledge might be deluded into deifying himself, I was able to remove once and for all. Caesar knew very well that when the herald announces that 'all those postulants who know in themselves any just cause or impediment why they should not enter the presence of the Gods should now depart' he would have to leave, for the death of Agrippina was public. Maybe he had as much provocation as Orestes, but Orestes himself would have been ineligible unless purified. As to delusions of deity, Nero had struck me as entirely free of them – he greatly enjoyed a rather heavy-handed squib on the deification of Claudius which some wag had attributed to Seneca (Seneca was furious, but because Caesar praised the work he seems to have swallowed his annoyance – one still hears *The Great Pumpkin Deified* read as one of his compositions.) The one reassurance I couldn't give them was how long Caesar would last, but in my view the odds on his getting through the next five or ten years, errors and accidents excepted, had improved vastly with the disappearance of his mother.

By and by, that being over, I went back to my work. I decided to devote more of my time to an aspect of surgery. Surgeons in Rome are, as you might expect, extremely good at trauma surgery: they get ample practice in tending swordfighters, charioteers, and other casualties of the Roman form of entertainment, to say nothing of their almost uninterrupted field experience in war. Like the rest of us, what they can do is limited by two things – pain, and the mortification of wounds. Now patching up gladiators is close to carpentry or tailoring, with bones and flesh instead of wood and cloth. But when I spent time in Egypt and saw, during the opening of bodies, how often mortal diseases come from a simple mechanical cause – one which could be snipped out with scissors, if only we could get at it, I found the death of such cases exasperating. I knew precisely what must be done to heal them, but I could not do it: how can one cut open a young girl's belly to ease an obstruction? Now in the arena bellies are cut open, and the Roman surgeons know how to repair them, often with success. That happens quickly, in the heat of combat, and the wounded man rarely complains of pain. It occurred to me first that if one could strike as fast and as surely one might be able to do the same, but I gave up the idea, because the closure of such a wound would be agonizing in itself, and sick men are not hardened characters like swordfighters – nor can one stun them with a mallet, as Roman surgeons do.

Pain was the first obstacle, then, in such cases, if one did not want to supervise a torture-chamber, and pain could be relieved, albeit not sufficiently for my purposes. Mortification, the second danger, is of course an old adversary in medicine, and thanks to Asklepios and his mouldy loaves I thought I might have a way of dealing with that. It is rarer in swordfighters when the wound is clean, the worst kind of moritification coming from earth or straw: Roman surgeons know this, and wash the wound, themselves, and their instruments with hot water and green soap. I said to myself that the first task I must tackle is to see if there is any pharmacon which will induce a sleep long and deep enough to enable a fast surgeon to do his office, for that was the first objective we must capture.

With this in mind I started a systematic examination of every drug in the books and on my shelves, both alone and in mixtures – after a deal of work (because one cannot take risks with patients, or, if one wishes to finish the research, by taking unknown drugs incautiously oneself), I have had some successes. I knew I was not wasting my time, because I knew that priests both in India and in Egypt can induce deep, unbreakable sleep by making the patient repeat certain words or gaze at a small jewel; if such skills could be acquired, they would be invaluable, but I had never been able to do this myself. It was, however, true, because I had seen it done. If such a priest ever becomes one of us, I thought, and we share other secrets, I hope to induce him to share this one with me. I also formed the opinion that whatever was done in the demonstrations I saw was being done by the patient himself, not by the priest. My patients, being unbelievers, did not seem able to achieve this.

This research occupied much time. Soon after my return to work I went to Anticyra to update my knowledge of hellebore, which was quite popular in those days as a painkiller as well as an antipsychotic. By doing so I missed an unrepeatable opportunity, because Caesar sent to Diodorus and asked if he would spare me to accompany an expedition then being assembled to find the sources of the Nile. Diodorus was delighted – it would be a chance to get herbs nobody had seen before – but through some foul-up I never got his message, and another physician went from Rome in my place. I think Asklepios had other plans for me. In any case I went back to my books and my dispensary. I was pleased about the expedition – the Romans under Caesar were being educated. You may not realize that although we have known since Aristarchus (and any fool can be shown with a ruler and pencil) that the Earth is a sphere, most educated Romans think it is flat, and if one expostulates they say, 'Who cares what shape it is?' Consequently, the one nation which today has the resources to explore Earth by sailing around it has no interest in doing so, and thinks it might be impious to try, or that they would fall off its other surface if they did. I might have been less happy if I had known that the Nile expedition was not interested in knowledge but in gold, slaves, and the supply of exotic animals! In fact, it was necessary for some of our Greek scientists to promise that these would be found, in order to get a grant for pure research.

When I went back the first time from the College to my office, Herondas, I was perfectly certain, from the moment I opened the door, that Acte had withdrawn herself from it. It was as if she had waited around, in some way, for my return, and now she had left. There was no replacing Acte, however, and I knew it. Over the next few years I lived with, and was looked after by, a number of women, both slave and free. It is bad for the health of a man or woman to abstain too long from sexual congress; it is particularly dangerous for the physician, who has to handle other men's wives while retaining correct behaviour. It was in any case against my inclination, and one cannot run a household single-handed and manage a practice. I avoided women in Rome, and boys as well, simply because it was too dangerous, and I ran enough risks there without adding to them. Probably I was overcautious. All my housekeepers were nice, some I was fond of, but there was never any approach to the sense of community I had had with Acte: some were not really able to follow what I was doing, for some real communication was hindered by the fact that I was their master, and others were far too gratified at having the attention of a rising local physician, and treated me as a social asset.

I had to ask Clea – whom you may vaguely remember – to leave for the last of these reasons, much as we liked one another. She had been telling people she was with child by me, and that I would shortly marry her, neither of which was true. This kind of thing did not stop my work, but it led to disruption, loneliness at times, minor bereavements when I lost friends I was fond of, and quarrels when I dismissed others. 'As Caesar could never be rid of his mother,' Diodorus said, 'because he hated her, so for a wholly different reason you can never replace Acte.' I had once asked her, before we went to sleep, why we were as we were, and she replied matter-of-factly, as always, 'Well, it's obvious – we've been together before.'

During that time I did hear once, and once only, from Caesar himself. A Roman packet delivered to the College a dispatch-box full of books, sealed with Caesar's personal seal, and labelled

'Reports of the Commission of Five on the Affairs of Lampsacus.' Inside was Petronius' book. He sent simply 'Greetings from the author.' There was another note with the scrolls. It ran:

> 'spurcum tibi misi libelliusculum – mihi jucundum; et Catonibus, et ipsi Caesari, nempe molestum. Tu risum da, etsi non plausum. Vale.
>
> L. Domitius.

No date. 'I'm sending you a dirty book: just a trifle. I like it, but it won't appeal to moralists, or, probably, to Caesar officially. You may laugh at it, even if you disapprove. Keep well. Lucius Domitius.'

Petronius and Caesar had written quite an extraordinary work. It was not, as I had feared it might be, a burlesque epic in verse; Petronius, who almost certainly wrote most of it, had brought off a tour-de-force. For a start, he wrote in prose. He borrowed the form of an Alexandrian novelette – the kind of thing which is produced for ladies by those teachers of rhetoric whom he so despised – mixed it with Menippean satire, and imposed the epic form on it. But instead of the heroes, tyrants, star-crossed lovers on assault courses, and the general hocum of popular fiction, his heroes were three Greek dropouts – 'Groper', 'Banjo', who had artistic and musical ambitions, and a violent yobbo called 'The Virgin'* with whom the other two competed for the attentions of a precocious small boy. There was also a rich, willing lady – 'Dainty Hotlips' – and you, Herondas, can imagine the rest. The plot turned on the wrath of Priapus, which is visited on Groper because he violated the Mysteries of the God and is consequently cursed with unreliable erections, as Odysseus was cursed with bad weather from Poseidon. The title of this confection was 'The Prickwort Papers'.

Here Caesar, who, I am sure, suggested that title, was having a joke at my expense, because I once told him that satyricon has no medical use – the association of the summer savory with satyrs is due to the little tails on the flowers, not to any

* Askyltos means 'not mauled' or 'not looted' – the allusion has to be sexual, knowing Petronius. Tryphaena ('swinger') is almost impossible to render. (A.C.)

aphrodisiac action, and clearly he hadn't forgotten. There were the usual poems inset in the text, and most of these I feel sure were Caesar's, or were workshopped by him with the Illuminates. As to the Illuminates, they were the subject of the whole thing: Groper was a combination of Otho and Petronius himself, Banjo was largely Caesar, and a skit on his musical and poetic ambitions: the Virgin was Tigellinus, and, of course, Dainty Hotlips was Poppaea. This programme, too, was probably Caesar's idea, and I imagine the characters were worked out in committee by the whole bunch of them. But Petronius was far too good a writer to be tied down. He mixes the characters, uses different aspects of the same model as separate figures, and generally turns a private joke into his own conception, the work about rogues and Romans he'd wanted to write. In the middle of the action stands a savage picture of one of his father's vulgar dinners.

I wrote to Caesar. I thanked him for the book, told him that I had indeed laughed my head off at it, and asked him to pass on to Petronius my opinion that he and Caesar had created a new literary form which might well continue to flourish when epics had become antique. He probably took that as flattery, I'm afraid, being used to favour-hunters, but it is still my opinion. I felt that writing the book had probably done both the collaborators good. It might wash the Illuminates out of Caesar's system, and let Petronius, who had got royally even with his father, move on to something else.

I was quite certain when I left Rome that with Agrippina dead, Caesar would divorce Octavia – probably marrying her to somebody harmless, or to one of the less scandalous Illuminates, to side-track any risks arising from her Claudian ancestry, and the chance she might, in bearing a child, bear a potential pretender. He would then marry Poppaea in short order. The reason he gave me later for not having done so – and he bitterly regretted it – was that he had been too busy, but I think we both knew that the real reason was the continuing presence in his mind of the Best of Mothers. A capable, intelligent wife would be too alarmingly like a mother for some part of Caesar to incur the risk. Caesar wanted Poppaea – but he had her already, so that incentive was withdrawn. Any pressure on her part or anyone else's was counterproductive – it raised the ghost, nightmares restarted, and the whole matter was put off.

And Caesar was busy – infernally busy. Not only did he press on with the mission of civilizing Rome by the introduction of Greek-style gymnastic games in parallel with the traditional blood sports – he was determined to develop his own artistic and sporting skills so that he could 'set an example,' and he worked like a madman to become, not only a Roman Emperor, but a singer, player, actor, orator and charioteer, all at a professional level. In a sense I think that Seneca's example of industry had set him a target, but behind it all stood the accusing, disapproving parents who still had to be satisfied, and were still unsatisfiable inside his head when everyone else applauded.

I think the Gods, and the Furies of Agrippina, destroyed Caesar through this delay. If he had been more decisive in imposing a quick divorce, or even if he had been a bigger villain, had listened to Tigellinus, and had accused Octavia of complicity in the concocted murder-plot Anicetus had arranged, the whole thing would have left a nasty taste, perhaps, but it would not have festered on. For if a crime is bad enough, a second crime adds little to its impact.

While Nero dawdled over Poppaea, moreover, something else happened, through no fault of his own, which sickened him with the position he held. Two years after I left Rome, the old Catonian Rome showed itself at its worst. The whole disgusting affair started when the Urban Prefect Lucius Pedanus was murdered by one of his slaves. There had been an altercation between them: the slave claimed that Lucius had promised to manumit him, and had accepted a down payment from his savings: Lucius said that he would decide in his own good time whom he would manumit, and when, and that if the slave could not be replaced by somebody equally competent he would have to stay on – if necessary until Lucius died. 'We'll see about that,' said the slave, and cut Lucius' throat.

Now in a civilized society the slave would have been tried for murder – and possibly escaped with banishment on the grounds of provocation, if his account of the matter were true. It was no more legal in Rome to cheat a slave than to cheat a free man, since slaves acquired the right to their own property. But in an evil hour one of the new race of prosecutors, smart young attorneys recruited by Tigellinus, who lived by competition with each other, took up the case – and pointed out that by law, whenever a slave murdered his master, all slaves in that household were to be deemed accomplices and all of them must be executed. He accordingly filed for the arrest and execution of some four hundred people, including women and babies in arms. I imagine he thought that he had supplied himself and his fellow lawyers with rhetoric to last several years.

Seneca was furious and denounced the prosecutor's opinion as a barbarous anachronism, which it was – the law hadn't been enforced for years, possibly centuries. It was a hold-over from the panic fear of slave-owning Romans that if they didn't make slaves act as spies on one another, there would be another Servile Rising. Nero told Seneca to cool down, that the whole thing was a legal nonsense, and that the Senate, even if they were Romans, would never tolerate such barbarity. But the Furies of Agrippina had turned against Rome as a whole. When word of the opinion leaked out, the population of Rome was outraged. What had been an academic matter turned into a general protest against the lawyers, who had destroyed dozens of innocent people during the last three reigns, and the obnoxious Establishment. When Caesar failed to intervene – and counsel advised him that until the Senate debated the matter, he ought not to do so – riots broke out all over town, and the debate itself took place with a rock-throwing mob besieging the Senate, causing casualties among Burrus' guards, and – finally – demanding a Republic.

The Senate could have defused the whole situation by repealing the law. Seneca himself decided not to intervene, or let Caesar intervene – Pedanius had been a friend of his and a fellow-Spaniard, and there was no need for panic measures. He left the Senate to a leading liberal jurist, Gaius Cassius Longinus, who could massage the frightened slave-owners, assure them that they would be safer in their beds if they substituted justice for injustice, and get the case settled.

Unfortunately, those same Senators found that they had to fight their way into the chamber through a particularly ugly riot. Backwoodsmen came from the countryside to vote for the Bad Old Days – many of them people who still kept their kitchen workers in muzzles to make sure they did not steal the food. When the liberal Longinus got up to speak and began to talk about the dangers of exemplary punishment, he suddenly turned tail, sensing the hysteria of his audience, or, quite simply, regressed to his military days in Syria, when every tenth man of a mutinous regiment was regularly executed. At first Seneca's staffer, who was monitoring the debate, thought Longinus was marshalling the old arguments to quiet the audience and would then refute them. Longinus harangued eloquently about the need for firmness, the thin ends of wedges, and the security of the State, in which civilization still depended for its necessities upon ignorant scum who understood only fear – strong stuff, of the kind upon which scum who should know better always rely to bolster their excesses. And then, to the horror of the staffer, he sat down. While the mob outside howled, the mob inside voted overwhelmingly for the status quo, and the execution of Pedanius' entire household.

Caesar was terrified by the riots already. Seneca was aghast – the men must be insane. Caught between Burrus and Tigellinus, both telling him that troops were being injured if not killed, and that he had to restore order at once, Seneca telling him that he could not let this monstrosity happen, and his legal counsel telling him not to interfere with the law, he lost his head completely. Shouting, 'If the sons of bitches want blood, let them have it – I disclaim all responsibility!' he sealed the warrant and locked himself in.

After that things went from bad to worse. When police attempted to remove the four hundred screaming, protesting servants and take them to execution, they were met by a determined armed mob. Burrus brought Caesar forcibly out of his private suite and said to him, 'You have let this go too far. Now you've surrendered to the Senate you have to let this monstrosity take place. If you surrender to the mob as well, I resign.'

So Caesar issued a Riot Act, and the Guards lined the streets to see the sentences enforced, while Caesar vomited.

It was Caesar's first open battle with old Rome, and he lost it. He was not the man to call the Senate to heel, as Augustus would have done, and still less the man to send word to the mob that the Caesar was on their side. And so among appalling scenes three hundred and ninety-nine innocent people were flogged, beheaded or strangled to death in relays to offset the introduction of civilization and gymnastics. Gymnastics had in fact contributed both to the venom of the traditionalists, and to the anger of the mob, who put down the decline in public swordfights to the stinginess of the Establishment. Caesar thereafter ostentatiously snubbed the Senate on every occasion which offered. I think the ghost of Agrippina must have been delighted, if not appeased, and I decided that I had been right to avoid settling in Rome.

While this was going on, Herondas, we were enjoying ourselves in Rhodes – you looking at the lighthouse, in the form of a huge man, I watching my son making pills out of beach sand, though I demurred when he wanted me to take some of them. Your father put a half-door on the dispensary to keep him from getting at the drugs, but he was strong enough now to look over it. Both of you loved the voyage in Arbaces' ship. I think he had been harder hit by Acte's death than I – for some reason he thought I might blame him for it – but recently he had taken a very pretty and affectionate girl from Chios; true to form, Arbaces had had a slight disagreement with her father, and had managed inadvertently to sail while she was on board, quite without his knowledge, since she had apparently stowed away. Her name was Gorgo, and before long she, too, had a baby, which I had the responsibility of delivering. Fortunately this time there was no problem, and Arbaces had a daughter who still lives.

When you two were in bed, I took the chance of visiting the reputed house of Apollonius, the poet, and in doing so, through the guidance of Asklepios (for such things never happen by accident), I met a namesake of his on the same mission. I knew nothing of him, but he introduced himself as if he recognized me – or rather, he sent one of his disciples to find me and invite me to a meal. This was one of the most interesting and productive evenings I ever spent in my life. Exactly as most people now think of Nero as a god or as a monster (chiefly the second), when he was in fact neither, I have heard sensible people say that Apollonius of Tyana was Hermes or Mithras in disguise, that he was a sorcerer, and that he could raise the dead. Absolute nonsense – the man was certainly an adept, a mathematician, and one of the most learned Pythagoreans of his time, but he was also a researcher who pursued his sources with incredible energy, and his originality was his only miracle.

The house where Apollonius was staying had become a kind of ashram. There were disciples, chiefly Greek or Roman, and of both sexes, but most of them affecting Indian dress. Apollonius sat on the floor, and we dined on Indian food spiced with coriander and cumin. I might have been back with Kapila. Apollonius had just spent three years in India and Tibet, he spoke Sanskrit fluently, and he had personally talked to all the most important Indian ascetics and masters.

'You'll have to excuse the disciples,' he said. 'You know how orientalia attract disciples. What doesn't attract them is the realization that yoga involves hard work. But I've winnowed out the chaff. Those who stay with me will probably get somewhere.'

I asked him how he knew of me – was that one of his siddhi? Apollonius said that it wasn't – 'If I showed you some genuine siddhi,' a very eminent yogi had told him, when he asked the same question, 'you wouldn't recognize them!'

'I wanted to talk to you because I never forget a name I hear twice,' he said. 'I heard yours twice, from Kapila in India, and from the new King of Armenia, Tiridates. I studied with his colleagues; did you know that in his country he is regarded as a leading esoteric philosopher? Then someone pointed you out and said, "That's Callimachus – Nero's doctor." Now we shall have another story about my occult powers!'

I cannot recount here all that we discussed. Apollonius told me one thing I didn't know – that Nero had written privately to Tiridates, as a Magus, to ask how he might be purified of guilt for the death of Agrippina. Apollonius' life work was to bring about some kind of dialogue between Hindu and Ionian philosophy, on the basis that if Pythagoras were right in regarding the observed world as a concretion of mathematics or quanta, then the next object of knowledge – and possibly the only one – was the observing brain. 'Zeno's denial of the reality of movement is really a very thoughtful statement of the conditionality of the "real",' he said. 'It will take centuries to address this through mathematics – Hinduism addresses it through inner experimentation: on the machine which is generating "reality", the human mind.' I began to see why the Greeks didn't follow him, and the Romans thought he was a wizard. When he started to explain that space, time and motion are not things but ways of seeing, I, who am not a mathematician, lost my bearings.

I asked him about the matter which was exercising me, the induction of surgical sleep. 'Oh,' he said, 'that's not magic either. Anyone can do it.' And he called in a disciple, and there and then showed me how such sleep may be induced. Under his influence the disciple felt cold coins as hot, and could be pricked without pain, and indeed, without drawing blood. Apollonius told him that when he heard a count of three, he would wake and recall nothing of the experience. Apollonius counted three, and so indeed it was.

More important, perhaps – though that lesson was one of the most important techniques I ever learned, and made my career as a surgeon – was something else. Apollonius used a bright object to concentrate the gaze of his subject – he told me it wasn't necessary, but that it simplified induction – and to induce sleep in his disciple, he borrowed Acte's pendant. When the disciple had left, he still held it. 'Who gave you this, Callimachus?' he asked. I told him the story of Acte.

'You won't take this amiss, will you, if I tell you that I would almost sooner have met her than you?' said Apollonius.

I agreed. I also asked him what he thought she had meant.

'Acte is saying in a very compact way, what I was trying to tell you very clumsily in mathematical terms. Time looks to us like a thread, but actually it's a block, and we see it a thread at a time. That's why the snake's tail is in its mouth.'

'But how,' I said, 'can the Pythagorean idea of recurrent lives possibly be right?'

'It isn't,' said Apollonius, 'any more than our impression of the linearity of time is right. Stop thinking about beads on a string. Did you ever see a Spartan message-stick? Well, you can't read the message when the paper is unrolled. If I could put that in plain, I'd be the greatest mathematician of all time. Or take this scroll – a worm has eaten into it while it was rolled. Is there one wormhole or many? One if you see the scroll, many if you unroll it. And the holes have no transcendental identity anyway – there is no *thing* called Acte or Callimachus: in fact, as I just said, there are no *things* at all. Democritus was right at the realistic level, wrong at the fundamental.'

'I think,' I said, 'Acte's exposition is easier to take in.'

'I agree,' said Apollonius, 'that's why I studied Hinduism.'

Since medicine is not practised in a thingless world, I am only now beginning to address what Apollonius was talking about. But I went home elated, and itching to try the sleep-induction he had shown me. On the first opportunity I did, and it worked. I set a leg for the first time without pain. It is moreover purely a physiological operation, like the action of poppy or nepenthe. It has no connection either with magic or with mathematical philosophy.

There was one final question I had asked Apollonius. I asked him if a man could be an avatar of a god.

Apollonius tipped out a bag of coins and chose all those which carried Nero's portrait. 'You have seen the Emperor,' he said.

'Now, is any one of these faces Caesar?'

I told him, no – some were better portraits than others, but of course every coin is different. In some the die has struck better than in others; some are almost unrecognizable. Some were cut from a badly-engraved die; others quite passable portraits.

'I agree,' he said, 'none of them is Caesar. But presumably there is a die somewhere, an archetypos, which is the portrait of Caesar. Dionysus is not a thing, Callimachus, as you and I are not things, but one might expect there to be many coins, of varying perfection, struck from that die, too. Personally, from what I know of gods, I doubt if most of them would strike us as godlike. The goodness of the gods is a philosopher's attempt to make them human – mythology and the Hindus are wiser, I think. If ever you were to meet a good likeness of Dionysus you'd very probably be scandalized.'

'Who mentioned Dionysus?' I said.

'Nobody,' replied Apollonius, 'but it's common knowledge that Caesar resembles him – and is a demonic force, both dangerous and propitious. And is an actor: and is not over-courageous: and may well on occasion play the rogue. Why not? Dionysus is in our heads, Callimachus, like all the gods. Why not in Caesar's?'

It would be unwise to comment further, Herondas. I will report simply what was said by Apollonius.

Apollonius and I have remained friends since that evening, though we rarely contrive to meet, and one never quite knows when he will remove himself to India or beyond. When I met him in Rhodes, he was planning another of these sabbaticals – like me, he had been started in Indian philosophy by a guru of the Vedic religion, which shares its origins with the Magians, but encourages subdivision of the One into Many, provided that the basic one-ness is recognized – rather as we for convenience divide 'healing' into medicine, surgery, hygiene, pharmacy and so on. This had been the model I had received from Kapila. I was a child at the time, and a Greek child, used to Olympian Gods, and Kapila was probably very wise to go this way, giving me the materials which would help me later to see for myself. Also, being a child, I didn't interrogate him about other schools, taking his observances for granted. Apollonius told me that there was a much deeper model, which goes beyond the Many completely and addresses the One, finding it to be both within us and experienceable as the Empty Plenum – a very Pythagorean idea, if you study what Pythagoreans teach about the Apeiron, which is both zero and infinity. The founder of this system – indeed, its discoverer – was a prince called Sacius, who abandoned his kingdom to address human suffering, and after much fruitless austerity and study under Vedic teachers, had the experience of waking, into comprehension. His disciples simply refer to him as 'The Awake'. This model was Apollonius' next target – not only because it was uncluttered with subdivisions and deities, but because it closely approached his own intuitions when working with Vedic teachers – and also because he strongly suspected that both Zeno and Pythagoras were aware of it, and had introduced some of its ideas into Greece. Apollonius says that though the vulgar of this tradition and the Vedic tradition have fought one another, as humans invariably seem to do, Vedic and Sacian adepts perfectly comprehend one another and have the same experiences, which they colour differently in interpreting them. Moreover the most adept followers of Prince Sacius, when they find themselves genuinely awake, swear to remain and awaken others, much as mariners in a shipwreck will not make their escape until all the passengers are ashore, an idea which appeals to me as a physician. I find myself increasingly having to look to my vows and *remain* a physician, not departing to become a disciple of some kind – you chuckle, Herondas, but the temptation is real. In India, it is traditional to do this when one retires through age: age, however, would prevent one going on arduous journeys of the kind which Apollonius says are necessary to find genuine teachers of these things – and I personally have no intention of retiring. Asklepios may be leaving this for some future assignment. Such 'assignments' the Sacians liken to 'a flame lit from another flame', a description of which one may say no more, but it is familiar.

Now all of us, Herondas, who have had certain experiences, know that what Apollonius says about Time is empathically correct. The point is that we have not seen it quite as he does – we have thought of that mode of perception as supernatural in some way, or at least I know I did. Apollonius' point was that things are in fact like that, and it is ordinary existence, not 'vision', which is artifactual and a special case. Moreover he worked this out first from physics, and only set about getting a direct experience of it later. We had the direct experience, but could not put it into plain even if that were permitted to us.

Without in any way decrying the importance of what we were shown, I rather think that Apollonius is the model for how in the future these insights will be taken into science, though it may take time of the order of centuries, and it is fortunately not our job to do it.

That took time for me to appreciate it. The new medical dodge I had learned didn't.

As soon as the leg patient thanked me and said, 'Wonderful, Doctor,' I rushed round to Diodorus and told him I'd discovered the secret of painless surgery, and probably the Meaning of Life as well (you can quit laughing, Herondas, because you'll inevitably do the same one day, if you haven't already).

'Splendid,' said Diodorus, 'you managed to set a leg under hypnosis? You know, I've never been able to make that work.'

Morale started to fall rapidly. 'It's been tried before?' I said.

'Oh, yes,' said Diodorus. 'But I agree with you, it badly needs re-evaluation. Half the trouble with the very few of our physicians who have tried it is that they either thought they were making magic, or didn't expect it to work at all. That's why it's not in the books. My problem, I suspect, is in being blind – I can't look at the patient, and the patient knows it. Did Apollonius tell you about the other things he does with it?'

I said I hadn't asked him.

'Well, Apollonius doesn't usually talk much to physicians – he's really a physicist and a natural-philosopher, and most of our colleagues treat him as naive, or a quack. He finds he can actually heal some conditions by suggestion. Did he tell you why hypnosis interests him? Well, he started it because a Magian philosopher told him it could be used to recall memories of former lives. It worked like a charm – Apollonius thought he'd got experimental verification of Pythagoras – until he started to look at the "lives". He found they'd all been kings, or heroes, or historical characters generally – the ignorant ones had "former lives" as some celebrity who was still living, only they didn't know that.'

'What did he do?'

'Chuckled,' said Diodorus, 'and started to be a bit more critical of his results.'

'You don't take him seriously?' I said.

'I take him very seriously. He's a totally hardheaded empiric dealing with an intoxicating and highly unpopular subject with strong doctrinal overtones. As a consequence he has to put up with disciples, cultists, abuse, people who think he's a magician – aside from an enormous amount of travel, and a lot of dead ends. *I* think he's getting somewhere. But he'll need several more of his Pythagorean lives before he can explain it to us. He says he may try to do it in poetry for a start. I think most of us have the wrong-shaped brain for mathematical physics – the people who can handle that have to be slightly insane in order to see things we don't. I think I grasp his main idea – that past-present-future exist en bloc, and we can congenitally see only a slice at a time. We know that's true, don't we? You, my lad, can probably explain the rest of it to me!'

I told him I couldn't, and left, muttering, 'Back to the drawing board.' Fortunately, as you know, Herondas, it wasn't as bad as that. When I started to find I'd been lucky in my first case, that not all parties could be put to sleep, and not all who were put to sleep could be operated on, I had the experience we all have with a new panacea, and nearly dropped it in disgust and went back to poppy and concussion instead. I took about a year to find out the limits. In minor surgery it works quite often, and even better in dentistry and for childbirth. For major surgery it works sometimes, as you have seen. Combined with henbane it works better still, since the patient, though feeling pain, does not remember it. Moreover, quite apart from the fact that I could make surgery less unpleasant, the whole technique – as Apollonius and Diodorus had tried to warn me – turned out quite ridiculously impressive to laymen, and indignation-making to colleagues. The first started to call me 'hypnochirurgos' – which I hated, but it has stuck. The second muttered about quackery. And the solicitations I started to get from all regions – far exceeding the repute of my baby-making practice – made them jealous, as well as leaving me no time to speculate about the conditionality of Time.

In fact, the atmosphere in the Faculty cooled quite a bit towards your former professor. Everyone was perfectly correct – as their interest dictated, because I made referrals, and I was getting more patients than they were, but one of my residents heard an illuminating conversation in the refectory between two members of the Archiatros Search Committee which Xenophon had set up to advise on his successor. Periander was telling Hermodorus that I'd ruined my chances. 'Pity,' he said, 'but we don't want an archiatros like that. Callimachus has an unfortunate taste for fringe medicine – first sex, now hypnosis.

Quite apart from the fact that being Caesar's physician at an early age has gone to his head. My vote must, you understand, go to a physician who is solid, not spectacular ...'

However, the College was quite ready, when in trouble, to send your former professor, the ex-Imperial physician, in to bat for them. When Thessalus of Tralles challenged Cos to a debate, they couldn't very well refuse (the Governor of Achaea was to be there), and the sacrificial victim was myself. 'He's an excellent talker,' Periander said, 'and he'll probably make mincemeat of Thessalus. On the other hand, if Thessalus makes mincemeat of *him*, we can point out that Callimachus is one of our younger Faculty and not, in some ways, fully representative of the school. Agreed?'

Thessalus had arranged the debate in Corinth, with a lay audience, as part of his campaign for self-promotion. He called himself 'iatronices', the quack destroyer, and his shtik was called The Rules of Health, or Methodicism. He arrived with P.R.O.'s, grateful patients to give testimonials, and a medicine show. His lecture was to the effect that orthodox medicine was a commercial fraud, that the Simple Rules had superseded Hippocratic mumbo jumbo, and that all of medicine could be learned by a common man in six months. And like most anti-medical quacks, he got an ovation from a big audience of hypochondriacs, some of whom were paying him through the nose for raw cabbage and inspiration to cure diseases they didn't have.

After he'd presented some of these testimonial cases, I had to reply. I complimented Thessalus on his frankness. 'He has learned the whole of medicine, he tells us, in six months. Six months into his training,' I said, 'every physician feels the same way. May I suggest that he now learns the rest of what there is to know?' And I went through his cases pointing out exactly what was wrong with his diagnoses – that the man with a persistent sore on his face, which Thessalus had 'cured', had in fact got a rodent ulcer. 'Thessalus tells us he has cured it with ground-up apricot pips,' I said. 'When it recurs in a few months, I strongly advise that patient to see a doctor – otherwise it will consume his left ear within a couple of years.' And so on. I don't much like this kind of knockabout before a lay audience, but it has to be done in the public interest. I pointed out that apart from the malignant ulcer, all the remaining cases were psychosomatic, or would have got better anyway, and I told them that that a fool and his money are soon parted.

When it came to the debate, Thessalus, who was rattled by the audience reaction, started by telling the meeting that I was a disgrace to a disgraceful profession, that he noticed I went where the publicity was, and that that was why I concentrated on sex and magic. The audience was now on my side, as I kept my temper, but Thessalus didn't see it. 'I wonder, Callimachus,' he said, 'if you would like to tell us what magical operation you are now developing to fill your pockets, and those of your colleagues?'

I said, 'Certainly. At the moment I'm thinking of developing transcephalic orchidectomy.'

Thessalus obviously didn't have a clue what that was, but I saw some physicians starting to grin. 'That's a fine example of big words to cover unnecessary surgery,' said Thessalus, buying the entire package. 'How much will this piece of carpentry cost?'

'Nothing,' I said, 'it will be absolutely free. I intend to demonstrate it now. Ladies and gentlemen, I don't share Thessalus' view that patients are fools. You are quite able to tell, now you have heard Thessalus in person, which of us two is a commercial quack. This man doesn't know his arse from his olecranon bursa: I wouldn't trust my dog to him, and if I were in your place I'd demand my money back. In my opinion, as a physician, he is totally unfit to be in charge of any patient whose sickness isn't recreational, and I personally happen to think even hypochrondriacs deserve the protection of our Governor against consumer fraud. If Thessalus had stayed another six months in medical school, he'd know a corny medical joke when he hears one. As he doesn't, I will here and now proceed in the interests of public health and safety, to perform a transcephalic orchidectomy on Thessalus, and I won't put him to sleep. He's insulted me and he's ripping you off. With everyone's permission, I'm going to kick his balls out through the top of his skull. Bend over, please, Thessalus. Now this may hurt a little ...'

The audience broke up laughing. ('This may hurt a little' was Thessalus' favourite phrase.) Thessalus left threatening me with mayhem, defamation, or both, and Arbaces (who brought his hands, in case Thessalus had a goon squad), took me back to Cos – only to find that Periander and the other old poultry thought my methods were beneath the dignity of Medicine, which they were. Diodorus said, 'Strong stuff, I agree. But in view of the provocation I think it was deserved. We Greeks appreciate dramatic confrontations and a bit of knockabout. Periander would have stood on his dignity and looked like a square – what *would* you have said, Periander? "No comment"? You know, I don't think Thessalus will be back.' Moreover, the Governor wrote the School a letter of appreciation for getting Thessalus run out of his parish, and saying how much he'd enjoyed the show. He had in fact been on the point of buying some expensive snake-oil from Thessalus for his wife's arthritis, but he didn't refer to that in the letter.

The physician's reputation, Herondas, is always a problem: he can't avoid getting one if he does his job. Quacks stage publicity-stunts to get one. The ideal physician ought to be both anonymous and invisible. But it doesn't work – even in Cos, where there are more medics than there are crabpots. There is no way one can stay out of the public eye, and one shouldn't bother about it.

For example, I worked exclusively out of the College, or my office. Then one afternoon I got a frantic call from Arbaces to come to the harbour. One of his best hands, his sailingmaster in fact, was holding a fender and had rashly put his leg over the stone edge of the dock. The incompetent in charge of the berthing vessel had overshot his moorings, rammed the dockside, and hit the unfortunate man's leg. If they moved the boat, it would destroy the leg – if they didn't move the boat, they couldn't move the man. When I arrived the entire waterfront was there. I could see, after I'd pushed my way in shouting, 'Doctor, stand back!' a tanned face gone pale, between the gunwhale of the grain ship and the stone dock, and Arbaces holding a hand which came up from the narrow space.

'Sorry to call you,' said Arbaces, 'he's done for. Kindest thing for Lampros would be to open his seacocks and scuttle him – he'll never sail again.'

'Hold your horses,' I said. I lay on my face and called down. 'Lampros, can you hear me? This is the doctor. I'm coming down.' And I lowered myself into the crack.

'Can you understand me?' I said.

'I hear you, doctor. Open my veins, like a good ship-mate,' said the casualty.

'We've got to move the ship to move you,' I said.

'Then finish me off first.'

'You need a pirate,' I said, 'not a doctor. I know

Thunderbolt's crew. It'll take more than a crushed leg to kill you.'

Lampros managed a grin.

'Hold on two minutes,' I said, and I gave him all the poppy I had. I scrambled back up.

'Are you set to warp that ship off?' I asked.

'When you say,' said Arbaces.

'Then tell them to stand by the capstan. That man will die of shock if you move her while he's conscious. I'm going to try something. I might be able to put him to sleep.' And I climbed gingerly back down.

'How is it now?' I asked.

'Pain's less, doctor. But I can't take more.'

'You won't,' I said. 'I'm going to try to put you to sleep. Can you still obey orders?'

'I don't ...'

'He's the Emperor's physician,' yelled Arbaces into the gap. 'Do what he tells you and be damned, Lampros.'

'Aye, aye, Sir,' said Lampros, and brightened slightly.

I was now going to officiate, I thought, down a crack between a ship and a stone wall, and persuade a badly shocked ex-pirate that he felt no pain. I took off Acte's pendant. 'Fix your eyes on that,' I said. 'Now, you will be able to hear everything I say to you ...'

And when I let go of his hand, it fell like lead.

'Warp her!' I called up.

'Not with you down there, Callimachus – she'll swing.'

'Warp her,' I said, 'and look sharp!'

The ship creaked, swung, pinched my ribs, and began to recede. I went on intoning, '... you are feeling nothing, your leg is no longer a part of you,' etcetera, etcetera, and all the time I could hear Lampros' tibia cracking. Then the gap opened, the sun rushed in, Arbaces and half a dozen hands grabbed us both, and Lampros, with his leg below the knee reduced to a pulp, was hauled up and put on a litter, still feeling nothing.

'He's dead,' said several people.

'He's sleeping,' I said. 'Now, Lampros, do you hear what I am saying to you?'

'I hear you, Doctor,' said Lampros.

There was a general murmur, but I wasn't bothered by the crowd reaction. There and then I performed an emergency amputation (luckily he had a decent stump and I need not disarticulate the knee), dressed the leg, taking my time, and said, 'Now, Lampros, when you wake, your leg will have been removed. But you will feel no pain. Do you feel pain?'

'I feel no pain. My leg has been removed, but I feel no pain. My leg is no longer a part of me ...'

'Lampros, when you wake you will feel discomfort, you will be ready to sleep, and you will remember nothing of this, except that your leg was crushed by a vessel. Now, I will clap my hands, and when I clap, you will wake.' I clapped, and he woke. Arbaces threw the surplus foot overboard into the harbour, where the patient wouldn't see it.

'How do you feel?' I asked.

'Foul, Doctor. And sleepy. That lubber has done for my leg. But it doesn't hurt much. Must have passed out when it happened.' And they carried him off to the College where Periander took him over. Later he went back to sea with a peg-leg the carpenter turned for him, albeit as a cook, not sailingmaster. Periander was huffy after. He said I'd ruined the stump, and I should have called him. But the waterfront, including Arbaces, stood there gaping like herrings. From then on I was a wizard, and Arbaces treated me with a certain amount of awe. I didn't like it, I didn't like the publicity, or being asked to touch people for luck, but what in Hades could I have done otherwise?

In fact, Herondas, for quite a while the two men on Cos with whom I felt I had most in common were a buccaneer and an alien – Arbaces and Bar Cochba. Bar Cochba's worries were increasing steadily as the temperature in Judaea went up. Moderate Jews had been quite unable to make Rome listen to an explanation of Jewish beliefs, and irredentists in Judaea launched a constant series of nationalist uprisings. Bar Cochba and the Jews of the Roman community were both running out of ideas, when they suddenly acquired a new ally – a young Jew of unimpeachable orthodoxy who knew personally the leaders of all the factions in Jerusalem, and who had, by the direct intervention of Providence, talked personally to both Poppaea and Caesar. He had come to Rome as an advocate, to defend some rabbis whom the Governor, Felix, had arrested (the charge was disturbing the peace, and the occasion, as usual, theological). They had had a hair-raising journey from Judaea, in the course of which their ship foundered; they were fortunately picked up by one of Acte's charters sailing out of

Cyrene, and put ashore at Puteoli. This young man had taken his religious education seriously enough to study in turn with the Pharisees, the Sadducees, and the Essenes, or Ascetics. His name was Joseph bar Matthias, or Joseph ben Matthias in Hebrew, though for convenience, since Roman officials never get the hang of Jewish patronymics, he took the name of Flavius.

Flavius not only got the arrested rabbis off; he started to explain effectively to Caesar what Judaism was about, and why Felix was at odds with it. The reason he did so well was that he went about it in the right way. Instead of besieging Caesar, Seneca and the others, he went straight to an actor called Aliturius. This Aliturius was a very good friend of Caesar. He was also a Jew, albeit too settled in Rome to take great interest in the troubles of Judaea. But he did welcome Flavius Josephus to his house, celebrate sabbath with him; then, taking him to Rome, he contrived to introduce him to Poppaea. Now Poppaea, in spite of her activities as an Illuminate, which might have suggested a lack of serious interests, was about the only Gentile in Rome who had an intelligent grasp of Judaism – as she had of Magianism, Hinduism, and many other religious philosophies. Poppaea went personally to see Caesar about the disrupting rabbis, taking Flavius with her. 'This, Caesar,' she said, 'is a prime example of the kind of ignorant administration blunder which is feeding rebellions. Let these perfectly harmless mullahs go home, order their own religious court to see they debate in private, not in front of a mob, and tell Felix to stop meddling in local theology. If this goes on, Rome will have yet another unnecessary colonial war on its hands.'

Caesar entirely agreed, sent the rabbis home, and said to Flavius, 'I'd entertain you, if it were not against your faith to eat Roman food. I want to avoid a Jewish rising as much as you do – you'll notice *I* haven't put my image in your Temple, and I have no intention of doing so. Rome will respect your faith if you'll respect Roman law, but if Jewish guerrilla movements keep on killing pro-Roman citizens and raising the devil generally, I'm going to be forced to send in troops, and the troops and our ignorant Senate between them will destroy your people. I'm in a cleft stick. Most of my advisers – Seneca in particular – see Jews as a nation of irredentists and seditionists, at odds with the whole of mankind, or as primitive fanatics like the Druids.'

'What can I do, Caesar?' said Flavius. 'If it comes to the worst, I will fight for my people.'

'I don't doubt it,' said Caesar, 'and if you do you will be defeated and lose the religious liberties you've got, and probably your life. What no Jew has ever done is to write an intelligible handbook on Jewish history and beliefs which my self-opinionated ministers will take seriously. All the Jewish literature they see consists of religious polemics and threats of judgment against Rome. These people of mine fancy themselves as philosophers. Don't you Jews have any philosophers apart from fakirs who snipe at sentries and set fires?'

Flavius told him that they had not only philosophers, but a scholarly tradition which was older than, and at least as interesting as, that of Greece – but most Romans couldn't read it.

'Precisely,' said Caesar, 'and nor can I. Poppaea reads it, but nobody else here does. Go home, stand up for what you think are your rights if you must, but don't join the losing side – Jews will need defenders at Rome even more if they fight us than if they don't. And write a decent study of Jewish history and customs for my civil service – in Greek: they always take Greek books seriously.'

Here was precisely the opportunity which Gershom and Bar Cochba had been praying their God to provide. Bar Cochba arranged for Flavius Josephus to come back via Cos and visit him. (I didn't meet him – this was an ethnic occasion, but Bar Cochba told me what he was doing.) So Flavius was sent home to write his book. Unfortunately events in Judaea went too fast for him, and he did not write it until later. By that time the catastrophe had occurred, and the Romans sacked Jerusalem, scattering the Jewish people, and destroying their temple, which they lack to this day, being forced to alter their manner of worship to a domestic cult. Apart from rescuing some old friends of his among the Liberation Movement whom Romans had crucified, he was forced to write his history from behind the Roman lines. The Romans regarded him as a possible spy, the Liberation Movement as a traitor, so his plea for a more intelligent Roman policy towards Judaea got him no credit, as well as coming too late. But it is a most instructive book, from which I, myself, learned a great deal about a people I have always liked as companions – and which, moreover, provided some of the world's best physicians. I sometimes think that if

Caesar had been able to marry Poppaea forthwith, this undeserved calamity might have been avoided. Fate, the violence of the Liberation Movement, and the Furies of Agrippina, destroyed Judaea, however, though not in Caesar's lifetime, and all such physicians are today forced to live as exiles – to the benefit of the rest of the world, but small comfort to themselves. I advise you, Herondas, to treat them with respect for their learning and compassion for their position, since any of us may be called upon to suffer exile one day.

One very odd thing about the Jews – in spite of their extreme zeal against images, which will not allow them to ornament their houses with statues, they for centuries kept in their Temple the emblem of our patron, Asklepios – a bronze effigy of a snake. Apparently the God of the Jews ordered their great prophet Musius to make it as a remedy against snake-bite. This snake-figure was eventually removed and melted for fear it would become an object of idolatry, but it seems to bespeak some friendship between their God and our Patron. Moreover it is a characteristic of their prophets that they are also healers – Joshua ben Joseph, the prophet of the Messianists, was renowed through Judaea for healing, and his followers keep up this tradition.

But Caesar was still temporizing in the matter of his divorce. As often as he began to reopen the matter, some new blow fell. First it was the Pedanius affair. Then a monstrous comet – probably that which the Babylonians tell us revisits us every 76 years – appeared in the heavens, and for many nights stood silently there like a menace, stretching from one horizon to the other. Comets are a touchy matter with emperors, owing to the belief that they predict the death of kings; it is not difficult to imagine, given the number of kings and the rarity of comets, that such a belief feeds itself. Moreover a second comet, equally bright, appeared over Rome only three years later. It is my own belief that the comet of the Babylonians had in some way divided itself into two parts, but the Romans saw in this double visitation only a threat of Divine retribution for the death of the Best of Mothers, and made no sensible observations that I have been able to find on either occasion.

Then no sooner had the comet departed, than a far heavier blow fell on Caesar, for Burrus his Guard commander caught an inflammation of the lungs and died. By his death Caesar lost his chief shield, though his headpiece Seneca soldiered on, talking constantly of retirement.

Caesar intended to replace Burrus forthwith by Tigellinus, but the colonels of the Guards made it plain to Seneca that they would not take orders from a horsebreeder. Seneca employed diplomacy – it was proper, he said, that liaison should be formalized between the de facto National Security Adviser and the Armed Forces; but of course he agreed that the Guards must be commanded by a soldier, not a civilian. He suggested a joint command, to be shared by Tigellinus and Faenius Rufus, and sold the idea to Caesar by stressing that with Burrus the professional gone, he ran less risk of a military coup if the command were shared. Caesar took this to mean that his henchman would keep an eye on the military nominee: Seneca himself intended that Faenius Rufus would dilute the possible ambitions of Tigellinus. And, said Seneca, if Caesar is wise, he will do well to settle the Poppaea affair and get on with the business of assuring the succession.

But still Caesar could not make up his mind. Poppaea was preparing to confront him with a choice – but unfortunately, by his delay, he had allowed public opinion – influenced originally by intensive campaigns of propaganda conducted by Agrippina, but now running under its own momentum – to crystallize behind the misused and longsuffering Octavia. On several occasions, passages in plays concerning reprobate husbands and long-suffering wives were ostentatiously applauded.

If Caesar could not reach a decision, Seneca did: having done his best to limit the damage which Tigellinus could do, he announced his retirement. He was going back to philosophy ('going to the forest', his guru would have called it) with Paulina as his Maitreyi. And retire he did, to write and practise vegetarianism. As a final rebuke to those who regarded him as the millionaire saint, and possibly an imitation of Yajnavalkya, he returned the entire proceeds of his official career to the Exchequer, saying he had only held it ex-officio. One rather unfortunate and unintended consequence of this piece of austerity was that in closing his positions he called in all existing mortgages, thereby setting a match to a bloody uprising in Britain – but that was unintended.

With Seneca removed, and the wheel taken over by Caesar himself, means were rapidly found by Otho and Tigellinus to end the dickering over Octavia's divorce. Out of a clear sky she was charged with adultery. The adulterer turned out to be Anicetus.

Having met Octavia – albeit not after the death of the Best of Mothers, which Andromachus felt had changed her from a neurotic child to a very self-composed woman – I have never been able to make up my mind about this extraordinary accusation. One very clear possibility is that Anicetus, who had never been troubled by his conscience, fabricated the entire affair to order – in which case he was an even bigger scoundrel than I know him to have been. But Anicetus' villainies in the past had been of the murderous or buccaneering kind. Another version, which I heard from a good source, is quite different, and it cannot be entirely ruled out, much as it conforms to the pattern of popular fiction.

Octavia never knew that Anicetus was the man who killed her mother-in-law. She had in fact absolutely refused to permit any mention of the affair in her presence, and physically stopped her ears when it was mentioned. One day, the story goes, Anicetus saw on the shore at Baiae a beautiful, lonely young woman walking with her maid. Coming alongside, he made himself agreeable to her, took her and her chaperone sailing, and introduced her generally to a style of manhood with which she was totally unfamilar. Nor did he attempt to take advantage of her immediately. Lacking all male company, and a little flattered by the gentle attentions and seafaring stories of this athletic Greek naval officer, twice her age, and a more exciting father-figure than Claudius, Octavia became incautious and ended by falling madly in love with him. This is unlikely, but not incredible. Anicetus looked like a stage pirate, as well as being a real one. At any event, I was told, at a suitable occasion Anicetus came alongside her and boarded her.

The two main reasons for doubting this story are that Octavia swore that it was false, and Anicetus boasted defiantly that it was true. I am inclined to believe her, and to agree that she was the victim of a particularly unsavoury plot. Her denials did her no good, though public opinion was thoroughly on her side – in fact, the Anicetus story only surfaced when rumours of a divorce caused public disturbances, and it was necessary for Tigellinus to blacken Octavia's reputation for chastity beyond all redemption. He had a great deal of trouble getting independent confirmation – Octavia's servants were solidly loyal. Tigellinus is said to have taken great pains to examine them under torture and in person. He failed in most cases to get his way – her personal maid, after a severe beating, and other torments, spat in his face and said, 'Scum! My mistress' cunt is a deal cleaner than your mouth!' On the other hand, there were other slaves, not so close to Octavia, who had either seen Anicetus coming and going, or who thought it prudent to have done so faced with unpleasant interrogation. The divorce was granted, Octavia was banished to an island – Anicetus, who was never under more than house arrest, boarded his ship, made sail, and left Italy for good, with a dishonourable discharge which caused him to lose no sleep.

Octavia was not on the island a month before she was killed. Here again there is a conflict of evidence. Caesar denied that he ordered it, which is in keeping, I think, with his dislike of formal executions. Others think that Tigellinus insisted, with or without Caesar's agreement, on grounds of the succession and of national security, the killing being done by 'spooks' from his intelligence agency. Arbaces told me that it sounded like the work of some of Anicetus' piratical friends, which may amount to the same thing. How she died is also unclear – according to one report she died of heatstroke through being locked in an overheated sauna. According to another, she was dragged into a bath-house and forcibly exsanguinated. It is conceivable, though not likely, that she opened her own veins, or – rather more plausibly, from my previous findings – starved herself to death. One wishes, for the sake of a very unfortunate lady, that the truth might be known for whatever it might be; few would think ill of her now.

Caesar's reaction was typical – he had had enough of Octavia: she was a standing reminder of his mother. He said, 'She could have been content with being the official wife of a Caesar!' and went ahead to marry Poppaea twelve days after the decree became absolute. The ceremony was theatrical, inevitably, but nearly ended in anticlimax, for Otho suddenly realized what he might have seen before – that Caesar would not extend to him the same courtesies in regard to Poppaea which he, Otho, had extended to Caesar. Now it was one thing for Otho and Poppaea to swing with Caesar and his Illuminates – quite another to see her married to Caesar and obliged to be above reproach. When messengers came to escort the bride, Otho refused to give her up. Finally Nero himself arrived, and found the door of the marital bedroom locked against him. There were recriminations through the closed door, threats from Caesar, and finally Poppaea settled the matter by pushing Otho aside, unlocking the door, and taking Caesar's arm, while Otho pursued them out of the house with remarks about wife-stealing, broken bargains, and the like. His temper was not sweetened by a rash of graffiti asking 'Question: Who was the first man in Rome to be charged with adultery for laying his own wife?' Poppaea made up the quarrel, however, and Caesar awarded Otho the Province of Lusitania – which he governed rather lazily, but with considerable ability – and it was he who, when Caesar was deposed, avenged his old Illuminate friend on the usurper – an odd story indeed, and worthy of the laughter of the Gods.

Anicetus, so far as I know, retired quietly to Smyrna, where he enjoyed the proceeds of his villainies undisturbed. His boatswain and accomplice, Cetus, however, did not retire; and thereby hangs a tale, for having received a good sum of hush money over various matters, he employed it in fitting out a corsair, and resumed his old piratical ways. His standard trick was to heave to, light a quantity of trash on deck to make smoke, and hoist distress signals. When an incautious merchantman came alongside to assist, she was boarded and robbed.

Unfortunately for Cetus, the first of his victims was one of Acte's charters, and in the affray two hands on board were killed and several wounded. Arbaces, who was now Acte's commodore, said nothing, but he decided privately that Cetus was polluting the environment beyond all bearing; so he readied *Thunderbolt* for sea and bided his time.

Now as luck would have it, there was a vessel refitting in Cos which had unloaded its cargo on the dock while bilges were inspected, and among that cargo was a quantity of Roman siege material destined for Judaea. Arbaces took the master of the ship out drinking and crossed his palm: while the master and the watch looked the other way, Arbaces' men borrowed, rented, or in plain language stole, a medium-range Roman missile launcher and five rounds: ten-foot javelins, carrying a charge of sulphur, asphaltum and Greek fire, and intended for use against wooden siege works. Arbaces loaded the ballista into *Thunderbolt*, aimed astern, covered it with tarpaulins, and set sail for the rocky north coast of Cyprus, where Cetus was last seen cruising. Once there he scandalized *Thunderbolt*'s mainsail, and sent his hands aloft with rope and marlinspikes as if they were repairing the rigging. He limped up and down for a couple of days and nights, until Cetus sighted him and gave chase. Arbaces let the pirate come up close astern, waited until Cetus veered to windward in order to come alongside, and as soon as the target opened he let fly. The long and short of it was that the astonished Cetus got all five incendiary missiles full amidships: the corsair burned to the waterline, the pirates abandoned ship and swam ashore or drowned. Cetus himself swam to *Thunderbolt*. But he was ill received there – Arbaces put a noose around his neck, threw him back, and towed him behind *Thunderbolt* until dead. He then set course for Cos, and returned the ballista, though not the ammunition, to its rightful owners.

Acte was in two minds when she heard of this buccaneering exploit. She was furious that Arbaces had gone looking for trouble, and had deliberately taken *Thunderbolt* into combat. On the other hand, when word spread in the ports, pirates started to give Arbaces, and Acte's flag generally, a wide berth – so he was soon forgiven. Acte wisely forbade a plan Arbaces was hatching to mount a commando raid on Anicetus' house in Smyrna, capture Anicetus, and hang him from his own rooftree for abetting piracy, and she strictly banned all other desperate deeds and private wars in perpetuity. But I believe the swashbuckling side of Arbaces appealed to her – she had a secret liking for desperate characters.

I think you know, Herondas, that the next time I actually met Caesar was in Corinth, when he came to Greece, and the Project reached fruition – that was when Xenophon retired and quit Rome to endow a new range of buildings for the College. I got only occasional direct word in the interval: Caesar was married, Caesar had now a daughter – he was delighted, and put it down to my ministrations on Poppaea – then that the daughter had died, and been accorded semi-divine honours, then that Poppaea's young son by Otho died (he was drowned fishing) – that Caesar had been advised by Andromachus that wine wouldn't hurt his voice, and had gone back to drinking it (that struck me as an officious piece of scientism: if anyone was addiction-prone it was Caesar, and so far he'd been sober for years). Andromachus was an expert on poisonous animal bites and wrote a poem – in rather unprofessional taste, I thought – praising his own antidotes, but Claudians and adopted Claudians didn't come into his field of study, and I never knew why Nero chose him: possibly he wanted to pump him about

Octavia – the snakebite reputation might have appealed if he had had to deal with Agrippina, but Andromachus only took over when I left. Luckily Caesar, though from then on he drank a good deal, never became a fullblown alcoholic, at least compared with some of his set. I'd have kept him on iced water myself. Celsus had retired from medicine – to write an encyclopaedia. What he thought of Andromachus I don't know.

A year later, as everyone knows, Rome burned down, exactly as Caesar, and the fire department, knew it would. Caesar was on his way back from Antium: when he saw the blaze he sent Poppaea back and took over in person. He did it rather well. The fire started in the Circus Maximus, among the stalls, as usual, but there was a stiff wind – by the time Caesar arrived it had burned right up the Palatine, and his palace was in flames. Instead of trying to rescue his property, he whistled up the Guards and plunged into a raving madhouse, full of people trying to salvage property, looters, kibitzers, sightseers, smoke, flames, and riderless horses. When it was obvious the entire town would go up, he set the Guards and his own retinue pulling down houses and starting backfires, telling them not to spare slum property – 'It has to come down in any case,' he said.

In the end it was clear that the men on the ground didn't need Caesar, and he was in the way, so he coolly opened his private gardens to the refugees, decreed compensation as Claudius had done, put Tigellinus in charge of relief operations – and incredibly but quite characteristically went to a music lesson.

In fact, as his staff said, he handled it for once as Augustus would have done. But the Furies of Agrippina were there to see that even that went sour. Augustus had no Furies to contend with, or if he had he defeated them.

Next day word was everywhere that Caesar's men had been seen actually starting fires, which was true – but in the aftershock, it was an incredibly dangerous rumour, and Tigellinus told Caesar he had to squash it. It also transpired that at the height of the uproar a procession of the Jewish Messianists I mentioned had paraded through the fire area, announcing that the vengeance of God had fallen on Rome, that their prophet was about to return, and urging people to join them and escape judgment. This unfortunate behaviour was suicidal, as it turned out. It was nearly homicidal as well, because word then went out that Jews had started the fire. Gershom ben Eleazer realized that what had begun as an anti-Caesar riot was about to turn into a pogrom. He went at some risk to Antium and implored Poppaea to explain to Caesar the difference between Jews and Messianists, before all his people were lynched. Poppaea rushed back to Rome and did so. Caesar at once proclaimed that Messianists, not Jews, were to blame, then realized that he had no evidence anyone was to blame, except people who store trash and have naked lights, and that if anyone was to blame, he wasn't – this was a typical series of Neronian improvisations. All it did was to divert the entire pogrom against the Messianists, whose only fault was premature eschatology and lack of tact, but the Courts joined in (Caesar had declared them guilty!), and there was a long and miserable series of judicial murders – including several Messianists whom Tigellinus allowed to be slowly burned, wearing the tunica molesta or tarred shirt reserved for slaves, as a diversion on the very occasion when Caesar appeared in a chariot to regain popularity by announcing the rebuilding of Rome.

Seneca was utterly disgusted, in spite of his dislike of the Jews, and furious with Nero for failing to stop the pogrom. He wrote to the leader of the Messianists, Rabbi Saul:

> 'As you can imagine, I'm deeply concerned and grieved to see innocent people treated like this, and still more that public opinion regards your sect as criminals and blames them for the disaster. There have been tyrants throughout history, and Caesar is behaving like one of them – the cause of these repeated fires is quite obvious.'

The Messianists later published this letter, and expanded Seneca's last two sentences into a specific charge that Caesar himself set the fire: the original was quite indiscreet enough, in my view. It shows which way Seneca's mind was moving. He may really have wondered whether Caesar had got tired of waiting for the inevitable accident and decided to assist the Gods – but I question if he would have been rash enough to put that in writing.

I won't dilate on Caesar's public theatricals – they were long since out of hand. Loyal audiences weren't permitted to leave while he was speaking, Senators wet their undergarments, babies were born in the stands. His famous organized clapping, which started as a rather original musical display, had long since been turned by his toadies into a claque, and Caesar loved having it. The more he performed, the angrier his Senatorial opponents got. Ever since Pedanius he had pointedly snubbed them, and he was said to have remarked that once rid of Senators he would have Rome ruled by the merchants – they weren't bloodthirsty snobs. The extremists among the Establishment party, fortunately for Caesar, struck far too soon with far too little support. The plot was idiotic. It failed to kill Caesar. Unfortunately it killed several other people, including Seneca, the poet Lucan, his nephew – and my old friend Petronius. Why Seneca allowed himself to be implicated, nobody is sure. Probably, being out of Rome, he brooded on Agrippina, on Octavia, on Caesar's neglect of administration, on the duty of the philosopher to resist tyrants – he also hated Tigellinus, and was afraid he would prove another Sejanus – the worst chief of police Rome ever had, who ran a reign of terror under Tiberius. In fact he gave Tigellinus the pretext to do as Sejanus had done.

The last straw was the rebuilding of Rome. Seneca and Caesar had planned this together. But when at last the chance came, Seneca found that Nero had added a touch of his own. He was going to build a palace which would outshine any other building in the civilized or ancient world. Seneca exploded. The man was not only a potential or an actual tyrant – he was a fool. I saw Nero's 'Golden House' and it was stunning – crisp, lively, and a splendid boost for Roman arts, sciences and manufacture; the least vulgar building, I think, that Romans ever devised, because it was witty. But Seneca did not wait to see the result – the prospectus was enough for him: he had a duty to take the helm.

The front man for the conspiracy was an odd, rich character called Gaius Calpurnius Piso, whose chief accomplishment was playing Roman chess. He was also, rather ominously, a good lyre-player. But quite obviously the man who would take over Rome, and possibly the empire, was to be Seneca. The man who recruited him was the soldier whose command he, himself, had arranged, to keep Tigellinus in check – Faenius Rufus. Of course the plot was discovered. Most of the people involved had as a motive fear of Tigellinus' intelligence agency, which constantly harassed and spied on patricians and commoners, but they underrated its efficiency. Nero was still against public executions, except for military traitors. The others, including

Seneca, were given the opportunity of an assisted suicide – or else. Seneca's death-scene was, as one would imagine, worthy of the Stoic (Nero sent to save the life of Paulina, who tried to go with him). Lucan the poet went the same way – probably caught in the crossfire: I never knew him. Petronius – who now had the title of The Critic, and was Nero's Master of Elegances – must have had his own motives. As with Seneca, suicide was an end he seemed to have planned. Guilty or not, he opened his veins, after smashing any of his personal possessions he thought Caesar might fancy, and writing a letter to Caesar setting forth a vivid account of the Imperial sexual peculiarities, and Petronius' true opinion of Caesar's artistic talents. This letter did not – naturally – survive, but it hit Caesar in a tender spot. He had thought that in Petronius, for once, he'd found an intelligent brother, and now Petronius had betrayed him twice. Caesar threw the most violent tantrum of his life, and had the house of Petronius razed to the ground.

For a while there was pandemonium. Tigellinus – who had compiled an enormous file of dossiers on 'enemies' – took the chance to level old scores. Finally Caesar, getting alarmed by the suicide rate which was being created in his name, appointed a soldier called Nymphidius as conjoint Guards commander, and Nymphidius stopped the massacre. Now our Emperor Trajan's secretary – who was born in the year Nero died – has written a history of this unpleasant period. In it he said that if suicides were slow in signing a consent to operation, Caesar, or Tigellinus, sent physicians to 'take care of them'. I think this gratuitous slander deserves refutation. The people sent in such cases were phlebotomists – mostly slaves. I know of no physician – certainly not from our College – who had any hand in the matter. Gaius Suetonius Tranquillus, whose history is mostly composed of tattle, though he writes well, should have consulted some of us who had knowledge of the period, and I have written him several times demanding correction. It is not necessary to exaggerate in order to underline the differences between then and now. I hope his work for our Emperor is less slipshod than his research.

The last blow was the worst. Poppaea died. She and Nero had a quarrel, in which she called him Lucius Ahenobarbus – he flew into the inevitable tantrum at this, and he pushed her or kicked her (I have heard him talk about it, but never questioned him). He then apologized. She seemed unhurt, went to her room – and was found dead from a ruptured ectopic pregnancy. Nero was heartbroken and guilt-stricken. Now to the Furies of Agrippina and of Octavia there were added the Furies of Poppaea. I heard the facts, though not the details, and wrote him a letter of condolence. He certainly received it, but he didn't answer it.

But the Furies quite inexplicably let him go, for four years, and Lucius Domitius, actor-manager, gave two of his most remarkable performances in the role of Caesar – and two of the most lavish productions. I missed the first of these, but I was lucky enough to get tickets for the second.

Caesar seems suddenly to have realized that you can't force-feed people culture. Given genuine swine, he was wasting his time casting artificial pearls. My patient, who wasn't a fool when he was free of his inner fauna of ghosts for a while, started to think operationally (if Seneca had been around, I would see his hand in this: as it is, I think our archiatros may have got Caesar pointed in the right direction). He'd failed miserably to freeze out sword-fighting shows by providing alternatives. All that happened was that the people grumbled, and the Establishment despised him. All right: they should have swordfighting: but with a difference. Romans also love military pageants – particularly triumphs. Nero hated war – partly through indolence, chiefly because to him both it, and the military establishment, were bloody ridiculous. However, to hold a triumph, you had to win a victory. In that case, the solution was to arrange a diplomatic victory, and celebrate it on an unheard-of scale – and producing spectacles with himself as actor-manager was Caesar's leading passion. That was to be Part I. The public ought to love it. If they did, he would go on to Part II – an even bigger triumph, but incorporating some civilized activities; having paid his dues as a Roman by playing Mars and Augustus, Caesar hoped to get a hearing in the role of Apollo. He meant to get himself proclaimed an Olympic victor, no less. One could hardly get more Greek than that.

As usual, once he had an idea – or a whim – in his sights, he pressed ahead with it. The new Domus Aurea was one of these projects, and that went ahead at top priority, with the best available designers and decorators, and with no expenses spared. But Caesar wanted it now not only as 'somewhere civilized to live, at last' after the rather draughty and very Roman palace which had burned, but also as a set for use in

Part I. All that was lacking was a victory to provide the plot. Bar Cochba and Gershom and Flavius Josephus were seeing their worst fears realized in Judaea – the country, incited by the Zealot Liberation Organization, had finally exploded against Rome and Romanization: Josephus, who had been afraid of this all along, and who knew how fanatical the Nationalists were, left them and went over to Nero's General Vespasian, in the hope of preventing a general Roman war against the entire population. Ultimately the Zealots would die bravely at Masada, and Vespasian's adjutant there, Titus, would sack Jerusalem, with Josephus looking miserably on from the Roman lines. But it hadn't happened yet – there was nothing much to celebrate, except a bitter Middle Eastern campaign against armed civilians. Nero could have resurrected Paulinus' defeat of the British uprising – but that was five years old now, it would have excited mirth, there had been one triumph on the subject already, and Caesar wanted something different – certainly not a parade of ruffianly tribesmen in chains. There was only one prominent feature of the nearby military landscape, and that was hardly a candidate for a parade: Tiridates and Vologses had outwitted a Roman commander, Paetus, made him look ridiculous, and provided the spectacle of a senior Roman officer abandoning his men under fire and running for his own skin. I think Nero had some sneaking sympathy – when Paetus got back to Rome, he was court-martialled and let off lightly. The Emperor found him guilty of desertion, cashiered him and – pardoned him. Paetus didn't even have to sweat while Nero deliberated. 'I'm giving my decision now,' Caesar said. 'It would be barbarous to keep a man whose nerves are weak in any suspense.' But in fact he had other reasons – Paetus had been sent to please the 'bring the Parthians to heel' party. Corbulo, Caesar's man, was still working for a settlement, fighting successfully when he had to, and keeping in touch with Rome. But the defeat of Paetus was still not a very promising subject on which to stand a triumph – so Nero, who was nothing if not original, decided he'd do the unexpected. Defeating Paetus had saved Tiridates' face, but he still faced constant Roman operations in Armenia; these were beggaring trade and agriculture, and he wanted to enjoy the throne in peace. Neither side could win outright. So Caesar sent Xenophon the Archiatros to negotiate. Although Xenophon was retired from practice, Caesar and Vologses arranged for him to be 'called in consultation' by a Parthian millionaire. The meeting was held in Ctesiphon, Volosges' capital; Tiridates came from Armenia to attend. And Xenophon secured agreement.

Caesar immediately prepared in person to direct the spectacle. He also sent me a ticket for the opening of Part I, but I didn't go. The ticket came in the form of a Royal Parthian Embassy request, on behalf of H.M. the Sovereign of Armenia, for my services on a journey by H.M. King Tiridates, 'this physician being known personally to His Majesty and to Caesar as being skilful, discreet, and worthy to attend princes,' etc. etc., and there was Xenophon's seal at the bottom of the tablet. This was sent to the College.

With it came also a personal letter to me from a 'merchant called Toxonices,' ostensibly about the supply of poppy resin (Acte by now had buyers in both Parthia and Armenia, and quite a few of them wrote to me).

In fact, Mr. Crackshot, whoever he was, wrote a far less commercial letter in excellent Greek.

> 'I am sure you haven't forgotten our brief meeting in Rome, and I certainly have not forgotten you. I have to go back there, to conclude the business with our old friend Lupus which was so unfortunately interrupted – Lupus will send physicians, and I will take my own, but I would be overjoyed, since you know all of the parties, if you will join us. Lupus promises good eating, good shooting, and a theatrical entertainment – a charade, if you like which we are now writing jointly. We will play it, for we both need applause. I am not given to play-acting – that is Lupus' hobby – but it is a small price for peace and quiet. If you are tired of being his physician, consider becoming mine, in another country.'

I sent my grateful thanks to 'Mr. Crackshot', told him that with a young son to raise I could not come, but I greeted him and congratulated him on his success in business (quite considerable – he was now officially a King), and wished his venture well. Diodorus sent my resident. The performance was terrific, and Caesar paid the entire bill for the production, running into millions. Tiridates, being a Magian priest, was not allowed for religious reasons to go by sea – so he and Caesar staged a nine-month Royal progress for him, from Armenia to Rome by way of Dalmatia. No Middle Eastern king had ever had this kind of exposure. If Tiridates wanted his legitimacy, and the authority of himself and his brother King Volosges confirmed, he got it right royally. All the way to Italy Tiridates had a maxi-triumph over Rome, with a large contingent of Roman troops riding behind the Parthian escort.

Once they arrived in Italy, the roles were switched by agreement. Tiridates rode in a carriage sent by Caesar – his wife, who kept strict purdah, exchanged her chador for a golden mask (Caesar said that she had to be visible; the mask was a brilliant theatrical compromise), and the monarchs met at Neapolis. Caesar was now to have *his* triumph, with Tiridates as the new vassal of Rome – the magnificent progress through the Balkans had been a trade-off. Tiridates would publicly acknowledge the endorsement of his crown by Caesar – as he had got it already, this was a formality, but it could be taken to mean that Caesar was crowning Tiridates. Moreover the two protagonists went about together – there were swordfights galore, on an unprecedented scale, with huge prizes. These were virtually non-lethal, however, apart from a few accidents – not only did the best professionals fight (for points, not a kill), but there were bouts between amateurs – Roman citizens who fancied themselves as gladiators, provided it wasn't too dangerous – a brilliant idea of Nero's to cut down on casualties. There were even martial-arts bouts between schoolboys, and a class for women to demonstrate swordspersonship (as there were, unfortunately, no Roman entrants, Tiridates laid on the Amazon body-guards of a Dahomeyan chief). Finally there was a *venatio*, or staged hunt in the arena. On this occasion Tiridates didn't smuggle his bow in – he stood up in the Royal box and gave the Romans a display of royal musketry which had the Guards – and his old Middle East Force enemies who had fought him in Parthia – chairing him round the arena. To show the lethal powers of the compound bow, Tiridates shot down one bull with an arrow which had gone clean through another, and out the other side.

It's astounding what can be achieved by public relations. Tiridates, who had been in arms against Rome, and humiliated its army, became a public celebrity, especially with the troops. Caesar, who had been quite unable to defeat him, had a triumph at his expense. So there were prizes all round. The quid pro quo for what Tiridates gained was formal submission. After a stupendous Guards parade, he had to march alone to the foot of the saluting base, mount the steps, and make formal obeisance to Caesar – who immediately took his hand, embraced him warmly, and replaced his turban with a crown. Tiridates addressed the crowd in Greek, with a Latin translation. He and Volosges would both send their sons to be educated in Rome – and, incidentally, as hostages, and a guarantee that the impulsive Volosges would observe the truce this time, in Tiridates' absence. The worst part of this for Tiridates was not the fact of the ceremonial kowtow, nor even having to sit through a pompous speech by Nero reminding him that he held his throne by courtesy of Rome – that was for the birds, and it was in the agreed script. It was probably the obligation to appreciate hours of Imperial lyre-playing, and suffering the indignity of crewing Caesar in a chariot-race (Tiridates banned all mention of this unroyal activity in Armenia). Finally Caesar, with Tiridates in tow, closed the doors of the Temple of Janus to indicate that Rome was at peace – one of the few occasions on which they were closed. The savage guerrilla warfare in Judaea was redesignated a 'police operation' for the purpose. Caesar was hailed as Imperator and Peacemaker on the same day; Tiridates decreed that the New Town at Artaxata, his capital, would be named Nero City, and borrowed Roman money and Greek architects from Caesar, interest-free, to erect it. On the return progress, he showed the Parthian and Armenian flags in a new series of cities, signing trade pacts all the way, and went home well satisfied. The only person who was furious was Corbulo – not at the settlement, which he had long advocated, but at the theatricals, and the fact that the astute Tiridates had got away with diplomatic murder at Rome's expense. So the Furies chuckled quietly, and Caesar lost another military friend he might one day have needed. My resident came back with a pocketful of Roman and Parthian money, a shipload of gifts, an eyewitness blow-by-blow account, and the recollection of having had a royal whale of a time.

No sooner had Tiridates left, than Caesar (who was delighted by the audience reponse to Part I) put Part II, *Son of the Triumph of Caesar* into production, switching directors – this time it was to be directed by our archiatros, since he had contacts in Greece – Caesar was to play the sole lead. Xenophon's patient work on the Project was to be rewarded at last. Caesar was to go to Greece.

The scale of Part II was to be unprecedented. For the first

time in Roman history, a Caesar would be out of Italy for a full year on a non-military expedition. Caesars had been out of Rome before – Tiberius rarely went there, and spent time, though never as much as a year on end, in Rhodes. There were obvious dangers – an empty seat attracts sitters. Tiberius dealt with this by leaving Sejanus in charge, with disastrous results. Caesar, who had got the measure of Tigellinus by now, and who was becoming scared of him after hearing about the office full of dossiers, was taking no risks, and made Tigellinus come with him, leaving Nymphidius in charge. He reckoned that Tigellinus could be kept fully occupied racing, drinking and whoring, and that he would be unable, once out of Rome, to keep hold of his intelligence agency, where the real danger lay. This, indeed, happened – and the Intelligence Agency went to pieces, at precisely the moment in his reign when Caesar was about to need undercover informants.

He also needed a consort for the progress. He was still missing Poppaea, grieving for her, and blaming his own violent temper for her death. For years now he had had a successor to Pythagoras, a handsome youth called Sporus, who had been Doryphorus' bed-boy. Doryphorus himself got rid of the sexual attentions of Caesar by training Sporus and introducing him to the unwanted lover: Sporus moreover was a pathic by personal inclination, and after Poppaea's death he was Caesar's habitual bedfellow. I thought him a very likeable young man – I have no grudge against pathics. It seems to me that their sexual preference requires no more medical explanation than the preference of certain persons for cooked brains, or blood pudding – which I dislike myself – or for red pepper, which I like, and other men find inedible. It is the attitude of others, who think them unmanly, which makes many of them difficult patients or colleagues. Perhaps, too, the elements are distempered in them, as they are in all of us, but here the result happens to be socially conspicuous. Knowing as we do, in Greece, that all of us are both male and female, and having most of us had commerce in youth with boys as well as girls, we are not specially hostile to people like Sporus: the Romans, who are no different in their tastes from other humans at heart, manage to be guilty about them and therefore indignant.

Caesar started by suggesting that Sporus should go to Greece as his consort – to show just how Philhellenic he was. The Roman committee put its foot down. If Caesar were to be accompanied by a male concubine the show would go on without them. They could not stop Sporus going as cupbearer, or something of the kind – even Zeus has Ganymedes – but Caesar had to be accompanied by a tangibly female spouse. 'Humbug,' said Caesar. 'You all have male concubines – why not Caesar?'

The committee pointed out that they also had wives, and Zeus himself had Hera – and that Caesar, having failed to keep either of his wives alive, would have to find another, real or nominal, in short order. Caesar started one of his tantrums, but Tigellinus saved the situation by pointing out that Sporus, for all his qualities, was unlikely to provide Caesar with an heir: did Caesar want to parade the fact that the succession was insecure?

In consequence Caesar took the matter under advisement, and within days he was rather quietly married – to a lady called Statilia Messalina, an experienced wife who had outlived several husbands (the last of these was a casualty of the purges which followed Piso's conspiracy, but she clearly bore Caesar no grudges). I, myself, could never make Statilia out – she was attractive in a quiet way, affectionate to Caesar, totally obedient to him, and in public at least she gave the impression of a mechanical Roman-ideal wife created by a magician for the part. What she was like in private I naturally don't know – except that Caesar slept regularly with her, which he would not have done if it had proved unrewarding. The odd part of this was that Sporus slept on Caesar's other side: on public occasions Statilia would hold one of Caesar's hands and Sporus the other – quite spontaneously, it seemed, for the same behaviour continued in private. I was never asked to see her professionally. Whatever the arrangement which kept Hera on good terms with Ganymedes as well as with Zeus, I was never in a position to probe it. As for the committee, Caesar had the last word. When they came to offer marital congratulations Caesar said, 'Well, I've taken your advice, so honour is satisfied. And since you think it undignified for Sporus to go as my bed-boy, I bow to the demands of public morality. After all, we have to set a good example. My wife and I have decided what must be done. I intend to celebrate my marriage with Sporus, too. It will take place shortly, and you are all of you invited!'

'What a damn shame,' said one infuriated committeeman afterwards, 'that Nero's father didn't marry somebody like Sporus!'

Sporus himself got a Mistress of the Wardrobe – a rather

disreputable lady who had some relationship with Tigellinus – and an expensive repertoire of clothes. Statilia got jewels and dresses which were the envy of Senatorial wives and the fury of their husbands, whom Nero continued to snub.

The Progress was launched in September. Caesar was to appear at every Greek festival, from Corcyra and Actium to Corinth, where he intended to hold court. Xenophon went ahead and talked to the Greek authorities. They, in the interests of the Project, were highly cooperative. The four great Games (Olympic, Pythian, Isthmian and Nemean) were rescheduled and held in a single year. This meant arranging an extraordinary Olympiad out of time, but even that was hastily organized. All these Games were normally athletic, but all of them added singing contests and other theatrical events to the programme. Our folk entered fully into the spirit of the production – after all, we have been the masters of the theatrical event for centuries: Caesar was a relative newcomer. Since this was theatre, Caesar had to compete – and win. That was what it said in the script. Compared with Tiridates' act of homage, it was a small price to pay, the Games would be a marvellous show, the gain to local commerce would be colossal, since all the contracts would be placed locally for stands, lodging, wine, musicians, jewels, transport, shipping, prostitutes, script-writers, sutlers and medical support. The lead player was donating his services. It would be the largest and most profitable trade fair in history, and the payoff would be the independence of Greece. Xenophon had found a way of securing, through the commercial revival of Greek history and art, what Tiridates had had to fight for. It was a stratagem worthy of Odysseus, and of our archiatros. Tiridates fought and won, the courageous and devout Jews fought and lost everything, and we merry Greeks took Imperial Rome to the cleaners, without firing a shot.

In fact there was only one sour note, to indicate that the Furies had not finished with Caesar. Corbulo, who had made no secret of his disgust over the visit of Tiridates, was secretly contacted by the Establishment and sounded to enquire whether, if the office of Caesar should through some unfortunate accident become vacant, he would be interested in the post. A meeting was arranged between the plotters in Rome and the disaffected group of officers in the old Parthian Theatre Military Force. The Intelligence Agency had a mole on

Corbulo's staff, and Corbulo received an Imperial message telling him to remove himself from this world, or face court-martial in it, an inglorious end to one of Rome's best officers. Possibly he was framed, like many others. But he did not complain. On receiving the order, all he said was, 'I won it fairly' – the phrase used by an Olympic winner when he receives the prize. Whether he meant 'I deserve my fate,' or 'Caesar should give me a medal, not a death sentence,' or whether he was mocking Caesar's stagemanaged Olympic victories we shall never know, but he locked himself up in his quarters with a glass of wine and his sword, and took his own life. If Caesar had had no Furies to misadvise him, he would have given Petronius' old post to Tigellinus and let him organize recreational activity, while Corbulo took over the Guards. The disgust and loss of loyalty of so professional and devoted a soldier was an unrecognized portent – it was lost on Caesar, in the ballyhoo attending his Greek visit. It was not lost on the Army, however. They were professionals, and they had no use for a performer from a different profession as Commander in Chief.

Our archiatros did not attend the show he had directed so skilfully. He came back to Cos and sent for me.

'Well, Callimachus,' he said, 'we have brought it off. At the end of this progress, Caesar will return to Corinth and declare the Province of Greece a free state, within the Roman Empire. I think you see why your visit to Rome was important. I wanted to thank you in person.'

'How about that problem you wanted me to investigate?' I said.

'It solved itself,' said Xenophon. 'Caesar will not go to Eleusis. In fact he won't enter Attica at all. He excluded himself when Agrippina died, and he knows it. Do you want to see the show? Caesar personally asked me to see if you would travel with him.'

'I have a small son, Archiatros,' I said, 'and a practice, and students; and I don't like crowds.'

'It would be valuable exposure for the College,' he said, 'if we provide the Imperial physician.'

'I doubt it, Archiatros: this is going to be the biggest hype in history. Wouldn't we be better standing back a little? Couldn't Caesar visit Cos on his progress and pay his respects to our Patron?'

'I did suggest that,' said Xenophon, 'but he won't have time. The schedule is far too tight. Caesar wants to appear at all the local Games as well as the big four. You need not tour Greece if you don't wish, Callimachus, but you'll have to go to Rome with him. I am retiring. We have to have somebody there. As to your family, you had responsibilities when you last travelled for the College, and I think you'll agree we met them adequately. Caesar will send for you.'

'How long for?' I asked,

'Until we are sure the Project isn't upset by his enemies,' said Xenophon. 'I'd say, about a year.'

'You know, Archiatros, that Caesar is accident prone. I don't want to be marooned in Rome again,' I said.

'You have my personal assurance that if things go wrong we'll replace you – or take you out,' said Xenophon. 'Now go and make arrangements. When Caesar sends, you won't have much lead time.'

No Acte to prepare for my going, this time – only my gentle, rather distant, but very nice housekeeper Selene. She'd be sorry, but she would find another job. You and Telesphoriades, Herondas, were too busy learning to handle a boat to miss me. Arbaces had tied two bladders to each of you, and taken you out fishing. Caesar was going from festival to festival, winning all the prizes, of course, and rather sensibly accepting them on behalf of Rome (which meant that the athletic committees need not have problems over the record books). At Olympia he won the four-in-hand chariot race on his own merits, tried in the ten-in-hand and took a bad spill; he was luckily only bruised, caught his team like a professional, tried to remount, and the racing connoisseurs were delighted by his gameness. He got the prize for 'most sporting performance' and the judges got ten million sesterces to support future games. A few weeks and eighteen hundred prize awards later, Caesar wrote to me, and I packed. It was precisely the letter I expected:

> 'Lucius A. greets the physician Callimachus. It is time we lunched together again. The programme required of me by Caesar, which has left me hoarse from singing, and covered with bruises from doing my own stunts, places me in need of a doctor – and still more in need of my old friend – who never applauds if I am not up to professional standard. This time I was good, and I'm sorry you missed the start of the show. You shall see the finale. Meet me in three weeks, on November 20th, for lunch at the sign of the Dioscuri, and we'll talk. Be well.
>
> Lucius Domitius'

I don't like Corinth much – it's the sailor's ideal liberty city, and with Caesar in residence it was even wilder than usual, and packed with tourists, hustlers, hucksters, people from the Imperial entourage, pickpockets, and pirates who'd gone back into the Merchant Service because of the boom in trade. I, of course, had been provided for, in one of the merchants' houses vacated to house the Imperial tour. This was a very different rendezvous from our first private meeting at the Wolf's Head. It was daylight, there were two Guardsmen on duty at the door of the inn, the food was Greek, not Roman. Caesar, however, was once more the only customer. He embraced me.

'Callimachus,' he said, 'Lucius Domitius welcomes you. He's had nobody to talk to for a very long time. That mask is heavy and those buskins are damned uncomfortable. Now, tell me about yourself. How's the boy?'

'Well, Caesar. One of Acte's captains is teaching him the sea. He's a Greek as well as a doctor's son.'

Caesar was fatter, less boyish – still strong, however, but looking weary.

'Are you married, Callimachus?'

'No, Caesar.'

'You mean, "No, Lucius." Caesar, damn him, is asleep – or dead drunk. Anyhow he's not here. I'm married, you know. You shall meet my wife.'

'Can we talk about Caesar, Lucius?'

'Oh, yes, we can talk about him,' said Caesar. 'Don't you take Greek wine, even? Waiter, bring hydromel for the doctor.'

'I think you told me, Lucius, that you and Caesar were agreeing to go into partnership,' I said. 'How has that turned out?'

'Very well, Callimachus. Lucius Domitius realized that the world wasn't big enough for both of them. So as soon as he was alone with Caesar – the week after my mother died, in fact, – Lucius stabbed Caesar and hid the body. Since then, Lucius has been impersonating him. Nobody has noticed, Lucius is enjoying himself, and his performance as Caesar is proving far better for Rome than if that idiotic young snob were still alive and taking his own decisions. Do you approve?'

'Lucius is sure the body won't revive? Or come to light?' I said.'

'Quite sure,' said Nero, 'it rotted instantly. I used to think "How can I satisfy Rome? The only skill I have is as an artist." As soon as I realized that an artist can play any part, if he's talented, I saw how to manage things. It's been hard going. The Senate and the Families are still trying to kill me, but I played the tyrant, and I don't think they'll try again.'

'How about your troops?' I asked.

'Rather naturally prefer parades and bonuses to killing tribesmen and getting killed by them,' said Nero. 'I suppose if I have to I'll give a performance as a general. You heard about my Triumph? That was something. There's going to be another when I get home, and you shall ride in it. How do I seem to you?'

'Tired,' I said, 'but better together as one man than you were as two. The problem will be what you do with yourself after the show. Actors have to go home.'

'I have things I want to do,' said Caesar. 'I have my music – in fact, if the Families ever throw me out I still have a profession to turn to – I have Statilia, I have Sporus: you must meet Sporus, you'll like him ...'

I wondered, Herondas, if this was a cure or a slow suicide. Lucius had killed Caesar, Nero told me. I would have been rather happier if Caesar had banished Lucius – but my opinion wasn't asked. Sporus came in, kissed Caesar, and was introduced to me – a pretty young man, beardless, about the age I'd been when I first met Nero, but with a sensible head on him and a non-Roman sense of humour.

A week later I was fetched in state, and took my place in the royal box, in the amphitheatre, with Caesar, Statilia, Sporus, Tigellinus, and a bunch of local notables. Tigellinus looked me over and said, 'You back, Doctor?' No executions this time, no sharpshooting, no singing by Nero. He rose to make his speech.

'Gentlemen of Greece,' said Caesar, 'I have the pleasure of announcing an unlooked-for benefaction (*cheers*). I think I have a reputation for munificence (*loud cheers*) as befits a Caesar, but even so, I think this time I am going to surprise you. What I have in mind is something which you have never asked for, and would not, I think have considered asking for. My only regret is that I was not here when Greece was at its zenith, so that more Greeks could have been Ceasar's beneficiaries, but better late than never. This is a gesture of goodwill, not a rescue operation. I thank your Gods, who have looked after me constantly by land and sea, that I now have the opportunity to make this announcement. Plenty of Caesars have awarded independence and tax exemption to cities. It is my great pleasure to be the first Caesar to award independence and tax exemption to an entire Province – that of Greece.'

The audience, who had a pretty good idea of what was coming, rose to its feet and yelled, as only we can yell. It took the entire Imperial Guard to stop them grabbing all of us and carrying us round the amphitheatre shoulder high – and a full hour to get the speech re-started. Caesar kept shouting, 'Gentlemen, let me finish! There is more to come!' and eventually he got a hearing.

'Thank you,' he said. 'Now to some commercial matters!' And he got his laugh.

'You Greeks,' said Caesar, 'are the world's best sailors (*loud cheers*) but you're insufficiently enterprising (*no, no*!) Oh yes, you are. Every time you want to sail from Corcyra to Piraeus, you go the whole way round the Peloponnese,' (and he made a pot-stirring motion) 'and all the way round Cape Matapan, where you are horribly seasick,' (he mimed that – *loud laughter*) 'and all the way up the East Coast (*laughter*) and where do you dock? Back here in Corinth, where you started from!' (*loud laughter and cheers*).

'Somebody has to call a halt to this circumnavigation. It's not only wasteful, it's exhausting! (*laughter*). It would be much quicker to walk, or ride a mule (*laughter*). So Caesar looked at the map – he's quite an original, is Caesar (*laughter*) and he remembered what his Greek tutor had taught him – "if you can't use the front door, you use the back!" (*laughter and cheers* – this is, of course, a proverbial dirty joke in Corinth). My predecessors have talked about cutting a canal here through the Isthmus. I differ from my predecessors, Greeks – I do not intend to talk about it. Six thousand Jewish rebels sentenced to hard labour after the recent disorders have been dispatched to Greece at my request by General Vespasian. Work on the Corinth Canal will commence next week. Now with regard to the expansion of trade between Greece and Italy ...'

But the lecture on trade was lost in total uproar, and this time the Guard let the demonstration continue until we were all deafened and made our escape. The following week the Jews arrived, the Roman and Greek engineers were presented, and Caesar turned the first sod with a golden shovel.

Now as you know the canal is unfinished to this day – the Furies of Agrippina, and possibly Poseidon himself, sent rock slides, accidents, delays and bad omens – then Rome, fighting in its own house, ran out of funds for the project. One might hope that our own Emperor will complete it – it was one of Nero's better ideas. The only tangible result of the visit to Corinth was the liberty of Greece, now lost again through our own inner divisions, a hole in the ground, and a crop of magnificent coins from every city which possesses a mint – plus the legend of Nero as another Prometheus, Apollo, and Dionysus rolled into one. Greeks still drink to him, exactly as Jews still curse the number which stands for his name in Hebrew (dozens of them died digging that hole).

I was concerned with the performance I'd seen – it was certainly effective. All the way back to Italy, Caesar bragged about it and we – Statilia, Sporus and I – listened to him.

'You have to hand it to him,' said Tigellinus, 'he didn't breathe a word about the canal – even my people never got wind of it. That I don't like – it shows they're slipping. Caesar must have told somebody. We know he told General Vespasian. I'll look into it when the circus is over.'

'You mean, it isn't over yet?'

'By no means,' said Tigellinus. 'That was simply Act One. You wait until we land in Italy.'

The same day we ran into foul weather, had some dangerous moments, and put back to Corinth. I was wishing to Poseidon that Arbaces, not some Roman bargee, was in command – I'd seen the weather building a full hour before our master saw it and took in sail. Then we started again. Tigellinus meanwhile got a courier, who had missed us in Corinth, and came aboard looking more worried than ever.

'Trouble,' he said. 'The Families are at it again. My people smell conspiracy. Caesar's been away too long and so have I.'

He tried to get Caesar to return immediately to Rome and postpone the pageant, but Caesar, who had grown his hair to his shoulders in order to look like an Olympian god, or a popular singer, told him to stop fussing. He rode into Neapolis, driving a silver-plated chariot, had a part of the old wall demolished to enter the city, as an Olympic victor should, and the parades began. I have never seen anything like it. It was indeed the greatest show on earth. After four towns, Statilia, Sporus and I were dizzy and deafened by flag-waving crowds bellowing, 'Hail, Olympic victor,' and waving olive wreaths, streamers and flags. They'd put a special jury gate in the walls of Rome itself. From there the oddest triumph in Roman history moved through even bigger and noisier crowds – not to the Capitol, which was the usual route, but to the Temple of Apollo on the Palatine. When we realized where Caesar was going Sporus shouted in my ear, 'Zeus will never forgive this!'

One can't see a procession from a car in that procession, so I am a poor witness. I was deafened, choked with saffron powder, and exhausted with military music. Instead of eagles and trophies, Phaon and Epaphroditus had had workmen decorating the whole town with athletic wreaths, wooden lyres, and similar cultural material. I was too whacked to appreciate even the part of the Golden House which had been finished. It had excellent doctor's quarters, a surgery, sickroom and dispensary (my old office had gone up in the fire), which I didn't see until later. Caesar appeared interminably on the balcony with Statilia and Sporus, until Statilia fainted and Sporus took her off to bed. Finally, when it had been dark for what seemed hours, the Guards got the crowd out of the street and out of the Palace entrance, Caesar came in from the balcony, olive crown, purple cloak with stars, the lot, and found his physician waiting to be dismissed.

'Hercules,' he said, 'I'm tired. How was I, Callimachus?'

'It was quite a performance, Caesar,' I said.

'My best. I'm as hoarse as a crow. But they liked it. Goodnight. I'll have some wine and go to bed. Boy, help me get my makeup off – you get some sleep, Doctor.'

That was really the final performance of Lucius Domitius in the part of Caesar. If he had dropped dead in the night, or one of the officers suborned by the Families had stabbed him, he'd have gone down in history as Rome's greatest actor – though if the second had happened, the assassin might also have decided to stab your former Professor, for luck. I went to bed and slept for fifteen hours.

Next day, Rome was back to normal, or almost normal. Caesar wasn't. I thought he was exhausted by a year of constant performing, and was not much bothered. He decorated his bedroom with the various prizes he'd won (they'd been given to Apollo, but he had them recovered so that he could look at them). He accepted a few invitations to perform privately or in public. Tigellinus was so furious at a rich Lydian who offered a million sesterces to have Caesar appear at one of his parties that he had the fellow waylaid and murdered, but I don't think he told Caesar about that – the invitation might have been accepted. Sporus and I played Greek chess, I checked my new office, wrote to Diodorus and Xenophon, and ordered supplies from Acte's factor. Phaon was accumulating papers for Caesar to sign, but Caesar didn't come out of his dressing-room and Epaphroditus had to borrow his seal to deal with them.

It was a week before I realized that something was wrong. What had happened was that Lucius Domitius was tired of the part. He had played it to the hilt. If he went on playing it, Caesar would come to life again. If he didn't play it, there was no Caesar.

The only person I could talk to was Sporus. 'You're absolutely right,' he said. 'The part has simply been too much for him.'

After a while Caesar came out of hiding. He called the usual meetings, caroused occasionally (there were no Illuminates now), held sessions with his staff to discuss the forthcoming Black Sea campaign, and – practised recitation.

We all had to put up with a good deal of Caesar's theatrical talent. Failing any other audience, he used to perform to a house of three – Statilia, Sporus, and me. For this purpose he had reduced most of the repertoire to monologues, and we had him as Agamemnon, as Phaedra, as Niobe – the lot. The first show of this kind I saw scared me rigid. Caesar was Phaedra – he did a noisy death scene, waving a dagger, and at the critical moment he plunged it into his chest and fell. Blood spouted out, I jumped up to give first aid – and saw Statilia and Sporus clapping. Caesar sat up. 'That had to be good,' he said. 'It fooled the doctor. He thinks I'm dead!'

'Don't ever do that again, Caesar,' I said, 'or at least do it in the theatre!'

'It unfortunately doesn't work in the theatre,' he said. 'This dagger only works for recitations. The effect's wasted unless you're close – in the theatre, a wooden one will do.'

What he had was a conjuror's dagger – it had been given him by the Jewish actor Aliturius, and one could in fact stab somebody with it, because the blade was perfectly rigid if one failed to press the button: 'But I do press it,' said Caesar, 'and I won't get carried away. I'd get carried away if I forgot.' When the button was pressed, of course, the blade collapsed. The handle was full of blood, or dye if one preferred ('It shows up and runs rather better,' Caesar explained), and moreover a groove in the collapsing blade deposited a strip of sticky wax, so that if you used it on a skin surface, it left behind what looked like a gaping wound. It wouldn't work on cloth: 'Which is why,' said Caesar, 'Phaedra bares her bosom – anyhow, it says so in the lines. I'm lucky in having a bosom to bare!' And indeed, being overweight, he had, and it didn't require supplementation for female roles.

Still the Furies held their hand. Nymphidius did his best with Caesar, telling him that he had to take measures to ensure succession.

'I'm doing that,' said Caesar. 'Give Statilia time,' – and went back to theatricals.

Tigellinus saw what was happening, too. He had found his Intelligence Agency in worse shape than he imagined. I think he realized that it was now or never, and decided that he preferred horsebreeding to leading a putsch – he started to withdraw, and eventually disappeared almost entirely from view, leaving the Guards to Nymphidius. I think Tigellinus was secretly writing letters to the military. Caesar talked about conquering India and holding another triumph in the future; he moved a few units and issued a new silver coinage – or rather Phaon did: we found out later that Phaon had been melting down Temple images to pay the expenses of Parts One and Two, and Nero's successor had to raise taxes to replace them. I realized glumly that we were simply waiting.

The Furies eventually acted. They had an Agrippina-like sense of humour, for their agent was called Vindex, one of the Governors of Gaul. Vindex started issuing coins on his own account (in spite of Phaon, Roman inflation was now out of hand, and the world merchants were steadily getting out of sesterces), inscribed FREEDOM AND VINDEX, or FREEDOM AND VENGEANCE if you preferred that reading. Finally he issued a proclamation denouncing Caesar's extravagance, Tigellinus' secret police, and the politicization of the Army and set about politicizing his own legion in Gaul. Vindex was smart enough not to get himself proclaimed Emperor. He offered the title to the Governor of Nearer Spain – an ex-consul and a septuagenarian, who could neither sing nor act. Galba sounded the Families, listened carefully for Tigellinus' police, and when he heard no sounds of burrowing he agreed. What forced his hand was a letter from another governor inviting him to support Nero against Vindex. Faced with that, he had to make up his mind. On April 2, he was proclaimed Emperor by his own troops, and raised his standard at Cartagena.

Nymphidius was sure that Caesar would be shocked into action. Caesar, when he got over the usual preliminary tantrum, smiled and said, 'Well, we've got the Guards, haven't we? And the German regiments will put down the rising. You carry on, Nymphidius.' And he went to meet a Greek inventor who was going to show him a new hydraulic organ. In fact, the loyalists defeated Vindex at Vesontio and killed him. But that did not deter Galba. The German Commander Vergilius was wholly loyal – he refused all temptation to accept the Emperorship, and went back to his post, with his legions. Someone had to hold the Rhine for Rome. The Senate asked Nero to confer with them – he replied that his throat was still sore: would they please take the approporiate measures against Vindex and Galba, and report their action to him? They issued a proclamation of outlawry and confiscated Galba's property.

Just before Vesontio, Caesar began to respond. He made some military dispositions, assumed the consulship, and held a council of war. I hadn't seen him for days, and I was shocked at the change – this was Lucius Domitius in his dressingroom. 'You know, Callimachus,' he said, 'I've a good mind to go up there in person. If an unarmed singer were to walk between the armies, they'd certainly stop fighting to listen to him. I'd better compose something suitable.' And if not, he could always make a living as a performer.

At the end of May, Nymphidius asked me for my medical opinion. It was a very awkward interview. I thought he wanted me to look at his foot, which had an old wound on it. Instead he shut the door of the office and said, 'Look, Doctor. In your view is Caesar fit to govern?'

I told him that I was Caesar's physician, and he was Caesar's senior commander. 'I can tell you if you like that there's nothing medically wrong with him,' I said. 'My first duty is to him, and so is yours.'

'I've also got a duty to Rome,' said Nymphidius. 'I hope they never conflict.'

Caesar had stopped talking to anyone, except Statilia, who showed absolutely no change of manner – she was still the Perfect Wife – and Sporus. At the end of April Caesar kissed Statilia and packed her off to Naples, talking about a concert he was going to arrange in July. That left Caesar, Sporus, and your Professor.

I suddenly saw what had happened. The female Furies had

left Nero to the Furies of Petronius. We were now three Greek rogues, Herondas, living in an immense palace which didn't belong to us. Very shortly we were going to be found out, and forced to leave by the back exit. We were, in fact, Groper, Banjo, and the pretty boy Giton. It was a shocking revenge, because the last Ahenobarbus production was not going to be classical tragedy. It was going to be the stage version of the Prickwort Papers.

Things went steadily from bad to worse. Caesar was still my patient, but I stopped arguing with him – he had given up and was letting things happen to him. On June the first, I reckoned something had to be done. There was only one person who would have kept her head, and who had some chance of being helpful. I went to Ostia to find Acte.

I hadn't seen Acte since my first departure from Italy. I found her walking her dog in the garden of her pleasant merchant's house in sight of the seaways. She remembered me.

'Callimachus,' she said. 'How is it with Caesar?'

'It's all right, Acte,' I said, 'he's still in position. I'm afraid I frightened you – he hasn't been attacked, or anything like that. But he isn't going to last – he seems paralysed, and I think it's only a matter of time.'

'How long have we?' she said.

'I reckon a week if we're lucky. Why doesn't he go? You could get him out of here.'

'Because if he goes,' said Acte, 'Rome will find him. Caesar can't run off and become a musician. That's his fantasy. I've just had to get rid of Arbaces – he wanted to get his ship's crew into the Golden House disguised as workmen, grab Caesar, and take him to safety. He was positively looking forward to a fighting retreat through the streets, in which he and his men defeated the entire Guard. I forbade it. I don't want him killed either.'

'So?'

'So Caesar can only get clear away if he's dead, and Rome knows he's dead.'

'So we give up?' I asked her.

'All I want,' said Acte, 'is to have Caesar safe with me. I've waited for ten years, haven't I? Thank you for coming, Callimachus, but this requires thought. Will you leave it to me, please?'

I told her I had to, and hoped she was too sensible to join Caesar by killing herself if they got him.

'Do I look the suicidal type?' said Acte, with a little of the old Madam in her manner. 'If I was, I wouldn't be here now. That's a Roman trick and we're not Romans, Callimachus. Stop asking questions, and you just promise me not to encourage Arbaces. I want no heroics. Men are born fools when they see a chance to fight somebody. Promise.'

Everything hung fire until June 8th, when the roof fell in. Word came that the northern army in Italy itself had gone over, or rather one of its commanders had. He was now fighting the other, so Caesar would get no help from there. Caesar suddenly exploded into activity. He announced to the surviving ministers that he would go immediately to Egypt. His agent there was Jewish, and a contact of Gershom ben Eleazer. Ships were to be secretly got ready at Ostia – Roman ships, of course. I decided this wasn't Acte's operation. In the afternoon, a signal came back that the squadron was ready (the telegraph had its last fling that day) and Caesar made a dash for it, but only as far as his villa in the Servilian Gardens. As soon as he had left the Golden House, Nymphidius told the colonels that Caesar had left for Egypt: Tigellinus kept quiet, and after a short meeting they resolved that since Caesar had left his post, their duty was to his successor. The customary gratuity was raised to an unprecedented 30,000 sesterces a head, and the Praetorian Guard proclaimed Galba. A centurion called Posthumius came to warn Caesar – and it was clear to my mind that his goose was cooked. He could not get to Ostia, and his total forces amounted to a handful of guardsmen who happened to be on duty. Caesar nodded his head, put Posthumius in command of the handful of loyalists, and went to get some sleep, and so did I.

So on the eighth of June – the day before the anniversary of Octavia's death, it so happens – Caesar went to bed as usual. He woke at midnight, got up, and found that there were now no guards. Nor was anyone else in sight. Caesar went round banging on doors. He found only two people left in the villa – Sporus, who told him to go away, because he, Sporus, needed sleep, and his physician. Epaphroditus turned up later – he had been alerted – and the three of us went to Caesar's bedroom. Clothes, sheets, and everything else movable was gone. So were a good many valuables, and Caesar's emergency cache of poison – the servants had waited until he left the sleeping wing of the building, and had then decamped with anything not screwed down. Contrary to the story, he neither threatened to jump in the Tiber, nor called for an executioner to end his life. What he actually said was, 'Rome has bolted from Caesar: I doubt if I could find a gladiator to cut my head off – no friends, and apparently no enemies.'

A move had to be made. It had been arranged that in total emergency Phaon would go to his country house and Caesar would hide there. Phaon, who'd spent the whole of Caesar's reign at the Treasury, arranged this like an efficient private secretary fixing a meeting. What he didn't tell Caesar was that he also sent word to Acte. Clearly, I told Caesar, this was an emergency in question. Luckily neither the stablemen nor the horses belonging to the kitchen manciple had gone. We were able to get them saddled, leaving word that we were going to Puteoli, so as to muddle any pursuit, brought them to the rear entrance, and took Caesar down through the kitchen. The whole place was as quiet as a grave – no ambushes, no assassins, no Furies, simply a party of four, getting out of the villa. Only a short way off was that enormous Babylonian palace – empty, except for mutineers.

It was an extraordinary exit. This wasn't Caesar and his friends – it was a party of unsuccessful players being run out of town, or Petronius' rascally characters escaping from the police. Nero himself had raided the property-chest – no shoes, tunic, an old cloak far too long for him, and a dilapidated hat. We got out of town, headed for the Salarian Way. Even the weather provided sound effects – there was a silent display of June lightning going on in the distance. Sporus was whistling between his teeth, and I remembered being told that pathics can't whistle, and noting that it was empirically untrue. Epaphroditus and he were nearly as nervous as Caesar – they were running some risk, particularly Sporus, if the soldiers caught them: I wasn't, or very little, for I never once in our College's history heard of a physician being killed by troops, though possibly there had not been too many of us in a comparable situation.

And the rest of Rome seemed to be playing its lines. As we passed a camp we could hear shouting, about what Galba would do to Caesar. Two people in doorways yelled to each other, 'What's happened? Do you know?'

'Caesar's bolted.' And as Caesar accelerated, 'Look, there

goes a posse in search of him!' A bit further on there was a stench of death, and an old man holding a torch. He was gingerly inspecting a corpse which lay by the road-side. Caesar's horse shied, his hat fell off, and the old man – a retired Guardsman, I imagine, saw his face. 'Hail, Caesar!' he bawled in a parade-ground voice, and came to attention. Agrippina couldn't have arranged it better.

When we got to Phaon's country house, it was dark. The door was locked. Sporus was trying to force it, with Caesar standing back and looking back anxiously over his shoulder, when we heard a peculiar, irregular step – more like a ghost than a man. Epaphroditus drew a sword, though he seemed to have precious little idea what to do with it, for he held it like a poker. The fellow who came in sight down Phaon's entry was one-legged, which explained the odd sound, but he walked briskly, stopped in front of Caesar, and said, with an accent, 'Are you Lucius Domitius?'

'Yes,' said Caesar.

'Word from Mister Phaon. You are not safe here. You go to the bothy. You know where that is?'

'Are you Greek?' I asked, in my own language.

'Sir!'

'Then talk Greek. Lucius understands.'

'My orders, Sir – proceed to the bothy. I think you know the course from here. You're to steer west by south for the drained marshes, and look for three poplars.'

'Yes, yes, I know where he means,' said Caesar. 'It's lucky I do – we'll all be killed looking for poplars in the dark. Who sent you?'

'Phaon, Sir, and Lady Acte.'

'This could be ...' said Sporus.

'Yes, it could be a trick,' said Caesar, 'but it isn't. Hurry, damn you! And thank you for the message. If I had anything of value I'd reward you. Hold my horse, can you?'

'Aye, aye, Sir,' said the one-legged man, and we left him.

'One of Acte's sailors,' said Epaphroditus, 'by the sound of him. That's hopeful – she may have brought us a bodyguard.'

The bothy was a fishing-hut of a tenant of Phaon, or it had been one, before the marshes began to be drained. It was in a thicket beside a drainage ditch between Rome and Ostia, and it was reachable by a series of abominable roads, made worse by the thunderstorm.

'Halt,' said Caesar, when we got close. 'Sporus, go and see if we can get in. If it still has a door, I don't have a key. Callimachus, go back and watch the road.' So Caesar stayed, trying to fill his hat with rainwater from a puddle, and saying that he'd better drink that, because there wouldn't be any ice-water for a while. He was scared but remarkably composed. I heard Sporus come back and tell him that there was a hole in the wall, and he'd have to get in that way. Then the pair of them went, taking the torch, and leaving me with Epaphroditus.

'I have the feeling,' he said, 'that there's something afoot.'

'It's afoot all right,' I said. 'I wish I knew what. Thank Artemis, there's a moon. We have to find that place. We'll start by hiding the horses, however. At the moment they're advertising where we are.'

The plain and marsh behind the coast here are malarial and full of thorn-patches and drainage channels. I reckoned we'd ridden almost to the coast. It was a good spot to hide – there were marsh people about, however, and by day it would be an equally good place to be conspicuous. I wondered why Caesar had got rid of us. At one point, blundering about among the brambles, we nearly fell into a drainage channel, where a ruinous-looking eel-boat was moored, draped with nets and eel traps, and some rather ruffianly men were plying their trade with a small, half-darkened fishing lantern. We gave them a wide berth. Something about the lines of that ruinous boat struck a chord, however. I realized as I followed Sporus what it was – the mast, which had a rough derrick stepped to it from which a square net was being dipped and raised, dipped and raised, was unusually tall, and it raked forward not back.

Wondering 'what next?' I shoved Epaphroditus through the hole in the wall, into a store full of straw and boxes. The torch was stuck in a hole in a manger-post. Acte herself and an old woman were standing by a kind of half-doorway which went into another store, but didn't quite reach the ground. Caesar was reclining on his cloak, talking to Sporus. By contrast with his composure before, he was now apparently in a bad fright.

'But how will they do it?' he said. (The whole conversation went on in loudstage whispers.)

'More majorum, Caesar – it isn't pleasant,' said Sporus.

'Cut my head off?'

'No, Caesar, the executioners will fix your neck in a tree-fork and flog you to death.'

'It seems,' said Caesar, 'that you are suggesting that I take the initiative and kill myself. If I do, Sporus, will you join me in Elysium? Will you come, too?'

Sporus didn't seem keen. 'Someone must preserve your memory, Caesar,' he said.

'Acte will do that,' said Caesar. 'I couldn't bear another world, Sporus, without you.'

'Caesar,' said Epaphroditus, 'I don't want you to do anything rash. But Sporus is right. You must not be taken alive.'

'I suppose not. Luckily I have a dagger,' said Caesar, 'two, in fact. Very well then. Callimachus, is death painful?'

'Usually not, Caesar,' I said, 'provided the first wound is mortal.'

'You wouldn't open my veins, I suppose? No, I thought not.'

'Quiet,' said Sporus, 'I heard something.' Outside there were three short chirps – an insect, probably, but it sounded like a boatswain's pipe. I was still trying to figure out what was going on.

'At least do it well, Caesar – not like Messalina,' said Epaphroditus. Caesar lay there, feeling the point of the dagger. Acte and the old nurse seemed to be making up the chorus. I had never seen a deathbed of this kind. It is true that not being a Roman, I had no practice with official suicides in general, but there was also something else.

'What hurts most,' said Caesar, 'is the appalling waste of talent. Sporus, my dear boy, kindly kiss me and go outside and keep watch. I suppose there is no point in hurrying this – or putting it off, for that matter. Callimachus, you've been a good friend. I'm grateful to you. I also hereby dismiss you as Imperial physician, and I order you to stay where you are and not interfere. Understood?'

'Understood, Caesar.'

'Then,' said Caesar, 'we can all relax a moment.'

Now Caesar, as I have said, suffered agonies from stage fright, in spite of his obsession with public performance. This was the phrase he invariably used before going on. I mentally tightened my girths, for I had seen Caesar play innumerable death scenes – they were his favorites, whether as Niobe, as Heracles, or as Lucretia. And normally he played them for all they were worth.

'We'll take it,' said Caesar, 'quietly. I don't need to forbid you to follow me, Acte, because you have more sense. I'll be burned here – make sure the pyre is kept well away from those fine trees. Mustn't destroy a sailing mark.' The performance, I thought, is going to be Paetus or Socrates, not King Cambyses – thank goodness.

Sporus stuck his head through the hole – it might have been, round the curtain – and said, 'Caesar, they're coming! Farewell!' And he disappeared. Then we heard noises off, horses, feet.

'I hear the thunder of Argive hooves!' said Caesar. He closed his eyes, and at the precise moment that a centurion's head came through the hole in the wall, Caesar struck. He gave a grunt, not a cry, Acte and the nurse bent over him. Epaphroditus covered his own face. The centurion pushed his way in trying to see in the smoky torchlight.

It was Posthumius. 'Caesar, we've come to...good Gods, he's stabbed himself.' Posthumius pushed the women aside and tried to staunch the wound with his cloak. Caesar's arms and legs began to twitch. The dagger fell among the straw. Acte dipped the sponge she held in a bowl of water, and the water darkened. As you know, Herondas, a little blood goes a long way. There was now a bowl of blood. Caesar's convulsion ended and he lay still.

Posthumius stood up. 'No good. Must be a poisoned dagger. He's gone. Callimachus, did you give him poison?'

'Doctor Callimachus had no part in this, Posthumius,' said Acte. 'The dagger is Caesar's own.' And she retrieved it. The light was bad, of course, but I had seen the dagger before. This was a different play from that which I had expected. Acte pulled the corner of the cloak over Caesar's face.

Then a much larger party arrived, there was neighing and shouting, light was shed through the hole in the wall, guards were posted, and three of them came in – Nymphidius, his staff colonel and his courier. Posthumius came to attention.

'Dismiss,' said Nymphidius. 'Greeting, Callimachus, Epaphroditus.' He went over to the body of Caesar, over which Acte was bending. 'Who are you, madam?' asked Nymphidius.

'I am Acte,' she said. 'Lucius Domitius is dead. I am his wife, and this woman was his nurse. We claim his body.'

Nymphidius uncovered the face, inspected the wound, put the back of his hand against Caesar's neck, and stood up. 'Dead,' he said, 'but we will make sure.' He started to draw his sword.

Acte placed her body firmly between Nymphidius and

Caesar. 'You can see Caesar is dead – I won't have him butchered, Nymphidius. Unless you make a practice of killing corpses.'

Nymphidius put his sword back in its sheath (the other officers had all come rather stiffly to attention, and it wasn't lost on him). 'Callimachus?' he said, and jerked his head toward Caesar. I uncovered Caesar's face once more, placed my hand on his neck, felt his pulse, inspected the wound. More correctly, I felt no pulse – my finger was placed not on the artery but on the pisiform bone, but Nymphidius was not to know that. I covered Caesar's face for the last time, stood up, shook my head with suitable gravity, and went back to my place. 'Didn't look to me as if he bled to death,' said Nymphidius. 'Was that blade poisoned?'

'Probably not, Nymphidius,' I said, 'he could have hit his jugular vein. In that case he could have been killed by an inrush of air.'

'Very well,' said Nymphidius. 'Acte, the body of Caesar is yours. You will accompany it to Rome. Four men in here, Centurion!'

'Caesar,' said Acte, 'will be burned here. It was his wish, the pyre is prepared, and if you carry him through Rome his body will be torn to pieces. Men don't attack an urn.'

'As you please,' said Nymphidius. 'My men will see to it.'

'Thank you,' she said, 'I'd like that. He was your commander, Nymphidius. You owe him a military funeral.'

That, of course, was the last thing Nymphidius wanted – for a start, it would take some explaining to Galba. The adjutant muttered something about getting back to Rome to inform the Senate.

'On consideration,' said Nymphidius, 'the cremation is a family matter. Can you handle it, Madam?'

'I think so,' said Acte. 'There are fishermen on the canal – we will ask them to help us out of pity to a widow. But I would appreciate your help in taking Caesar into the other room so that we may prepare him.'

In the end four German lancers carried Caesar out on the cloak, into the front room of the bothy, while Sporus, who had been hovering about outside, was sent to ask help of the eel-fishers. It was dark in the yard – the beginnings of a pyre had been set well away from the trees, as Caesar had directed. Nymphidius came over to me.

'I need,' he said, 'your certificate.'

So while he held the torch I took out a tablet and wrote as follows, with Epaphroditus trying to read over my shoulder:

> 'June 9
>
> 'I today examined the body of Lucius Domitius Ahenobarbus, also known as Nero Drusus Germanicus Caesar, who had in my presence struck himself once in the throat with a dagger.
>
> 'No vital signs were observed. There was a incised-punctured wound two inches below the tip of the left auricle and overlying the left external jugular vein. Patient was right handed. There was considerable effusion of blood, insufficient to cause death. Wound was not probed.
>
> 'Patient was pronounced dead at the scene.
>
> 'In the absence of exsanguination, death from a wound in this position would most likely result from air embolism. It is my opinion unnecessary to assume that the weapon was poisoned.
>
> 'Body of patient assigned to next-of-kin for cremation.
>
> Callimachus, Iatros of Cos.'

All of the above, Herondas, being true and sustainable. Although Caesar had very considerately discharged me from the professional relationship, the obligation to act in the best interest of a former patient persists. It may on occasion be met by economical, though preferably not false, certification.

Nymphidius took the tablet, snapped it shut, and handed it to the courier. 'To the Senate, and look sharp,' he said. 'Geta, fall those men in. I want three lancers and you, Barbatus. Stand guard, see they burn him, don't interfere, and don't allow trophies. The widow is to have the ashes – if she is the widow.'

So we were left in the dark yard with three German auxiliary lancers and a young NCO, the beginnings of a pyre, and two torches. In minutes the fishermen arrived. They were surprisingly well organized – without orders they formed a line. Like sailors loading cargo, they quickly threw on the pile, first faggots, and then when those ran out, old nets, oakum, fishboxes, worn fenders, and finally two tarbarrels. Epaphroditus and I watched the pyre grow. The Germans, standing behind us, were distinctly uneasy: these tribesmen are not very comfortable with pyres, darkness, or the spirits of the dead. Finally four fishermen were called into the bothy, and came out carrying Caesar's body on an improvised bier, wrapped in the cloak. With some difficulty they got it on the pyre, covered it with nets, and jumped down. Acte and the nurse had followed the bier, Acte upright and cool, the nurse in tears which rapidly became hysterical. Taking the torch, Acte walked three times round the pyre and touched the faggots. I think the Germans behind me thought that she was about to jump into it. The wood blazed up, and the old nurse, increasingly distraught, suddenly tried to do just that. She was held back, and Acte put an arm round her shoulders. It struck me that though bent double she had extremely broad shoulders for so old and frail a lady, but at that moment the oakum caught and enveloped both the body and us in dense clouds of choking smoke. Then one of the tarbarrels exploded with a thunderous bang, scattering burning pitch and setting fires on the thatch. Two fishermen swarmed up to put them out. In other words, total confusion. The whole macabre business was too much for the Germans. Somebody shouted, 'Da kommt der Kaisergespenst! Hilf, Wotan!'

They broke ranks, and it took the noncom a great deal of cursing to get them back in line with blows from his stick. In the middle of it all stood Acte, like a businesslike Valkyrie. Meanwhile two of the fishermen helped the old nurse away in the direction of the eelboat. They returned without her, and stood round the fire, caps in hands, until it began to die down, and when it became no more than a red circle, just before dawn, we noticed that they had gone. As soon as she could come near enough, Acte, with the traditional ladle, filled the urn. The young NCO, mopping his brow, lined up his detail, saluted, and marched them off to their horses. The eelboat was warping off towards the marshes.

'It's over,' said Epaphroditus. 'He died well. Farewell, Callimachus. I'm taking Lady Acte back.'

And she left with him, bearing the still hot ashes of Caesar, with a grave look my way, and I was left alone.

It was getting light, and the circle from the pyre was white not red. Sporus came out of the shadow of the bothy.

'Explicit comedia – vos plaudite,' he said. 'Just for a moment I was afraid the Nurse had the bit between her teeth – it was getting dangerously like that scene where Deianira leaps into the pyre of Herakles. But the effects were terrific.'

'Speak well,' I said in Greek, between my teeth.

'Where will you go, Callimachus?' said Sporus.

'To Cos,' I told him, 'but I have to stop in Syracuse for a consultation. What about you?'

'The climate in Rome,' said Sporus, 'may be a little unhealthy for pathics. Probably Corinth. I hope they didn't take our horses – let's go and see. Do you fancy a ride, to settle our minds?'

'We might go down the marsh road a little way,' I said. 'I'd like to see where that eelboat went, and reward the fishermen.'

'I wouldn't,' said Sporus, 'they looked a rough lot to me. But there's no harm in watching them leave.'

As we rode down the towpath we could see the boat moving through the levels, draped in nets, seeming like a barge of the dead. By the time we reached the point where the drainage canal debouched into a salt lake, she was out in the fairway, scattering birds, and poling steadily to the break in the dunes where a sandbar separated lake from sea. There was a little customs post with a jetty, and a picketboat moored at it. Beyond that was white water, with a stiff breeze rising offshore.

'This way,' said Sporus, 'we'll see her shoot the bar.' So we rode round the lake shore, our horses' hooves splashing in salt, and on, over the dunes to the beach, where we could gallop and reach the point ahead of her.

We drew rein on top of the endmost dune, above the hut and the jetty. She was coming slowly to the bar, on the far side, something dredged up from the sea, trailing spent cables, fish traps, nets. Her men poled her noiselessly, almost stealthily, like a ghost ship. Then she crossed the bar and reached open water, where she paused. At the same moment the door of the hut opened, the boat's crew tumbled out and into their places, and a voice hailed, 'What ship, and whither bound?'

'Thetis, Antium, washing my nets,' came back.

'Heave to for inspection – coming aboard you. Give way together.' And the picketboat pulled out. At the same moment the eelboat began to undergo a sea-change. She was like a woman who strips off her clothes. Two hands aloft cut the lashings which held the draped nets. The polemen jettisoned their poles and ran from fore to aft casting off the fenders, fishtraps, camouflage netting and hamper and sending it astern, across the picket's bow if she held course – and Venus emerged naked, with smart blue sides, brass trim, and a great golden eye at her hawse. Still she dawdled, then a voice sang out in Greek, 'Out barges! Set her!' and the long, light yard ran up, made of a single reed from China, too frail-looking for the outsize leg-of-mutton sail. 'Set she is, Sir!'

'Give way, and pay her off!'

She leaned gracefully as the breeze caught her, the sail filled like a wing, and with the picket half-a-cable away she tucked up her feet like a seagull and sprang into the wind. One minute she was standing aback, the next a white bone appeared in her mouth, under the golden eye, and she was at full speed. The picket coxswain called, 'Way enough!' The picket stopped rowing and came half-about to watch her, trying to unfoul their sweeps from the rubbish she had jettisoned, and I saw the receding caique's two helmsmen looking back over their shoulders – and giving the picket the finger. Leaning against the galley, a sea-cook was drumming derision on a pot with a wooden peg-leg.

'Smugglers, evidently,' said Sporus. 'It's a good thing we didn't try to talk with them. Lucky, in fact, they didn't cut our throats last night.'

The customs officer on the jetty greeted us when we went down. 'What was all that about?' I asked him.

'Smugglers, Sir, or pirates I shouldn't wonder. They had us fooled, and they know it. I hope the devil chokes them and Neptune sends them to the bottom. But Zeus, what a craft they've got! I wish she were mine. If I ever find a ship like that I'll marry her – too good for cut-throats and rascals. Do you have word from Rome, Sir?'

'Caesar, they say, is dead by his own hand.'

'So. Bid you good-day.' He went inside.

'Rome,' said Sporus, 'may not be too pleasant now. If we follow the shore we'll come to Ostia. Shall we ride?'

I did not remain in Rome to see Galba take office. He sent me a courteous letter telling me that I had nothing to fear from him, since by all accounts I had been a conscientious officer, and offering me a joint physicianship with his own man. 'As to Nero,' he wrote, 'he will be missed – by the riffraff.' When I demurred, pleading business in Cos, he made no effort to dissuade me.

The riffraff included, as it fell out, Poppaea's husband Otho – as the new Emperor was soon to find out, for Otho returned and cut Galba's throat. They were not alone, however: an embassy arrived from the two brother-kings, Vologses and Tiridates, expressing their grief at Nero's death and requesting, in terms amounting to a demand, that his body and memory not be insulted by the new regime. The Greeks, too, though they sent no messages, were profoundly unhappy at the new turn of events.

Nero was given an expensive funeral by Acte. As his body had already been cremated, Galba's freedman Icelus, who had been imprisoned by Nero, but had now taken charge in Rome, and who was anxious to impress on the public that the tyrant was visibly and irrevocably dead, ordered that his image, stuffed out with straw, should be publicly cremated once more. It was placed on the pyre, wrapped incongruously in a tinsel-edged theatrical robe, and Caesar was burned for the second time. A very composed and dry-eyed Acte followed his ashes with both his childhood nurses; one of these had been with him at the end, the other had lately refused to speak to Nero because he had sacked her son (for using the Imperial bathtub, of all things!), but she relented and was prevailed on to attend. It was a subdued affair. The urn was placed in the family mausoleum – of the Domitii, not the Claudians – and that was that. As for Acte, she returned to Ostia, and a few weeks later took passage to Rhodes on an ordinary merchantman.

I left light, and with few goodbyes. Seneca, Petronius and Burrus were dead – Xenophon was back teaching in Cos. I had sent away my effects and cash ahead of time. After being driven into Antium by a summer thunderstorm, and watching it die out over the Tyrrhenian Sea, we set course for Syracuse.

The patient there – old times – was an infertile lady, married to a Greek merchant. Her physician was Roman, trained by Celsus. We talked over her case, and I asked him his name. It was Lucius Geminianus. 'And your wife's name is Hippolyta,' I said. 'What is your daughter called?'

It seemed she was called Acerria in Latin, Alkestis in Greek, the second of which was her mother's choice. So I dined with them, not knowing how to take the meeting, and saw her – a grave, darkhaired child of eight years, and when she saw me she smiled and waved, then, rebuked by her father, came forward in time to childhood again and was sent to bed. I, for my part, could hardly eat my meal or make conversation. 'She's a strange little thing,' said Hippolyta. 'When she was three, she used to insist that she had a son who would be a physician, and asked after his father, who was a physician. But she's forgotten that now. Children play strange games.'

I, for my part, wrote to Diodorus and arranged that Lucius should join us in Cos, bringing his family with him, for there was little good teaching at that time in Syracuse, the Methodici were turning Medicine upside down, and I needed a colleague to help me carry my clinic load.

I had, of course, seven years to wait – starting as Acerria's godfather. I thought she would grow back into a duplicate Acte, but she did not: for a start, she had an easier girlhood: this time there was less street wisdom. How are the two faces of the coin alike? Roughly as a woman resembles herself after she has changed her hairstyle, her garments and her face – but actually the difference is rather more, because it involves a good deal of forgetting to make room for re-learning. Apollonius says I am uniquely lucky to have actually seen this and observed the changes. Have we two discussed it ever? Not in so many words. Alkestis isn't what my guru called a jatismara – that is to say, after the first few years of her life she wasn't bothered by any carryover. If I probed now she'd retreat, and in any case what would be the point? The most I did was to bring her surreptitiously about the age of twelve to try her hand at healing, with pets for a start, to see if the gift carries over. She undoubtedly has it. Probably she will have the other Acte gifts – dreams, foresight and so on. At the moment she is quite wrapped up in the new child, and I will not probe here either, having waited for her to become a woman again (that was a weird trick to play on her lover!) I can wait a little longer to satisfy my curiosity.

It is an extraordinary experience, and a privilege rarely accorded by the Goddess, to be the lover of the same woman twice over: but I must admit that I am enjoying it. It is perhaps more extraordinary to possess the same woman, first as a woman and then as a virgin. It was the guile of Acte, perhaps, to let me have this remarkable gift.

I leave it to you, Herondas, to interpret the plan of Asklepios. As to me it seems quite clear. He has not revealed any more of it – that I became archiatros on the commendation of Xenophon in his will was an unexpected (and, you may rightly think, unmerited) favour on his part. The Sybil has been no help – all she can tell me of the future is that my son's son's son will be a physician, which is hardly prophecy, and will be called 'Weasel,' which I think most unlikely. Galenus was never a name in our family, and who would trust a weasel as physician? However, the Sybil probably knows what she is talking about. My wife Alkestis greets you, also our child, or she would do so if she were of age. Telesphoriades has moved of late to Pergamon.

One matter I did not mention is that in the year of my return, someone unknown sent me as a present from Rhodes, an inlaid lyre. Not being a musician I cannot play it, but it is an interesting object which you may one day see. May Asklepios guide you.

Callimachus, Archiatros, your friend.